Some day the earth will weep,

she will beg for her life,

She will cry with tears of blood.

You will make a choice,

if you will help her or let her die,

and when she dies,

you too will die.

-John Holland Horn

Oglala, Lakota

This book is dedicated to all who have felt the pain of the

Mother,

all my relations and

all creatures great and small

The Red Path Way

Beginning of the Past

The silence of a new day's morn was broken by the paddle's gentle stroke through the still waters. A loon's call brought forth dawn's dappled light through the shadowy mist that sat upon the river.

The young brave, Wahweyho, gently laid the paddle to his side and drifted downstream with the current chanting his song of praise for the beauty of another day.

The spirits of his ancestors listened in respect to his blessings for his people, the land and all creatures great and small that formed the intricate web of life.

Wayweyho was lost in reverence for the awakening of nature. The scents of pine and cedar, musty soil and spring flowers invaded his senses as the mountains of Kananaskis Country rose towering in their grand majesty above him. The screech of an eagle's cry pierced the air with the glory of its flight, as small forest creatures scurried upon the detritus of Mother Earth's floor.

The Great Mother bestowed her protection upon this man who embraced the future of the first ones. He held the heart of humanity in his firm grasp.

His path was laid out before him: a fine ethereal thread that shimmered through time and into the present.

Present

Willow pulled the green, battered Dodge van into the caretaker's stall. The van was a sweet deal she'd found neglected and covered in a growth of weeds, struggling to draw existence out of old things long forgotten. She pulled the weeds from the bumpers, oiled and greased the wheels, serviced the engine and converted an ancient gothic velvet wall hanging into curtains. Her summer home was complete.

This new job was every naturalist's dream position, caretaking a piece of paradise in a pristine valley in the Kananaskis. The valley was in the foothills of the Rockies where nature was as she had always been: untouched, sacred and whole.

Mother Earth fed Willow's soul and the gifts of knowledge she held inspired her very essence. The book of Gaia's wisdom lay vast and open at her feet.

Willow jumped out of the van with a whoop after trying to align and level the ¾-ton van. Parallel parking had never been her forte.

Her partner, a suave, techno, "city-ized" English gent,

stepped cautiously onto the soft pine-needle-strewn ground with his black leather dancing shoes. He gazed across at Willow with trepidation, it was time for him to step into his new role, that of "Ranger Bob."

The universe seems to give us roles to play and the ideal situations to do so. We put on our masks and dance to a tune orchestrated in the cosmos, though the steps are our own. We spin and turn, seeking the primal state of being. Where bliss is freed from our souls and we scream out the ecstasy of being, if blessed enough to touch self. At least that is how Willow tried to manage life as it unfolded, always believing in her path.

Willow unloaded their gear: ax, propane stove, dishes and water cooler and then proceeded to set up their new home. They would begin work the next day.

The job entailed driving around the 137-site subalpine forest collecting fees, cleaning five double outhouse stalls and selling firewood. Weekdays were to be spent cleaning the 200-acre parkland that bordered on an endless sea of nature's blessed existence, after the weekend's pack of city folk had returned to their slave barracks leaving mounds of garbage behind.

Ranger Bob worked on the inside of the van, straightening his clothes and setting up his toiletries. He had to rummage through his clothing to find "the outfit" that would fit his new persona. Once an ecstasy-popping London raver, he was now to be transformed into Grizzly Adams, roughing it and living with the bears. This was a dream of his that he held in the recesses of his mind, an essential part of his initiation into manhood.

Ranger Bob had never even held an ax. All was new,

frightful and exhilarating.

Bob had followed Willow back to Canada after they had met working in the jungles of Mexico. Willow had been building a health retreat along the Caribbean Coast and he was running a fly fishing camp. Bob had always dreamed of the wilds of Canada, the mountains and the animals. Now that he was immersed in it full on, a panicked excitement set in. "Lions, tigers and bears, oh my!"

Willow had just finished setting up the kitchen on the end of the picnic table when Bob jumped out of the van. His long, dark curls were tied neatly into a knot at the nape of his neck. He wore the official forest-green camp attendant t-shirt and his own matching green tights, cut off and rolled up his dark hairy legs.

She laughed and smiled at the beauty of his boyish nature. He was such a handsome diva-ish man with big blue eyes edged in long thick lashes. He was slender as a dancer and brilliant as a star, but he was definitely no woodsman. He smelled like a well-perfumed buck. Scented musk is not such a good idea in the wilderness, even though it is tamed by man's footprint of development.

They hung a bright blue tarp above the improvised kitchen tying it among the trees for added shelter and then started a fire in the campground pit to bring the warmth of its hominess to their new lair.

Willow thought happily to herself, "Well this is it, the big dream, becoming one in harmony with nature. And to find a job that pays for such a blessing seems like perfect synchronicity."

The Sun began to set upon the mountain, the darkness of night bringing in the eve's chilling breath.

Willow and Bob settled in, they were excited about their new home. They lit some of the sacred herb, giving thanks to the experience of nature in her purest sense. Willow also lit a sage bundle to smudge their campsite, cleansing any remnants of the habitat's old energies and drawing forth protection from beneficial spirits.

The chirping of the birds faded as the sound of a distant creek whispered to their senses. Relaxation soon settled into their bones like a heavy wool blanket upon their shoulders.

Willow lazed back in the reclining hammock chair she had hung trancing out as she gazed into the star-strewn sky.

The newly transformed Ranger Bob was eloquently sharing his knowledge of the stars, pointing out the Big Dipper, Orion's Belt and the Pleiades when a voice called out, "Hello!"

Willow and Ranger Bob were startled that the wind had covered the man's approach so well. They thought they were the only ones in the campground as neither had bothered to do the rounds. Officially, their contract did not begin until the next day.

Bob jumped up and extended his left hand introducing Willow and himself to the man.

The tall, elderly Native man smiled a warm and welcoming grin. "Hey there, I'm Joseph. I am set up over on site 20. Been there about ten days now and it's been cold as hell. I'd have to say it feels like summer ain't ever gonna come. Damn climate change! It sure is nice to have some people around after the scare the other night. I didn't think they'd be able to find another caretaker so fast!"

"What scare?" Bob asked. He looked at Willow with a fearful gaze.

Already Bob had a little more trepidation than excitement in his bones. When it came to living on the land without the luxuries of electricity, the peaceful silence of nature was a little more intimidating to Ranger Bob than the metro city boy wanted to acknowledge. The two of them had lived with only the use of generators in Mexico, but there was the open expanse of sandy beach with no dangerous animals to encounter unexpectedly in that scenario. And now it appeared that he may have a new story to add to his epic "bushing it" adventure in the wilds of Canada.

Willow asked Joseph to sit down and poured him some herbal tea that she had brewing on the fire pit's cast iron grill.

Joseph sat down and began warming his gnarled, weathered hands upon the clay mug as he stared into the fire. The flickering flames beckoned forth his journey back to the eve in question. He took a long sip of the warm elixir and cleared his throat, "Well, you should have seen the panic! No one knew what to do, with the campground being so isolated and all. It takes three hours to get to the city limits, as you know. You can't even use those cellphone contraption things. They don't work out here. It sure is a good thing that you have radios to contact the warden if you have to deal with an emergency like the past weekend."

"Like what? What emergency are you talking about?" Bob asked nervously.

Joseph looked at Bob and Willow with shock when he realized they had not been informed of the past night's events. "Well they should have let you know what happened before you were hired," stated the old man. "I even saw a write-up in the paper about that missing woman. They still haven't found the body. There are a lot of people who disappear from parks you know, many more than are ever acknowledged or spoken of."

"Could you please let us in on the mystery?" Willow asked. "I didn't get a chance to read the paper today before we arrived."

So, Joseph began from the beginning. "Well, I guess it was around 8:30 or so, two nights back. The camp was pretty full, being the long weekend and all. I was sure glad I got here early! Anyhow, I heard this awful bloodcurdling scream over in section E by the trailhead. Well, everyone was concerned that maybe someone had been hurt bad or even murdered by the sound of that painful scream, I tell ya! But I'll be damned if I know what happened. A few of us decided to investigate but we couldn't find any lady in duress and there was no evidence of foul play at any of the sites. Harry, the camp attendant called the warden's office on the radio and they sent out some park security officers. There were 80 registered guests and every one of us heard that scream, something I'll never forget, I tell you that! A lot of people just up and packed up 'cause they were so scared. The park warden even called the police and they brought in a helicopter and scoured the mountains thinking maybe there was an accident, but nobody could find the elusive source of that horror-filled cry."

Bob was pacing the campsite chewing the side of his thumb, it was a nervous habit he had. Willow casually suggested that they call in on the radio and talk to their boss to see what the story was in the morning. They thanked Joseph for enlightening them as to why it had been so easy to get this job so late in the season and without any previous experience.

"Well, I'm sorry kids, I didn't want to scare you or anything but you know Harry, he's been caretaking the Elbow here for eight years and never had he heard such a sound! He said he would never come back again. That man felt this here place had become haunted by evil spirits or something. You should talk to him, he has some interesting stories to tell you," Joseph finished, as he rose from the chair.

Bob picked up the bottle of Blackberry Smirnoff that had been this evening's aperitif and a nerve calming aid throughout most of his adult life and proceeding to pour himself a stiff one. "I wonder what that was all about," he said. "Maybe there is some kind of bush-whacking maniac running around the forest out here or something? I believe we should reconsider this job Willow." Bob's voice wavered shakily over the tinkling of ice in the tumbler.

Willow lit up the remainder of the spliff and took a deep haul. The aroma of a heady skunk fragrance lingered in the air as calm filtered through her mind. She casually passed the smoke over to Bob who inhaled deeply, letting a tranquil ease relax his growing anxiety.

"Let's watch the stars again babe and get lost in this beautiful evening. No noise pollution. Just the whispering of the wind in the trees," said Willow. "Tell me more about the stars and their proceedings across the universe Bobby. I love getting lost in your narrative sweetheart."

They talked for a few more hours, enjoying the peaceful solitude of the gentle forest in the foothills of the Rockies.

Willow stretched her arms to the heavens while she rose from her chair. The smoke from their fire was well entrenched in her denim jeans and jacket. She loved the scent of a campfire as it seemed to bring back a sense of sacredness and gratitude in her. Some deeper part of her bowed to the symbol of this element and the safety of survival it evoked in the primal self.

Willow came out of her reverie and sleepily asked, "Hey, are you up for a trip to the bathroom before we crash?"

"No, I'm fine. I am going to mark the boundaries of our campsite with copious amounts of urine. I read that is how to keep animals at bay in the Farley Mowat's *Never Cry Wolf*, I hope it is based on scientific research."

She smiled and said, "Okay, I'm gone but I'll be right back." Willow grabbed her shit-kit and headlamp and headed off in the direction of the rather modern "baños" that were just a short jaunt down the camp's gravel road. The bathrooms were modern in the sense that the outhouses had running water in the sinks with mirrors overhead to check you were presentable while on your campout. Appearance is important even in the woods for some, something Willow never quite understood. Her ego was frail and looking in a mirror to find faults was low on her priority list.

The night was refreshing with a slight chill in the air, the scent of pine and cedar was strong around her and she was aware of the sound of scurrying in the bushes. Her footfall upon the gravel was distracting to her heightening senses, and she found herself drawn into the loudness of her steps.

She tended to walk through the world with her eyes to the skies always trying to see beyond the hidden. She was seeking answers to the mystery of understanding a person's place in the cosmos, and the place of the human race in the vast evolutionary picture.

Willow tripped and fell heavily onto her knees in the gravel as her right hand landed directly upon the bloody remnants of a dead white rabbit. She pulled her hand back quickly from the dead animal's remains and looked around to see if there were any signs of its predator. The scent of fear and a fresh kill still lingered in the air. To her left, she heard the faint sound of pacing padded feet. The cooing of an owl pulled her attention away momentarily from the sounds in the bush, its symbology significant as she recalled the stories told of animal totems and their messages. The sight of an owl and its call can be interpreted as a sign of foreboding, a sign of imminent death and present death, so it appeared. "Maybe the rabbit was the owl's kill?" she thought. Taking a deep, centering breath Willow reached into her pocket and pulled out her small pocket knife. She drew her attention into a concentrated and focused intent. A prayer of love, respect and gratitude was then whispered to the small creature: "Blessings for your existence, my sacred friend. I give thanks for your offering. A'ho." Then she grasped the dead rabbit by its still warm foot and proceeded to cut it off at the joint, throwing the other remains off the path and into the brush where she knew the slayer lay in wait. Whether a four legged or a winged one, the bush was a better place to consume the carcass.

Willow felt blessed for this gift from nature. She now had a lucky rabbit's foot, it could help her become more sure-footed with any luck. The rabbit after all was her sign in the Chinese Zodiac and much like the rabbit she jumped around from home to home. Willow was always searching for a way to exist while still showing adoration for nature, which meant that much of her time was spent seeking her next form of seasonal employment. But destiny seemed to be telling her she was exactly where she was meant to be.

"When I set up my altar tomorrow you will have a place of honour nestled in a bowl of salt. You can lie to the North among my quartz crystals," she thought as she stroked the soft fur. Then she rose to her feet and after dusting off her knees wrapped her small specimen in a handkerchief and put it away in her jacket pocket. She was just about to continue on her way to the outhouse when a chill ran up her spine raising the hair on the back of her neck. The wind seemed to get cooler, whispering a small moan.

In a moment of trepidation Willow hurried on, she kept a firm grasp of the small blade's handle. "You never know what's out there after that story! I am just being cautious, and it is important to be conscious when in the woods alone," she thought. Bob was a short jaunt away, but he would probably run and hide in the van if she were to scream for help so relying on him was a no-go. She alone would need to face her fears.

She could see the bathroom just ahead. She picked up her pace as the wind increased and began swirling around her. Small bits of gravel and twigs whipped up against her face and dust blinded her eyes. She scrambled for the door handle and when she found it she threw the door open. Once inside, she turned quickly to lock the door behind her, while breathing a small sigh of relief. "Wow, that was weird," she thought.

Willow threw cool water on her face and brushed her hair and teeth after relieving herself. She looked around at the cobwebs and dirty floor of the outhouse and saw the promise of a huge workload. The place was a mess, and something was building a nest right in between the two stalls. Judging by the smell, it was probably a pack rat. "Yuck, they are a bitch to get rid of," she thought. "We'll have to get a live trap and bait it. Bob will love that!"

After the blithering of her mind calmed, Willow put her toiletries away. Keeping her knife handy on the side of her belt, she turned the lock and headed out the door and back to camp.

"Hi hon, look what I found on the road just in front of the bathrooms," she said upon her arrival, holding up the sinewy end of the foot.

Bob looked somewhat appalled at the specimen but replied, "Nice, what are you going to do with that thing? What is it anyway? It looks like part of a dead animal."

He should have been accustomed to Willow hacking off the limbs of animals as she had often made him pull over when they saw roadkill birds along their drive here. In Mexico, it had been dead snakes that she'd call for a stop to skin and dry. She practiced the ritual of preservation to show respect to the animal whose life had passed without a blessing of gratitude. She'd incorporate the acquired roadkill parts into jewelry, smudge fans and sacred trinkets to support herself in her travels.

"Weird chick," Bob thought. He believed Willow was a witch, in truth she scared him in ways and awed him in others.

"It is the foot of a rabbit," Willow replied. "I'm positive the kill was fresh as I sure had a weird sensation when I was in the process of amputation."

"Well I'd guess you'd feel weird, you're sawing off the limb of a poor little bunny," he balked.

Willow smiled and continued to recall how a chill had overcome her with the sensation of a predator being near. "I was a little nervous for a moment, an odd jangling of the nerves," she chuckled. "My overstimulated senses are about to crash. What a strange night. I'm exhausted. I think I'll hit the sack. Are you coming to bed babe?"

Bob glanced around the site. Unable to see past the dwindling fire, he decided that he as well would lay his head to rest.

They opened the van's side door and climbed into their new home. The scent of pine in the air, fresh sheets and wood smoke invited a deep sleep.

A dense cloud of sweetgrass smoke that had lingered behind the forest's cover began to slowly permeate the van's interior through the open door. The thick mist of the sacred herb enveloped Willow like a shroud inviting her into another world as she closed her weary eyes.

Willow was a romantic at heart and loved Bobby dearly, but she knew that the love they once shared had changed and this sadness had filled her sleepless nights. They had met in Mexico at a little isolated resort. Bobby was a superb entertainer that had the guests and Willow laughing endlessly at his antics. He was a brilliant, witty comedian and such a wonderful diversion from the quiet Mayan village Willow had immersed herself in. They fell in love quickly and things moved along very fast. They seemed like a perfect match at first; strolling on endless white sand beaches, making love under the starry skies completely lost in the splendor of their new lust.

But as the years rolled on they both knew their differences were not compatible. Bobby was a hip, metro type of man and Willow seemed to have been born in the wrong century, she was happy without the luxuries of the modern world. They danced to different tunes and as their lust fell away there was only their companionship that held them together and Willow was quite sure it was not enough.

They were not on the same page. This place they now found themselves in was the embodiment of the life Willow sought and Bobby was up for the adventure as he had romanticized the wilderness since his childhood, but this was the big test to figure out what their future was. Willow knew she had no desire to live in the city, to play the game of an ego-driven society, whereas Bobby excelled in the bright city lights that seemed to shine just for him. They were both at least true enough to themselves to know that to try and change for one another was not an option. Opposites attract, but that is where it should end; that truth was a hard pill for them to swallow for they truly cared for one another. And that's why they were there sleeping side by side in the middle of the Canadian wilderness. Breaking up can be hard to do but hanging on when things are over can be even harder.

Into the Past: Spring 1890

Wahweyho smiled and waved to his people as the canoe drifted into the reed-covered bank along the river's edge. The young children ran up to him, overjoyed at the sight of the young spirit man.

Wahweyho's path had been chosen for him since the coming of his first cycle of seven, when his gift of seeing became apparent to the elders. Each passing cycle of seven, in the young man's circle years, was celebrated with a challenge that was given to test his worthiness and hone his skills. The young brave had mastered all challenges, from that of warrior to that of healer. His bravery was unsurpassed. His being combined with logic and a compassionate heart made Wahweyho a much-celebrated healer and visionary among the people.

He walked through the throng of gathering children, playfully rubbing the heads of those within reach. The young women batted their eyes as they offered him dried pemmican, tea and hardened wheat biscuits. Wahweyho nodded with lowered head in acknowledgment of their gifts, but he quietly refused them, unwilling to break his fast until he had spoken with the group of elders awaiting his arrival.

When he reached the gathering place at the center of the village he called out a greeting at the entrance of the hide shelter. Upon acknowledgment, the tired seer parted the flap and entered the tepee.

The buffalo-skin shelter was dark and filled with smoke,

the only light coming from the embers of a coal bed glowing in the central hearth. The purifying smoke of cedar bough and the scent of sacred sage wafted in the thick, cloying smog.

The elders had been chanting and assisting the young spirit warrior on his journey to the other side for many moons now. They had known since the season of darkness (Winter Solstice, and the time of Wahweyho's last vision quest) that the vision of the Paiuteto holyman from the southeast lands who predicted that the unification of all souls from the spirit realm would join with their brothers on this plane through the ritual of the Circle Dance was manifesting. The calling forth of all nations was being fully realized, even as some tribes were still in conflict over the precise meaning of this vision.

Many wrongly sought to interpret Paiuteto's vision in the image of the gods and practices of individual and varied regions.

What the weary warrior foresaw in this vision quest was

also based on his own interpretations, biases and influences and he had thought long and hard about how to proceed with the story of what he had seen on his latest journey.

The young seer was casually trying to seek the eyes of his mentor and teacher, Red Hand. He was afraid that he had somehow read his vision wrong and needed the reassuring nod of his wizened guide. He could feel his teacher's life force in the crowded darkness giving him the affirmation to trust in himself.

Red Hand watched the young man, sensing his apprentice's self-doubt. He could see the weakness that the week-long fast had wrought upon the seer's sinewy body.

"The little teachers have taken him far this time," Red Hand thought, as he observed the weakened young man he held so dear to his heart.

The council had been afraid they were going to lose Wahweyho a few times on this journey, but the whispered chant for the homeward heart and the rhythmic pounding of the drum brought the warrior back to their realm of existence.

An elder shuffled his behind upon the buffalo pelts and gave a small "huff" to encourage the boy to begin his foretelling.

The young apprentice had never been wrong or misguided in interpreting his visions, even though the heaviness and fear of self-doubt still lingered. The gods spoke directly to the visionary, a heavy burden to bare.

Have faith my son, Red Hand emitted with the silent love of pride and encouragement toward his apprentice, shining his intent forward through his heart to the young brave. Wahweyho humbly began, "Tunkasila (duen-kah-shee-lah/Grandfather), I have come from the Cave of Light bearing the vision of our people's path and future. In my spirit quest I was visited by all representatives of the Twelve Nations, our ethereal bodies connected across the vast fields of dream-time.

In the mindlink with our brothers from the South, the traders

of the blue-feathered macaw, one came forward and spoke of

the wisdom in the stars and the whisperings of our Great

Mother. These builders of the vast mountain altars have spoken

that our time to unite is now. The universe calls forth our

awakening into unity.

"Tribes from the East, the ones that lay beneath the

spiral mounds, prepare for a famine of body and soul. They are

challenged in practicing the dance through their repression.

"The plague brought by the pale skin is aggressive and

their people are dwindling fast. Their ways are quickly being

buried in an attempt to save the Mother's knowledge before

their end is upon them.

"Our brothers, the Anasazi, Ancient Puebloans, Zuni

and Hopi, the keepers of the balanced core center, spoke of the

coming of the spotted illness and that of a deep hunger. A dark

cloud of treachery is upon them, and they too are hiding their teachings and dancing in the dark of night.

"To the North and the West, they follow our lead to lie low and live peacefully with the Mother. They are trying to dream away what is an eventual reality, as peace is strong in their hearts. They seek to protect their ancestral hunting grounds and their ways of culture but will join when the calling comes. They know that they too will be confined like animals in a pen to uninhabitable, plague-ridden ground and that life as they have known upon the Mother for eons is about to change."

The wise man, Red Hand, trembled as the boy's story unfolded. He was wearied beyond his years, old in heart beyond many cycles of Sister Moon. He was a seer, from an ancient lineage. He held the gift of power to communicate to all animals, great and small. His wisdom had been passed down from his ancestors since the beginning of time. A wisdom enhanced from communion with the plants of the field, their teachings and remedies. All those of his lineage were keepers of the Sacred Way. He knew the gods and their names, those from all the directions: North, South, East, West, above and below.

Red Hand knew as well, that there was much more to the story from beyond the foreseeable future and that of the unforeseen. For he too had journeyed to the other side and knew what his people faced.

The old man's vision and strength was failing now. His mind was no longer strong enough to continue the crossover through the portal, past the world of the dead and into that of creation. Red Hand had always known, as the stars had shown, that Wahweyho was the awakener whose arrival had been predicted by the Twelve Nations. This young, powerful soul would bring unity throughout vast lands with the wrath of the Mother incarnate by his side. Yet not in their time but in another. A time where the lands would have changed, and his people would have all but vanished.

The young traveler from the worlds beyond continued,

"Our ancestors are awakening as we speak due to their being called forth with the Circle Dance. Many of the seers, healers and wisemen agreed the time to dance in the new world is now. We, the people of the Sioux Nation, see no place for the takers.

"The tribes of our brothers from the South agree and are concerned as they have lived through the rape of their lands, the assault and murder of their people and culture, three centuries past. They barely survived long enough to hide their wisdom from the invaders. They advise we make haste in raising our power, without hesitation, before it is too late.

"I am afraid, my elders, that this separation from the varied interpretations of the holyman's vision will divide the power of the Dance from the unity necessary to fulfill the destiny of our path and the veil will not part for beyond a thousand years.

"Tunkasila, my elders, I wish to ask for guidance from my mentor, for all I have seen has left my heart weary. I have tried throughout my week-long sojourn, through my meditation and prayers, to grasp an understanding and find the direction of the course we must follow. I will need to gather strength from all our gods to ask for their assistance in keeping the portal open, as it waivers through this dissent among our brothers. I fear our people's chance of survival beyond the present and into the future is at stake!

Present

The sweet melodic sound of birdsong greeted the rising of Father Sun. Willow graciously rolled to her side and stretched her arms above her head, smiling to herself at the beautiful awakening of nature's song.

She decided to try and incorporate some form of discipline in her new routine as campground host. Structure was something that awoke a small rebelliousness in herself, so she would begin greeting the day gently with the yoga Sun Salutation asanas to try and quell her nature that lay in opposition to compliance.

She brushed and braided her long dark hair into the traditional braids of her ancestors, one falling down each side of her head. Willow shared the features of her grandmother, who was from the Iroquois Nation. A long, slender and regal nose and intense, close-set dark eyes. A mirror image of the healing woman she had never met, but one whose guiding presence she often felt.

Willow was raised in an orphanage until the age of four, after being taken away from her mother as an infant by social services. When she was adopted she took on the name of her new family, so any of her relations that knew of her existence could not find her due to privacy laws. As a young adult, she tried to trace her family and it was then that she discovered her mother's lineage.

Her mother was a drug addict who had purposely lost contact with her family, from Willow's understanding. She disappeared like thousands of other Native American women, lost in a system that didn't quite care enough. She was hidden in a file shelved away like many of the victims of drugs and violence that were deemed not worthy of society's time and money.

Willow was angry that women were made disposable, easily used for sexual gratification, then disposed of in North American society. Those of colour, more so.

The young woman felt that the women's rights movement of days gone by that had taken huge leaps and bounds forward had been pulled backward, due to the marketed solicitation of the feminine. Willow had decided long ago to drop out of a world that made a woman feel inadequate and undesirable if she did not wear high-heeled shoes and makeup. She was completely buried in a past she desired, one where the Goddess was recognized. Progress and technology were evil addictions of the ego in her mind.

Willow's father was a mystery, as he was marked as unknown on her birth record, but she knew he must have been white by the caramel colouring of her skin. When she finally found her mother's family, her grandmother had passed beyond to the other realm and there were no other relations alive that she could find. She was the last in her mother's lineage and her wise-woman grandmother had known this.

Her grandmother had left a gift behind for the granddaughter she had never met, yet somehow knew existed. An old hand-hewn cedar chest had been stored at an ancestral archival site of the Iroquois Nation and it held Willow's cherished family heirlooms. A book of ancient secret wisdom was hidden among the treasures of her culture, all of which had been secreted away for years awaiting Willow's discovery.

Stories of oral tradition had been written down in an old leather-bound diary, part of her inheritance from the wise-woman healer. Her grandmother spoke in the book of her responsibility to pass on her knowledge through her bloodline, from daughter to daughter. Since Willow's mother had been lost to the ways of the broken spirit, the responsibilities of the wise woman's teachings now fell upon Willow to embrace. The rituals of honour and respect, of how to follow and find one's path and direction along the web's weave, gave Willow faith in her destiny.

The old cedar chest held various sacred tools of power that were to be placed upon one's sacred altar to assist in journeying. There were intricate weavings and faded pictures of her ancestors, the long lineage of healers that came before her birth.

Willow threw cold water on her face from her water bottle and brushed her teeth. She placed her purple yoga mat upon the ground in a small clearing to the South of their site and began her affirmations facing the rising Sun in the East.

She recited a prayer in her mind: "All is as it should be. I am a radiant being filled with light and love. Everything I need is already within. I release all that no longer serves me to the universe. I am a servant of the light, fill me with your perfection. Blessed be." With this she evoked the spirits in unspoken prayer. A prayer said to self and Gaia for upliftment.

Brilliant sunbeams fell upon her face as they crested over the horizon, bathing her in healing light as she arched her back in the downward dog. The stretch felt amazing as her lower back released. She could feel the blessing of Father Sun caress her skin, the sensation of the warm liquid light of awareness pouring upon her brow seeping into her soul.

A cool gentle breeze blew down from the mountain tops and spoke in whispers, drawing Willow out of her reverie. She drew herself up from the position she had been in and listened intently. The birds were no longer singing. A deep profound silence had descended upon the surrounding grounds.

A raven swooped overhead, landing in a large cedar, the branches swayed gently upon its landing. Willow caught the eye of the coal-black bird and they fell into a hypnotic gaze, seeing each other, their true selves: her minuscule and him all knowing. In folklore, he carried a message of warning. The raven was known to be a trickster in the stories of creation, but he could be a friend as well.

"Well, Brother, what are you here to share? I am listening," said Willow.

The raven's eyes pierced into the depths of her soul. Willow shivered with apprehension as he relayed his message, he wanted her to pay attention with her intuition, to watch within the shadows at play.

She intuited that her grandmother had sent this bird as a friend and guide. He meant no harm. He was a bearer of the message to bring attention and be present. Her lessons were to begin, and her teachings would be utilized.

All this Willow absorbed in a form of trance, she had an almost out-of-body-experience type of knowing. She smiled in reverie and thanked the bird with a nod. "I think I shall give you a name," she said aloud. "How would Hermann the Harbinger be, since I believe you to be a prophesier of woes to come, my friend? Blessed be that you are sent from Grandmother Fading Dawn. I believe this to be so and so it is," she said with affirmation and a smile to herself.

The wind calmed, and the sound of nature's abundance renewed her with the calming elixir of life unbound.

Willow bent down and picked up her mat before returning to the small outdoor kitchen to prepare a breakfast of fresh fruit. She needed a strong black coffee; the morning had brought many surprises to her half-conscious dream state.

Willow felt secure that life was calling her forth along a predestined path. She had been preparing for many years to be called upon after discovering her ancestry. After opening the trunk she had been left from Grandmother Fading Dawn, she had discovered a responsibility to the heritage of her family's ancient wisdom. Purpose had been awakened in her.

Grandmother Fading Dawn had known from her messengers and guides that she had been gifted her long-awaited granddaughter. But the girl was kept hidden from her heritage for to be of Native descent was considered a disgrace in Canada.

Fading Dawn had decided to write down her wisdom, the rituals, prayers and chants to the Mother, even though it was forbidden by tribal law. The knowledge of the plant kingdom and the vital energy points for healing would be lost, if she had not written it down.

This child was the last in the line of the Red Path Way. All other healers of the lineage had been destroyed and the links of empowerment broken.

Young Willow had been her only choice, but the right one as she was chosen from the Mother herself to bring forth the awakening. The respected elder had been ostracized by the Tribal Council and eventually the reservation, because of her desire to share the sacred ways with a halfbreed not of their way.

Fading Dawn had tried in vain to share with the elders that in a vision she had been shown that this granddaughter of hers was the incarnate of White Buffalo Calf Woman. She would be the light force behind the coming of unity in the Lost Tribes. The old ways would become respected and revered once again, and the matriarchal society would become whole and one, as before.

When all was in alignment with the Sacred Mother the web of life would shimmer throughout all the worlds, a gossamer thread entwined between the realms to strengthen the whole.

The elders would not listen, and the sweet heartbroken wise woman died alone in a little sod-roofed cabin in the Kawartha Lake Region of Ontario.

Willow placed a pot of coffee to brew on the cook stove. The fragrant aroma drew Bob out of bed. It was 7am.

"Morning sunshine," Bob said, before he gave Willow a quick peck on the lips. "There is nothing like the smell of coffee in the morning!"

Willow poured and sweetened his brew, and they discussed their day.

First off, they needed to speak with their boss about this so-called murder and then proceed with the park cleanup as they had noticed quite a bit of trash left at and around the sites on their drive in, probably due to such a hasty retreat of campers.

After breakfast, Bob radioed the office and asked Carlos, the head honcho of the operation, about the scare from the long weekend.

Their boss, Carlos, was a short burly Italian. He guffawed boisterously over the radio at the Joseph's account of the situation. "Well that old fool is just trying to scare you! Yes, the police helicopters were called in. A waste of taxpayers' money, if you ask me! It was only a cougar. I am 100 percent sure. They can sound just like a woman screaming and scare the hell right out of you," he said. Carlos continued to reassure them, stating that they had rangers looking for the missing woman as they spoke. "No one should ever hike alone on these trails," he continued. "It isn't our fault if something happens to someone off-site. It is not our responsibility to monitor everyone in this park and it is impossible anyway! You just need to be responsible to post an alert if there are any bear or cougar sightings on the trails. Maybe you'd better go put up a cougar warning first thing, just to be on the safe side. There has also been a report of a three-year-old male grizzly a quarter of a kilometer up the river from the swinging bridge, on the Powder-Face Ridge Trail. This is the beginning of the most used trailhead into the backcountry, so you'd better put up the posts this morning before your rounds."

"Okay, Boss, I am just finishing my coffee and I will

get right on that. Out for now," replied Bob.

"Keep your radio on as I'll be checking in later. There will be a truckload of firewood heading your way. You will need to unload some bags at the check-in station and keep about 20 at your site to sell. I'll radio you sometime this afternoon. Carlos out."

"Well that is a relief," said Bob. "Where is that trailhead he is talking about anyway?"

Willow pulled out the park map and discovered that their site was just 100 yards from the trailhead. Maybe her uneasiness from the previous night was due to her instinct of danger with a grizzly being within close vicinity?

In truth, Willow had no real fear of bears after working one season in Alaska. She had stayed at a camp in the Clarke National Park, on the Cook Inlet, that observed the great bear. She had learned that the grizzly was called a brown bear if it lived within a certain range of rivers full of salmon. The brown bear was not as territorial.

Willow recalled the time when she had observed 26 female brown bears with their cubs suckling teat and pulling up roots of tall sedge grass in a vast green meadow. They reminded her of a herd of cattle. Her fear dissolved at the sight and beauty of the great and powerful sacred brother bear, at watching their majesty.

Willow learned from Dave, the guide, in his lecture upon an observation deck, that the herd was usually very calm unless a male came around looking to mate. The male grizzly would ruthlessly kill a cub just to bring a female back into heat.

She remembered how her guide swaggered with confidence, after years of experience with the bears, beaming

when he noticed her astute fascination. He had suggested
that in the morning they could take a hike to get a better view
of the females with their cubs. Dave mentioned how there
was a natural land bridge that became exposed when the tide
was out and how they could have a better view of the bears'
lair in the morning, a much better interaction than observing
from the lofty heights of the lookout they stood upon.

Willow excitedly agreed to the hike. At dawn, she and
a group of tourists gathered to head out and get a closer look.
Willow reminisced how the thick morning fog had slowly
began dissolving into fine wisps of wet moisture that chilled
the air.

The group of five tourists along with Dave, their guide,
headed out excitedly with their cameras in tow. There was a
local squatter at the camp, Johnny, whose pet border collie led
the troop frolicking playfully ahead of the sightseers followed
by three goats.

Willow retold the story the pilot on her flight in on the
bush plane had told her about how Johnny had come to
reside in such a pristine place. It appeared that he had been
the only permanent resident of the camp situated alongside
Chinitna Bay when it became a protected park. The
government could not legally reclaim the lands and remove
Johnny from his site, as he held squatter's rights dating back
to when he had made a gold claim some 50 years earlier.

The company Willow worked for had leased the
property from him for the bear observation camp, a lease
that had been a lifesaver for the old miner.

Willow remembered Johnny like it was yesterday. He
was a funny little man and the stereotypical image of a
hillbilly bush-whacker, just like someone one would imagine
from the Gold Rush era. He only had three yellow, tobacco-

stained and decayed teeth peeking out of a gummy smile that remained mostly hidden among the bristles of a couple of days' stubble growth. His greasy auburn hair was shoulder length and hidden under a well-worn, brown felt cowboy hat. Thin black suspenders held up faded and ripped Wrangler jeans over dirty grey long underwear and his pants were tucked into rolled down rubber boots.

Johnny lived with his animals in total isolation throughout the long dark Alaskan winters until the spring, when the tourists would begin to arrive. The only way off his land was via bush plane, an expense he could only afford with tourist dollars.

A half-century enduring extreme isolation and the many years of cabin fever had left Johnny a little strange in the end. His fortitude must have been incredible, Willow thought, to be able to endure alone for so many years. A great northern guru who preferred moonshine, goats and a dog to the foibles of his fellow man. Willow at times felt much the same, so her respect instantly ran deep for the crazy, old gold miner.

It appeared that all the tourists that ventured to his lands were as impressed by him as the grizzlies themselves, for they left him alone, most of the time.

The group had just finished slugging through the still muddy banks of the now exposed crossing, when the crew realized that trailing a few hundred yards behind the pack of goats was a momma brown and her three juvenile babes.

Dave was familiar with the family, as triplets were a very uncommon occurrence. This was the cubs' last year with the sow, and since they were now three years old, they were being trained to survive on their own. Mamma bear had not run them off yet.

"Perfect, we are all part of one big walking food train," thought Willow at that moment.

Dave instructed the group to stop and gather close together, as a young male from the trio began showing signs of being the curious sort. He was coming much too close for comfort, which was not a good sign as juveniles are very unpredictable. The group quickly gathered together.

Willow remembered how they had to haul one German tourist off his laurels when he continued to take pictures with his wide-angle lens apparently caught up in a National Geographic photo-op moment he could not resist.

Dave had straightened to his full height of five-foot-two-inches, thumbing the cool steel of his 45-caliber pistol held in its holster at his side for reassurance.

The young "juvi" male began swaying his head, sniffing the air, and huffing with an open mouth. A maw full of teeth was in full view as he began to lumber forward toward the tightly huddled group coming to a stop within a mere ten feet. He stood four feet at his front shoulder and appeared to weigh in at minimum of 300 pounds.

Dave began to wave his arms above his head and yell, as Willow and the rest of the group of tourists tightened their formation as instructed.

The bear was startled when Dave took a large, aggressive step toward him shouting aggressively. The brown jumped three feet back, turned tail and ran.

The mother, standing on a ridge farther back while observing her rowdy son, casually turned and followed her youth's path of retreat with the other cubs in tow.

A deep sigh of relief escaped the mouths of all present. No one had wanted to see the agent of death pulled from Dave's belt. He had reassured them that in his 17 years as a guide he had never needed to use his side-arm, it was there for precautionary measures only.

Willow and the others were in awe of the small man's bravery and intelligence. He did not overreact, despite the possibility of a "food chain" event. The group decided that the bear viewing had been plenty close enough. They happily decided to turn around and hike back to the safety of the electric-fenced enclosure of camp, just in case momma and the trio decided to change their minds.

Willow drew herself out of her reverie and back to the present. She found the warning sign for "Bear in Vicinity" from the official park folder and hand wrote one for the cougar as well.

After the signs were posted, Ranger Bob claimed, cleaned and marked his domain, while Willow planned where to set up her altar.

Bob was thrilled, hoping beyond hope, that he would get a sight of the beautiful and powerful beast, the grizzly. A beast that inspired bowels to loosen, honour among men, great vodka and was worshiped as a brother god by the Keepers of the Earth. "Shall we see if the great bear spirit will bless us with his presence, Willow?" Bob joked, as he trounced off with a twinkle of childlike innocence in his eyes, a pen and his poetry book to write in, his red beatnik shades in hand.

"It's always best to see the world through rose coloured glasses, and they help hide bloodshot eyes," he would often joke.

Bob tended to make funny little jabs at Willow's philosophies about animals and the Earth's living consciousness. They were things that he wanted to believe in. But being that he was younger than Willow, he had not yet found a need to satiate the empty vessel of self. He had the vision and faith of the young, as well as a tendency to find his awakening in a pill or bottle. That was sufficient at this point in his life, he did not seek or desire the depth it took to look beyond the ego and into the true self.

"I like to observe the grizzly from a safe distance, Bobby, as they can be a little unpredictable," Willow replied to his jibe. "We need to make sure we make lots of noise, so we don't startle the bear if it's around. This is their home, one that we should be asking them permission to share, not the other way around," she continued haughtily.

Willow's mind went off at warp speed as her inner ramblings continued, "It is not as if the animals can read the 'Do Not Cross This Line' boundary signs drawn up by the ever-expanding presence of man's quest and conquer attitude. I don't understand the need to invade and conquer all lands. Never have and never will." She always felt protective of the animals of the wild and an inner battle raged as to where one should draw the line between observation and the space to let life just be, left to unfold in peace.

"Thank God we can escape the rat race for a while. Wouldn't it be great to just spend one's life running campgrounds in the summer and working in a fly fishing camp down South in the winter? What a perfect existence, living in nature's bounty endlessly. Life is so good," said Willow as they reached the foot of the trailhead. Willow would try to find a positive perspective after one of her frustrated internal rants. It was a personality trait that made her seem a little mad.

Willow decided to take the lead to look for any telltale signs of the bear, such as tree markings, torn up roots or piles of jam-berry shit.

Ranger Bob was in Disney-fantasy mode, believing bears to be somewhat like a big dog, or the character Baloo from the Jungle Book. "Wow man, nature is awesome," said Bob in his other alter-ego, that of a surfer jock. He had the lingo down, he just lacked the physic of the buffed beach bum. The words were barely out of Bob's mouth before the joy was snatched from his improv act.

The couple stood in awe at the litter-strewn ground. Garbage was piled high, juice tetra packs, straw wrappers, and cellophane from cigarette packs were just a few things that lay among the debris. They felt sickened and saddened beyond belief that in a developed country such as Canada people still had the audacity to be so clearly unconscious and lazy as to not deal with their own refuse. And in a park? In nature protected for one's use? It was absolutely disgusting!

They had both seen a profusion of garbage in Mexico where environmental education lacked and the reality of no garbage pick-up men, or any laws or people to enforce penalties for polluting played a role. In Canada there really was no excuse for littering accept for that of truly not caring.

They had to walk on past the mark of man for the meantime as they did not think to bring garbage bags along. And the further they rambled along the trail, the more garbage they spotted. The smell was like that of a refuse pile, a sweet, cloying stench of rot drawing wildlife closer to the worst predator on the planet.

"Welcome to Parks Canada where we protect the land for you to enjoy?" Willow thought.

Toxic cigarette butts were everywhere, beer cans (nicely burned to ensure proper recycling) were piled in the bush along with mounds of ass-wipe, diapers, beer caps, gum wrappers, rope and twine. There were white plastic bags of the I'm-so-environmentally-conscious-I-will-pick-up-my-dog's-shit-and-put-it-in-a-plastic-bag kind, but they were left behind on the side of a trail, or, better yet, hanging from a tree where they could swat passing mountain bikers or hikers in the face.

Ranger Bob had his first case of hiker's rage. "How can people do this!" he screamed.

The tear in Willow's aching heart throbbed painfully. The tears she suppressed were hard to swallow past the well-formed lump in her throat.

"I'll head back and grab the company truck and some bags to clean up this mess, you put up the signs," said Bob when he noticed Willow's glistening eyes.

Willow nodded her head. Speaking was not an option at that moment.

It was obvious to her why the bear had wandered so close to the campground. The wide hiking trail created a nice path directly to the stink of man.

"Oh, Mother, please forgive those who forget that you are all and that we, your mere children, are blessed to walk upon your grace," she murmured aloud. She turned and looked up the trail to where Bob had just gone and noticed the crow observing her from the treetop.

"Hello, Hermann, my friend, maybe you are here to show me the ways of man. I am sorry that we have forgotten the teaching of gratitude. I promise I will return our Mother to beauty once again. If only on this small parcel I have been blessed to caretake."

The raven flew up from his perch and began to caw and circle ahead in the distance where a small overgrown trail led up the mountainside to a plateau. Willow noticed that the Sun seemed to penetrate the mountainside where Hermann flew, almost as if it was lit from within. She put down the signs and followed to where the bird directed. Willow realized shortly after commencing that the path she was bushwhacking through was probably an animal trail and her thoughts wandered back in time.

Once, in Mexico, she and Bob had decided to take a shortcut through a mangrove swamp to find the one road leading to the closest village, which was five miles away. Bob had assured Willow when they headed out that he knew the trail and there was no way they could get lost.

Three hours later, after following numerous animal paths deeper and deeper into what seemed like an entrance to hell, Bob began yelling at Willow to get them the hell out of the swamp they were in. "Christ, you're a Canadian bush woman, you should be able to find our way out!"

Willow was frustrated and had already searched to see what side the moss grew on the trees, which she remembered from Girl Guides was on the North side, the moistest side, but moss surrounded the whole tree. They were also surrounded by water, crocodiles and the poisonous chechen tree! She decided the only way to figure out where they were would be to climb a tree. When she reached the top, she could only see the mangrove swamp stretching on for an eternity. Father Sun sat directly overhead and had taken a path they had not been observing.

Willow came down from her perch and listened to the sound of a vehicle, the engine noise barely reaching them. Few cars passed through the treacherous beach road to the small Mayan fishing village. She could not decipher where the sound came from. In a moment of despair Willow just sat down and prayed for guidance. She could hear the ocean. The sound of her gentle waves rhythmically caressing the shore called to her above the mangrove's cacophony. The womb's waters would lead them home.

With that experience behind her Willow decided to trust the bird and her ability not to get lost, moss grew on the North side of trees in Canada after all. She continued following the bird's flight until she reached the plateau. The Sun's light splayed in iridescent rays and reflected off a piece of glass, or something, in an open clearing just ahead. The beams of light were coming from within what appeared to be the entrance to a cave. Its dark opening was hidden among a flurry of bracken fern.

The Cave of Vision

Past

Wahweyho sat in silent contemplation upon a bed of warm pelts awaiting Red Hand. The fire in the center of his teepee had been kept burning in respect for his journeying to the beyond: an enticement meant to lure his spirit home from the other realm. "Red Hand will help me understand the variations of the messages I've retained from this journey into the dream world in the Cave of Light," thought the seer.

Red Hand's twisted, weary body limped across the village square, an ancient oak branch supported his gait with its strength. The old man's eyesight was feeble due to thickening cataracts from his many moons in the darkness of smoke-filled caves.

Those who were not busy working at the tasks at hand cleared a path for the elder to pass: a sign of respect in the Native culture.

The wizened healer felt as ancient as the trees that surrounded the small band of Stoney Indian, Sioux. Their people had always been nomadic, following animal migration patterns and nature's bounty of fruit and greens, since the time of memory; until the white man came.

The more the rights of the brothers of the Indian Nation were infringed upon, the more the old man lived within the world of his visions, on the other side.

It was hard for him to stay present and be in his body when one had to live within the restraint of borders and laws that buried the Mother under a mountain of disrespect.

The wise man was called often to stay within the web, for he needed to rest his soul. His guides bespoke of his future path on the other side and his need to gather strength and allies in preparation to help Wahweyho when the time came, a world away from now.

The flap parted, and Red Hand stepped into the teepee, fragrant sweetgrass blessing him with its sacredness. He smiled with fondness, as the plant was favored by his young apprentice. The old man always knew of his apprentice's approach from the sweet smell that accompanied him.

Red Hand knelt at the feet of his apprentice awaiting his words, the last of his story while still a human being, a two legged on this plane.

Wahweyho spoke in a hushed tone, "Tunkasila, I am afraid that I have not been able to come back whole and intact this time. I have left much of my being behind with our ancestors and brothers. Many others who have passed through the portal are choosing to stay where endless herds of pte (buffalo) roam free; where abundance pours forth, as crystal waters from the great fall. The worlds beyond the living are losing definition. The brothers say that we need to build a path of light to keep the gates open for all the Mother's children to unite." The brave visionary continued, shaken and weak from he had experienced, "I do not understand all I have seen. I journeyed to the cosmic circle and entered the center. I sat as if upon a mountain top, with a bird's eye view of what was to come and what is unseen yet manifesting. I did not want to share all of the visions from the quest with the council grandfather, and my heart is heavy with the unspoken truth," said the young seer.

"My son, do not doubt what you have been shown, for you have been blessed with the honour to light the Red Path's Way," replied Red Hand. "As you have seen, Wahweyho, the web is torn and fragile. The dancing of the Circle Dance for five consecutive days to raise the Mother's vibration and unite all with our ancestors will never blossom forth, not in this lifetime, nor the next."

"A new cycle began my son when those with the pale skin came across the great universal waters. There are those of this race that speak with a forked tongue and have yet a paler, green skin. They know and fear the power our healers possess. They have been diminishing their own people's light for hundreds of years, by murdering those that remembered the Earth's magic; horrors even beyond what the foreigners have done to us my son" spoke the shaman, Red Hand, to the seer.

"We, as well as they, have continued to face the

annihilation of our holy people through the killing of the wise ones this passing season. The pale ones have lost their way and their teachings thousands of seasons past; just as we will lose ours. But we shall return!" stated Red Hand.

Wahweyho stared off into space, into the other realm. He was revisiting the vision where a troop of blue coats slaughtered a whole tribe of Sioux, half-starved women and children lying upon the blood covered ground. They had just celebrated the Winter Solstice, eight days past, and were planning to continue praising the Mother with the Circle Dance. They danced to help bring about the peace and beauty in abundance the vision had promised and ecstasy in the awakening to come.

The horror of the killing broke the link of power within the movement, just as the cold-hearted lizard men, Red Hand spoke of, had planned.

Wahweyho's eyes began to tear as he saw the coming

rape of the Indian Nation. Their loss of council with the Goddess and the breaking of spirit. The locking up of children, the claim of ownership upon the Sacred Mother leading to a plague of dead and brokenhearted people. The genocide of his nation's people.

The seer knew he would die soon, even though he was just in his fourth cycle of seven, at the peak of his strength. The recent journey upon the web's matrix was the last chance for the Twelve Nation's seers to connect and take council across realms.

The veil was thickening in an attempt to correct a tear upon the intricate web of life. All portals were being closed; caves and entryways were made hidden and sacred knowledge buried until the coming of White Buffalo Calf Woman.

Her coming would portend that the time of awakening was upon all nations and unity with the Mother would shift into a new consciousness of love, respect, gratitude and peace.

"Tunkasila, I am wearied and broken by the vision of our people's demise. I have seen that we will return only after many cycles of seven, past the counting of three hands plus three, only then will the opportunity arise to re-open what we, and all nations, have hidden. This is the time of my great confusion Grandfather, when my vision from this quest becomes unclear. "I enter a period of time far ahead, beyond all our lives. A time when the white pte calves are born in great number. But White Buffalo Calf Woman does not come forth, for our people are still broken and they no longer believe in the Dance of Awakening.

"I knelt at the feet of Wakan Tanka (Great Spirit) and he spoke of my need to cross over from the plane of the ancestors back to that of the Sacred Mother at a time when the Crystal Cave of Light is reopened. Through the fields of time and the mist of manifestation I can barely see my path through the fog of the web. There seems to be a silhouette of the Wiyan

Wakan (Holy Spirit) and she stands holding the wicapasaca (wee-chah-pah-shah-chah, meaning buffalo skull) high above her head. It is composed of a thousand tiny crystals reflecting a great light that blinds me so I cannot see beyond and into the outcome," said Wahweyho

"What is it you need me to help clarify, my son?" asked Red Hand.

"As I have spoken of from the vision, Grandfather, many holy brothers stay on the other side. The web thickens, and spirit easily gets lost in the delight of that life never to return without enticement. You know how weakened the spirit becomes for soul travel after a lengthy time upon the other realms of dimension, my honoured teacher. I do not see how I can sustain power for the return the Father asks of me, nor how I can help in the ethereal form I shall become. How will I find my way back to the Crystal Cave without the Tribal Council's guidance to call my spirit back home?" Wahweyho continued after a pause, "I am afraid that I am not strong enough to hold the field's weakening vibration and retain my life force long enough to cross the veil alone when I am called. I am afraid I am not worthy enough to be a servant of Wakan Tanka," choked the young man through tears of exhaustion.

"My son, you will not be alone," spoke Red Hand. "Although the nation of our brothers will fall there will still be those that will retain the teachings and hold the sacredness of the Mother in esteem. There is to be a testing of spirit on this realm as well, my son, and many, many lessons will need to be learned. Our Mother will suffer greatly before she completes another full circle of life, and she too will be reborn, as will her children, as will all creatures great and small, as will you, Wahweyho, with my help." The healer placed the palms of both his hands upon the energy centers of the Wahweyho's forearms and rested his head upon the questing warrior's brow. He began a low guttural chant from deep within his throat, calling upon Earth and Great Spirit, animal totems and guides until the young man's body relaxed and he fell safely into the dreamtime.

Red Hand stood, and while cursing his legs and age he began to gather herbs to throw in the deerskin bladder that lay beside the fire's dying embers. He whistled to the raven that hid in the rafters among the drying medicinal plants.

The sleek, black trickster "ka-cawed" in rebuke, as he flew down to perch upon the old man's shoulder.

"Quiet, the chosen one is at rest. I don't want your squawking to enter his dream. I've put him in the realm of darkness for rest; his soul body is very heavy. I need to prepare a recovery broth and begin an elixir for the journey to the end world. Bring me the pouch that contains the serpent vine and chacruna leaves from my brother, the shaman that inhabits the lush, green jungle of the great winding river tribes of the far South. It will take three days to prepare the elixir and all must be ready for the rising of the Wesak Full Moon, the time when the peonies shed. This is the time when she, the Great Mother, illuminates rebirth and opens the door to the twelfth crown chakra. A time that will allow the spirit to stay intact when it leaves that of the human being," commanded the holyman.

The raven did as he was asked and gathered the embroidered cloth bag in his beak. He knew the demands put upon Red Hand from the gods would kill the old man for the raven saw all, through all the realms, and through all of time.

A fine tentacle thread—a mindlink with the essence—allowed the raven to continue to be a messenger for time eternal, a harbinger of woe and a bringer of dark night and dawn.

Present

Willow, slightly winded, perused her surroundings. The
prickly heat of electricity filled the air with the scent of ozone.
The wondrous spectacle of Hermann in flight, soaring
directly above, verified that she had reached the place of
beckoning.

He swooped down and rested upon a cedar bough and
began to nod what seemed like an affirmation.

Willow was in awe at the beauty of the small opening
that lay among grandiose cedar and fir trees. The vista
beyond the trees oversaw Sheep River, a small tributary of
the larger Elbow River. She had a sense of being transported
back in time to when the Great Mother was untouched by
greed and exploitation, free of the footprint of man, free of
those who had forgotten to walk softly upon her beauty with
grace, gratitude and consciousness. The scent of vibrancy
filled her nostrils, blossoming forth life and singing the birth
of spring. She breathed in deeply and stood in wonder while

her eyes devoured this Eden.

Willow began to turn in a small circle within the center of the opening, noticing how the fern-covered cave was facing directly East into the sunlight. Sun rays were reflected in a plethora of blinding rainbow hues that bounced off something brilliant hidden within the cave. "I wonder what is causing that light?" thought the lithe adventurer as she headed directly toward it and pulled back the plant matter that blocked the cave's entrance.

"Wow, magnificent! I can't believe it. Look at the beauty within your womb, Mother!" exclaimed Willow, as she ducked her head and entered what appeared to be a cave made entirely of crystal stalactites. Her heart began to thump heavily, and her breath came in short gasps as dizziness overcame her. "Woah, I need to lay down," she thought. "In and out, follow the breath, the stomach rising gently with every breath in; the breath out, slower and longer," she mouthed the words silently in a meditation of presence.

She laid still on the ground, her ebony hair flowing in a fan about her head and her hazel eyes turning the green of a mountain lake. She could feel a throbbing deep within the Earth, their heartbeats becoming one with every breath. "Oh, blessed Mother, thank you for your existence. I have missed you," murmured the young woman. She caressed the red, sandy dirt she lay upon, letting the fine texture pour through her fingers. Willow felt like she had found her awakening, finally, in her 27th year. "I have been guided here, so it seems. I shall build my grandmother's altar at the foot of your entrance and I will honour the sacredness of this path you guide me upon," stated Willow.

Finally feeling grounded, she opened her eyes to stare into the cave's natural luminosity. In the far recesses she could see what must have been the markings from a fire as a coal-black mark was seared upon the roof.

She rose slowly from the hard surface. Standing fully erect she could just reach her fingertips to the highest points of the natural quartz ceiling—a chandelier encrusted upon the dark night of the cave. The width was double the height, about 14 feet across, with what looked like smaller crevices in the North and South corners.

To the right of the hearth she could hear the trickling of water, which added a cool, fresh smell to the musty space. She ran her hand along the walls feeling for moisture. When she found it, she squatted and followed the source into a natural alcove where crystal waters pooled. Cupping a portion of life's sweet elixir into her palms she drank and baptized her face. The smell of sweetgrass clung to Willow's fingers as she ran them over the markings surrounding the ancient earthen hearth.

"I can see you have been a place of honour before. Wise men and woman would come here to this sacred center for a spirit quest in days past," she thought. She knew this region had been home to the Stoney Indians, a relation of the Sioux, before they were put in reserves and park boundaries were designed and implemented years later. "Broken promises made once again in the tradition of government and her men," Willow mused. "How could such an obviously ancient site of worship lay hidden and forgotten all these years?"

The cave held a natural luminosity and as Willow's eyes adjusted, she noticed the rise of a small mound. There appeared to be something buried within it.

The mound was surrounded by etchings and dried herbs that lay among the remains of old nests and vermin feces. She reached her hands down and began smoothing away the dirt of the rise. She soon discovered a bundle and gently began dusting away years of the Earth's passing remnants. An old leather hide lay beneath. It was bleached white and tied with a worn leather thong. She blew across the delicate relic and a fine white ash took to the air, swirling into a dancing cloud of various formations. The hide reminded her of the sacred bundle her grandmother had left for her: a bundle for spiritual relics and tools.

"Willow, where are you?" Ranger Bob's voice drifted up from the trail.

Willow jumped, almost dropping the ancient bundle. She gently put it down, deciding to leave it where she had found it and turned to exit the cave. She looked behind her into the dancing pixels of light and particles. She decided she would keep the location and her findings to herself. This could be her place of refuge, her place of discovering and implementing the teachings of her grandmother's diary.

"I'm coming!" Willow shouted, as she ran down the twisted trail away from the mysterious cave.

"What are you doing? I left the truck parked up at the trailhead. Hurry and help me pick up this garbage. Then we can go and meet the boss and unload the firewood. He radioed me and said they would be up here in an hour," said Bob.

"I was just wandering around checking out some trails," she said as she popped out of the forest behind him.

The young couple ran along the trail gathering the garbage that lay about. They filled two bags within minutes and then they ran back to the entrance of the hiking trail.

"Okay, we better get to the truck, Bobby, where did you park? I thought you said you parked at the trailhead?"

asked Willow.

"I did. Damn, someone must have stolen the company truck!" cried Bob. "I know I left it here." He pulled the camouflage bandanna from his head and wiped the forming beads of sweat from his brow.

They both stood on the road and looked for the truck. Eventually they spotted it only a short distance down the campground road in a ditch. The blue Toyota truck was embedded in the trunk of a trembling aspen.

Bob dropped his bag and ran ahead. When he reached the truck, he peered into the cab expecting to find the culprit. But, it was he, himself, for he had forgotten to set the brake or leave the truck in gear. When he yelled the reasoning back to Willow she could not help but laugh hysterically at his cursing and frantic antics making the matter worse.

"Thank God the tree isn't damaged," said Willow, once the giggling subsided.

"Fuck the tree. If it wasn't there the truck would have just rolled to a stop. What's the boss going to say!" cried Bob.

"It's not the tree's fault, Bobby. Let's just get her back on the road and explain what happened. It was an accident and there's nothing we can do about it now," said Willow calmly.

Willow and Ranger Bob jumped into the truck. Ranger Bob put the truck in four-wheel drive and skidded his way back up the road in reverse.

They drove the four loops, section A through E, and met up with Carlos at the entrance of the Elbow Valley Campground, "our new home," thought Willow. "That is, as long as they weren't canned immediately!"

The boss and another man sat parked in a one-ton truck that had a Kananaskis Park logo on the side. They were in front of the chain-link fenced woodshed, waiting patiently while they both puffed on cigarettes.

Bob pulled up beside the registration booth that sat behind and to the side of the woodshed and they both jumped out as the truck rolled to a stop. The booth also served as a small store, carrying brochures and essentials like cigarettes, pop, junk food, ice, matches, lighter fluid, cheap rain gear and marshmallows.

Bob stood nervously, rolling his headband between his hands about to mouth an explanation for the dent in the bumper. He was prepared for a blast, thinking the look of shock on the little Italian boss's face was due to the sight of the damage to the truck.

Carlos yelled, "Get out of the way!" Bobby looked over his shoulder and quickly jumped to the side of the road, as the truck went rolling by, driverless again.

Ranger Bob ran hell bent for leather desperately trying to reach through the driver's side window to pull open the door and jump in so he could throw on the hand brake as the truck rolled toward another ditch.

"I take it that is what happened to the bumper?" said Carlos to Willow.

She nodded, her face beet red from trying not to laugh aloud at the Charlie-Chaplin-like spectacle.

The group unloaded 150 bags of firewood to sell on the upcoming weekend, keeping 20 in the back of the truck for on-site sales. Carlos instructed Willow that she would be the one delivering wood and left. Bob was permanently banned from driving the ground's truck, which infuriated him.

"I'm sorry that you are not able to bomb around with the truck, babe, you can use the Nissan Sentra. It might be a shitbox, but it is good enough for around here and we won't even need to register and insure it if we don't leave the grounds," Willow said.

"I'll look ridiculous driving around in that. I'm supposed to be a park official. How can I get any respect in that shitbox?" he shouted back.

"Well sorry, Bobby, it is not my decision. What did you expect? You were the one that didn't engage the brake, twice! There is over a thousand dollars in damage to the front end of the truck. You should be happy they are not taking this out of our wages!" she responded in defense.

"Yeah, well you are so fuckin' perfect, aren't you? Of course, *you* would never have made that mistake!" He carried on, stomping around, "Don't say a fuckin' thing to me. I'm going to check and clean the sites, alone!" He stormed off with a couple garbage bags stuffed in the band of his tights.

"Well, here we go again," thought Willow breathing through the painful welling in her heart. The two had been cycling through bouts of frustration with each other for months now. She had known for a while that they would not make it. There seemed to be some sort of hatred or frustration that Bob directed at Willow, possibly due to her confidence and ability in nature, which exceeded the young Englishman's.

Maybe it was due to her independence, her inability to be needy or needed without becoming resentful and her tendency to shut down when confronted. People are complicated. She had learned a long time ago that in the end there is only self and one's path in the universe and lessons, lessons, lessons.

"Walk the talk," was the path Willow tried to follow. If you wanted to live on the land, go live in the bush. If you want to be self-sufficient, learn to live in harmony with the land. All was written in the scrawled words of Grandmother Fading Dawn's diaries, her Red Path Way teachings. She was on the path of the warrior to maximize her human potential. The gods directed that path: growth from childhood to adulthood, ignorance to wisdom, irresponsibility to responsibility, arrogance to humility, fragmentation to wholeness.

Willow found her place of center recalling the teachings of Black Elk, who said: "The first peace, which is the most important, is that which comes within the souls of people when they realize their relationship, their oneness with the universe and all its powers. Then when they realize that at the center of the universe dwells the Great Spirit, and that this center is really everywhere, it is within each of us."

"Okay, let go and move on," she coached herself. "I should have stayed in that place of silence instead of speaking," she thought. "Oh well, I spoke the truth," her mind blathered on in defiance. "Stop it! Think positive. I am going to focus on the cave and setting up the altar, it's perfect that Bob is gone and hopefully it will be for a few hours," she huffed.

Willow drove back to the site with Van Morrison easing her back into the mystic.

Old Joe was at his site across the way splitting wood when he noticed the young woman pull into her camp. "That couple sure are an interesting pair? I bet that young buck will be high-tailin' it out of here before the blossoms fall. The girl, however, she has some fire in her, she'll stick it out," he thought to himself.

Willow waved to the old speaker of high-tales thinking: "I wonder what he knows about the history of this region. I think I'll go talk to him to see what he has to say, what stories he can weave."

"Afternoon, young lady. How was your evening? Did you happen to get the chance to talk to that boss of yours about those screams the other night?" questioned Joe.

"Well, it seems that it was all a misunderstanding and the official story is that it was a cougar that created all the noise, supposedly they are said to sound like a woman screaming when they get going. Carlos said, there is no missing woman. The lady mentioned in the papers is on a five-day hike along the Nihahi Ridge, and not due to check in 'til tomorrow. The Rangers are verifying where she is now," responded Willow.

"Everybody overreacted, I guess," said the old Native, who was smiling at Willow. "Though, I know the sound of a cougar, and I believe it was just not quite the same. There was somethin' not right about that sound. Somethin' unnatural about it; it sounded more like the screaming and yowling of a banshee spirit," he continued.

"Are you originally from around here, Joe?" asked Willow, changing the subject.

"Yes, I am, my dear, and my forefathers before me. I am from the Stoney Tribe. My people were placed in the reserves around here. I follow the nomadic ways of my ancestors and stay here, in the woods, where my spirit is at home," said the proud and stoic man.

"Well I am very, honoured to meet you, Joe. I have always had remorse for the way governments have treated the Natives of this nation, and of all nations, for that matter. It is disgraceful! I really wish that someday we will all awaken, and listen once again, to the simple wisdom and wise teachings your people have shared. It is such a sad story, one whose truth is still not taught in schools. We have so much to relearn," said Willow.

"True, daughter, but here we are. And the circle of life continues," replied Joe.

"Do you know anything about the opening in the forest with a cave, just above the Powder-Face Ridge? I discovered it this morning."

Joe's dark, leather-skinned face turned pale. "She saw it! She discovered what is hidden. Is she the one he's been waiting for, they've been waiting for?" he questioned himself. "How did you find this place?" the old man asked cautiously.

"Well, I know that this is going to sound strange, but I was led there by following the call of a raven. I believe he was sent from my grandmother, who is of Native descent as well." Willow had decided to try and justify some of her heartfelt mysticism to the old man, to try and gain her perceived loss of respect, due to her paler skin.

It was well known to her that the Native people were not very accepting of the whites, with good cause, nor were the whites of them, with no cause. All was lost to racism in this life, even for those with mixed blood, something almost all share if one chooses to explore their ancestry.

Willow continued with her tale after her bout of insecurity. "The raven kept circling above the trail, drawing me to the clearing, and I saw the cave's darkened entrance illuminated by something glittering in the sunlight. It beckoned me in," she said.

"A raven you say, do ya? What tribe was your grandmother from?" queried the cautious guardian.

"She was of the Iroquois Tribe, from the Great Lake

Region. I never had the honour of meeting her, but she has passed on her knowledge in spirit and writings," Willow said in solemn respect.

Old Joe harrumphed and rubbed his chin while he thought, "Well, I never expected a halfbreed to be the bringer of the awakening, but the signs are here, they appeared long ago at the beginning of the fourth age. I have been waiting for what seems like an eternity, since the discovery of the crystallized buffalo skulls at Uluru, Ayer's Rock, in Australia. The last in the cycle of the prophecy has finally come to manifest."

Joe narrowed his gaze, squinting through rheumy eyes to see through the veil, and there the young woman's essence stood in the glory of a golden, luminous light. The spirit she would become opened her arms, as the Madonna in recognition, with a dazzling smile and a nod; it was the affirmation he needed to embrace the girl.

He was honoured that he was the one out of a long line of guardians to be granted the grace to assist in the opening of the Crystal Cave of Light, the last of the twelve portals.

The girl did not seem fully aware of her purpose, for the adornment of her shroud was still ethereal. "I will have to walk gently with the teaching ways to ensure the novice is prepared for her journey along the red road to the center of the lost realms and back again. She must be prepared to secure the knot in time upon the sacred web; one that shall unite all nations and all people across all the universes," the Native elder surmised to himself.

"Yes, I know of the Crystal Cave of Light. It is held in high esteem as a sacred space among my people. The dwelling is a journey cave and I am the guardian. It is one of many sacred sites that we have hidden since our people began to lose our ancestral grounds.

"The cave is the portal to a vortex that has been hidden throughout the mists of time by a thin veil. One that you have clearly been chosen to see through and into the beyond. I have been waiting here, living at this campground, to guard the cave since I was a youth. I have the great honour of preparing you for your journey, before parting the sheer curtain between worlds," Joe said in reverence.

Willow swallowed and lowered her head, "I am so sorry, Joe. I already went inside and looked around, but I left everything where it was. I could not help myself. I was curious where the reflection was coming from. It was just so beautiful."

"That is fine, little sparrow, for the Crystal Cave would not have shown you her light without you being ready to see it," said her new-found guide. "We will start the proceedings from the beginning, as has been foretold from the tales of old, since the time of my great-great-grandfather, Red Hand. He hails, as do I, from a linage of seers that have joined in an oath of protection. guardians of the path to freedom and the awakening of our people. You are the Way, little lady. And I am here to be the strength in your limbs, young Willow, to help you reach into the beyond and bring about the shift. But, I must admit," he continued after a pause, "I thought the chosen one would have been a full-blood. Oh well, only the great ones know the reasoning of her ways."

"I am honoured, Joe, that you feel I am involved in some form of destiny that will help bring about equality and recognition for Native teachings. I have always believed that the lost religion of the Keepers of the Earth has been the demise of mankind, and the slow death of consciousness. My heart has been heavy ever since I was a child. I have always tried to beautify the path I walk upon, at times that being the only peace I've ever found."

"Tell me of your grandmother's teachings. What your soul sings. Then we can decide how best to proceed. Time is short, for the full Moon is almost upon us. The luminosity of Sister Moon will light the path to be taken," added Joe. "Where is that young man of yours, has he seen the cave?"

Old Joe sighed with relief, when Willow stated that he had not.

Something within her knew not to divulge what she had discovered to Bobby. She felt the cave's desire to be kept a secret, for its sacredness to be held close at heart.

"I have an old wooden chest that contains all Grandmother Fading Dawn's words of wisdom. Come over and I will show you her diary, so you can see what I have learned through her written words. I have practiced all the ways entailed: all the rituals of respect. I have prayed, and I bow down daily in reverence to all things great and small. I know of my minute place in the universe and the fragility of the web of life since the breaking of unity in the Circle Dance and the movement was destroyed," said Willow.

Joe and the young woman chosen to awaken the lost ways walked across the dirt road to Willow's site, a luminous glow embracing them through layers beyond the seen.

Willow pulled the old cedar chest from its home under the bed in the back of the van. Joe sat back as she opened the fragrant little chest and his eyes fell upon a sacred bundle. He now knew beyond a doubt that the young woman came from the highest lineage of healers and seers. A buffalo symbol was stitched in seed beads upon a bleached, white buckskin, it was the surest sign of her heritage.

She was the one who would be called to manifest into White Buffalo Calf Woman. A tear of joy came to his eyes in reverence for the young woman that stood before him, her path and the finality of the outcome of what was to be.

"I honour your grandmother for her wisdom in knowing what lay hidden in you, Willow. We will begin by preparing the site for a sweat. Hold fast to what your grandmother has left you—her wisdom and her teachings. I can see her power was great, and you will need all her tools for your journey. We do not have much time, only three days before the Wesak Moon and I have much to prepare."

Willow grabbed her backpack and quickly placed the makings for her altar inside along with the sacred bundle, sage and sweetgrass. She hastily packed matches for lighting and evoking the element of fire. A vessel was brought for water and her crystals for honouring the Earth. An eagle feather, for what blows in creation's thought, was laid gently upon the top of her sack before its contents were secured.

"I have a few hours to spare before I expect Bob to return. And then we will need to find a way for me to explain my time away from work, as it will be hard to hide this from him," said Willow.

Joe just gave a solemn nod, but within his mind he was making a list of preparations needed to call forth the four leggeds and close the camp once and for all.

"They could not be interrupted once the ritual for opening the vortex began. Nothing would stop the awakening of the Red Path Way. Not this time. Not ever again! We shall call forth the cougar, great bear, wolf and coyote. The banshee spirit's call to rise will ride upon the wings of spring winds once again," thought the seer, strong in his resolve.

He felt foolish, for not recognizing the animals' call the

previous week; the call that brought their long-awaited Goddess home to bring about the shift.

The Journey

Past

The raven flew down to perch upon Red Hand's shoulder as he prayed over the blending of the chacruna leaves into the serpent vine decoction. This was day three in the preparation of the medicine used to help one's journey to the land of the dead.

As the brew neared completion, the wise man grabbed his walking stick and prepared to seek the "little friend."

The plant would strengthen Wahweyho's ability to keep his spirit intact upon the web, and through the Underworld. The healer would need to harvest the fresh, red flower that grew forth from the patties of pte to feed the young seer while in trance. It would help the brave hold fast upon the serpent's back and to ride it back again when the time came. After the purging of worlds was complete the next level would begin.

The delicate mushroom flowers Red Hand sought were once abundant. The gift was a blessing used for the return of spirit that kept the Red Path Way upon the web intact. The sacred fungi were becoming diminished due to the slaughter of the buffalo by the alien invaders. The power of the great animal's entity was energetically transferred into the medicinal aid and was the only ally the great nations had left to protect and strengthen the web's weave, which was their duty upon this plane.

The lizard people, those that retained the reptilian mind, knew of the power inherent in the sacred medicines. They were doing all in their power to break this link of knowledge, to thin the delicate, ethereal web of time and to kill those that walked upon the fragile thread that linked worlds, upon worlds.

Wahweyho had recovered from the previous quest after sleeping through a rising and setting of Father Sun.

He was famished upon his awakening but knew to feed his lean, muscular body only fresh fish, greens of the field and water from the clearest spring. His next journey, his last journey, was about to commence with the rising of the full Moon the next evening.

Wahweyho walked through the village in reverence, gently touching all that he came upon with impassioned eyes. He knew that he had to remember the sacred beauty of this realm, his people, the quest and his path home.

When the Sun cast rainbow hues of pastel pink with the red of blood upon the foothills, the two men of the sacred teachings set out on the Elbow River and onto the tributary that led to the Cave of Light.

The hand-hewn dugout canoe was shoved off by the last of the Native braves to grace the land as free empowered men. They had protected with their lives and freedom the Way from the infringement of the white man for as long as they could. Their genocide was near complete.

The tribe was being forced into yet another treaty. The

new treaty broke their present reserve into five smaller ones and claimed ownership of the lands that housed their sacred grounds: that of the Crystal Cave of Journey.

Red Hand was solemn as he said goodbye to his wife, Snow Flower, and took his son in hand. The young boy had not had his naming ceremony yet. Names were not relevant, as his lineage was intact. The boy still wore the smear of his father's blood from the crown of his center and down his forehead, representing the division of sides. He had become two—child and man—but one with his father and destiny as a guardian of the gateway. As would his son be and his son's son after that, beyond time until the prophecy was fulfilled.

Neither of the men spoke through the winding river's course. Both focused on the shimmering, emerald-green abundance of the Mother.

They sat in the contemplation of profound gratitude, the canoe seeming to guide itself intuitively upon the current. They floated quietly onto the gentle inviting waters of the Sheep River, scents of ozone-fresh, birthing life wafted on the cool breeze.

When they reached the path access Wahweyho jumped upon the bank, with the agility and stealth of the mountain lion, and pulled the dugout into the shrubs.

"Woah boy, let us take our time to walk gently upon the Mother, so we can feel her heartbeat beneath our feet." Red Hand paused and then continued, "Let us feel the harmony in the rhythm of our unity. As you have seen in vision my son, this will be your last journey, the one of no return for a long while. You will need to preserve all you have seen, all you have learned, from this time upon the web. You will need to lie in wait of patient embrace, until the time when the door shall re-open through the call and beckoning of White Buffalo Calf Woman," said Red Hand. "And little does he know, my last journey as well," thought the tired, old guardian.

Wahweyho smiled at the old man whom he looked upon as his father.

The young man had been abandoned on a mountain top after the death of his mother at birth. He was found by Red Hand, swaddled in a fresh pelt of pte, the warm membranes of blood keeping the infant alive.

Through the cold of evening's frosty breath and the dangers of hungry forest dwellers, the child lay protected between the horns of a crystallized pte skull, his keeper.

Snow Flower, Red Hand's wife, embraced the babe as son when he was brought home by her seer husband. And as soon as the child could toddle about, he was apprenticing alongside the shaman.

Red Hand remembered the discovery of the child. He had been searching for the web-walker over mountain tops for days. When he found the boy, he fed him the milk of the great roaming buffalo. Snow Flower later sun bleached the hide the boy was wrapped in a brilliant white, as instructed from guides beyond.

The shaman had known for many cycles of Sister Moon the path that the young, noble man would be called upon to walk; his destiny and place in the web was one whose calling could not go unheard.

Wahweyho did not know about his mountaintop discovery.

When the warrior mentioned the dream-story of the crystal skull any doubts the old man had held about his interpretations of his own vision quests were dissolved.

Red Hand's strength wavered at the task of the duties to follow, duties he did not relish. The taking of his own life meant nothing to him, for his crippled body sought rest in the arms of the Mother. But the taking of this brilliant soul, his son, was an act of ritual he could not embrace.

He knew he would walk alongside the visionary, protecting him—this boy, this man—through realms in time far beyond a century, until the time of awakening. And this knowledge alone was his fortitude.

Did the seer that became his son know their death was the only way the elder could assure his return, when the time came, through the web of realms?

The weight upon the fragile, whisper-thin threads would be immense and only one could walk the path home.

All that was to be known could not be taught in the short life of the young warrior. He would need to continue his teachings along their journey across the worlds, upon the Red

Path Way.

"Tunkasila, my teacher, I will remember the words of wisdom you have bestowed upon me through all of time. I honour you and all of my relations for all guidance. Now let us proceed with ceremony. My purification is complete, and I am ready. You have taught me well," said Wahweyho, as they entered the clearing at the mouth of the Crystal Cave.

The two shamans, apprentice and wise man, put their wrapped belongings of ritual upon the ground and began the whispered calling and whistling in of their guides, for each had his own.

They swept the site clean and both went to each corner of the site, facing and giving praise to the four directions, their elements and their representatives.

Other forces were beckoned forth, those whose strength would need to be called upon throughout the journey in time.

A fire was lit inside the Crystal Cave of Journey from

young cedar bows, releasing a smoky aroma that cleansed the cavern and crackling heat waves shimmered upon the quests of past.

Wahweyho stripped down to his deerskin loincloth and proceeded to rub a paste of ground sweetgrass, ocher and bear fat upon his skin.

Red Hand laid out in ritual order: a rattle, a buffalo horn, the sacred pipe, journey plants, the serpent elixir, and a shimmering ebony blade of obsidian.

The sacred pipe was made in accordance with the teachings and instruction from White Buffalo Calf Woman's first appearance.

The bowl was hewn from stone, with seven concentric circles upon it, to represent Earth. The stem was carved from wood to represent all growing things. Pte was etched upon the surface of the polished wood, to represent all four leggeds. Twelve feathers of the eagle hung from sinew to represent all winged creatures, the Twelve Tribes and the doorway to the twelve energy vortexes hidden upon the Earth.

Wahweyho spoke, "I am ready, Father."

The old visionary shook the gourd rattle over the elixir as the young warrior sat in meditation. Then he filled the pipe of peace with the "little smoke": a combination of thorn apple, tobacco and peyote. These magic friends of the field were gifts shared among medicine men from across vast lands and nations before recorded time.

The shaman puffed on the pipe with his mind in the sacred zone of prayer, slowly rolling the acrid smoke around his mouth then blowing out blessings upon his son and over the elixir.

When the presence of the ethereal helpers appeared, the old man poured the thick, black, oily liquid into the depths of the polished buffalo horn. He then asked for their guidance across the realms for the savior's way.

The holy pipe was passed to the brave. His prayers to the Mother were already perfected in his mind. He inhaled deeply and felt the mind-altering tendrils wisp through and into his thoughts.

Wahweyho was then handed the elixir that had been empowered through the three-day ritual. The bitter taste of brew upon the brave's mouth made him gag as he swallowed a large gulp.

Red Hand continued a whistling chant and the singing in of the helpers. The song lulled the seeker into a realm of colours as little lights danced about his eyes drawing him into the luminosity.

Shadowy forms of the ancients appeared at his side, the soothing sound of trickling water drawing him into the depth of the Mother. Wahweyho's mind began to spin.

The serpent uncoiled and then began wrapping its body around thought's creation.

"Hello, Mother Creator, show me the way to the beyond. I am requesting your help for my awakening to the purpose I have been born unto upon this plane. I am ready, along with my guides and teachers, to embrace the path of light that leads to the worlds beyond. Let me ride upon your shoulders into the depths of the Underworld and through dimension's gateway," said the brave's mind thought.

Endless faces of the dead appeared before his eyes. Flesh falling off their skulls in layers of decomposition. The skulls of man began changing into that of apes, friends, mentors and enemies. He was passing through the realm of evolution, into the hole the First People had crawled through. Its walls began pressing upon the center of his solar plexus, causing the purge that would open the door to the next level. Many entities awaited the calling brought forth upon the warrior's arrival. The elixir evoked images of its origin: a vast green of jungle plants spoke of their healing gifts. The flickering tongues of serpents licked at his face before crawling into his mind through the sockets of his eyes. The serpent consumed all on the ride into the Underworld.

The walls of the council hall began to form from the coils of a giant boa as Wahweyho was belched forth from the serpent's mouth.

Sharp fangs became the pillars of a doorway. Scaly flesh transformed into the cylindrical center of a shimmering quartz crystal room. Spirit formed into his mentors and a multitude of healers that lived within the vortex.

They had chosen to stay in the void since the time of the slaying of the wise ones, eons past, to be of assistance in the heralding in of the fifth planetary shift.

The ethereal forms of members of the Twelve Nations gathered around the young warrior seer and council began.

The head of the tribe of Atlantis began by speaking first. "Welcome, brother, we have been awaiting your arrival in great anticipation. We have all worked in unity to prepare for the Earth's future transformation. We have opened the vortex at our place of origin in what the people of your lands call Antarctica, well over 10,000 years ago on your plane of linear time. Of course, we have veiled her passage through a mile of ice until the time when the Great Mother sheds this cloak. The sleeping human mind cannot yet embrace the awareness our light of consciousness brings: the story of our becoming.

"The enemy—those of the lizard-mind—will continue to control the physical realm until all the centers of awakening are open. You are the keeper of the last doorway and we have gathered in force to help you in the quest to activate the portal and keep the doorway hidden until its opening, for we know you walk alone our young, brave warrior," the ancient Atlantean finished.

The second portal keeper stood, and bowed in honour. Wahweyho remembered this fierce, great hunter from the far

North. He was a powerful shaman. "Blessings, my son. We have jointly guided you here for you to learn the truth of the red man's purpose. I am the keeper of the way to Middle Earth. Her vortex shimmers in the green of emerald lakes and hues of the setting Sun. One whose doorway I protect, hidden among towering mountains of sheer ice to the North."

The third council member then stood and began his introduction. His skin was coal black, his nose broad and his lips dry and thick. "I come from the land of Uluru, in Australia. An isle that lies far beyond the reach of Turtle Island's shell. My ancestors are walkers in time. We, the Aboriginal peoples, are to be destroyed upon the linear line. Our culture buried, as yours too will be. We hold eleven of the crystal skulls of pte. The twelfth was gifted to your people as a sign of the one who protects the Red Path Way. When the skulls are uncovered, in a time beyond your own, the divine entity of White Buffalo Calf Woman will alight upon the twelfth portal. A sign that portends to the bringing in of the fifth world," finished the Aboriginal time walker.

"I am from the lands of the South, beyond the turtle's head. The bringer of the serpent vine to our brethren," said the keeper of the fourth energy vortex's door. "Our people were destroyed centuries before your own, over the conquest for the gold that honoured our gods. I have watched this epic betrayal from atop the mountains of Machu Pichu, the home and realm of my gods." The representative of the Incan race continued, "We are a fierce nation of great warriors, as you and your people are. We rejoice in the joining of all mystic forces to bring about the calling forth of the First People."

"Greetings Wahweyho, warrior son," spoke the Uro chief of the ancient race from Lake Titicaca, high in the Andes Mountains. "I have closed the fifth door's access, that of Aramu Muru, long ago when our ancestors from galaxies and the worlds beyond this foretold of the need for secrecy to protect their race and our becoming. Access to the portal has only been attained by shamans of great discipline. Those who can sustain the vibration long enough for the long journey across dimensions."

"We, the Tribal Council, upon this visit, will help you raise your vibration high enough to allow access of all brethren, all brothers and sisters of all races who awake in time, to pass through the portals when the shift arrives upon the physical plane," another spoke.

The hypnotic dialogue of Earth's story flowed like song through the journeyer's mind.

"I have been instructed by my ancestors, those from the seven-sister star system of the Pleiades," said a squat Mayan elder. "The Mother's resonance has called us all to council. The Keepers of the Earth are failing due to the movement of dark forces from within the black hole's void. We have observed through times' knitted mists, your tribal councils of past. The lizard-mind's recent discovery that the swirling Circle Dance of Awakening is activating the twelfth portal presents an ominous time. The present repression from the cold-blooded ones shall endure beyond a century. They do not want to transcend into the fifth world. They prefer the reality of the material plane and are afraid of the power in creation. They reside in the dark place of greed and destruction," the Mayan's voice rose, resonating his heart's passion.

"I represent the keepers of a cluster of raised portals in the lands known as Guatemala. In Tikal, my center, we cover the entrance way to that of the Underworld. I am known as the keeper, Hol Box (bosch), head priest of the spiral decent and the sixth portal's doorway. One of the energy activation centers in the Pyramid Triad."

"I, as well, am a shaman priest from the Pyramid Triad," spoke another muscular Mayan. The glimmering spectacle of quetzal feathers created an aura of magnificence that awed Wahweyho, as the man continued his intro. "I protect the planetary passage to the star system, and am keeper of the seventh gateway at Palenque, in the lands of Mexico," said the Mayan priest.

Another man with the stature of a god said, "I am the third keeper and guardian of the eighth vortex, the spin of creation. Our joint activation in the Pyramid Triad, sustains our great Mother Earth's vibration. Us three aligned support the energy in the formation of the matrix: the web of life upon this plane." The regally adorned man shimmered n the precious metal of gold, his eyes outlined in thick, black kohl.

"Our activation centers have been buried to protect the knowledge those on your plane are still yet too primal to embrace. Fear is suppressing the higher path to consciousness. The lands of the East will awaken when the call of reactivation from our founders shoots forth from a temple mount. The place will become known as Israel. This place holds a smaller vortex, one in a line of many, that will bring upon the beginning of the call to awakening," he said.

"When the center of the Pyramid Triad, that of my people's land in Egypt, is activated, you will be awakened from the deep sleep, Wahweyho. You are to be the link across all realms, to form a knot in time. It is the only way the Mother and those upon her will survive the awakening into the fifth world," said the man known as Pharaoh.

"The activation is far along the linear line on the thread of your time," said the guardian of the ninth vortex. "We have stood watch upon the belly button of the Mother, the connection to the womb of creation, the lifeline to physical entities.

"Our brothers will start a movement upon the Earth as predicted," said a Hopi elder. The Kachina will reappear dancing in our new existence. White Buffalo Calf Woman's spirit will be called forth to manifest with the red man's awakening to their inherent power and life purpose when the lizards try to contaminate life's giving waters. When she finds a vessel, strong enough to sustain the energy grid of the Red Path Way, the shift will begin. This being, in the physical manifestation of a two-legged woman, will reopen the passage of the twelfth doorway with your help. With all our help, even that of your father's father, and all creatures great and small."

"I know what we speak of can cause great confusion to the mind that dwells within the physical shell," said a shriveled, bearded, white elder. He continued, "Warrior of the chosen race, know that we have faith in your ability to be the awakening! There is much you cannot retain until the crossover, like that of my people, the Druid. We built great stone circles to attest to the Mother's inherent and living energy. The call forth to activate our center upon the isle of

England, the tenth of the twelve, is when the Earth herself swirls out the message in symbols upon fields of grains and grasses," said the magical high priest, twinkling stars swirling about his flowing robes of midnight blue.

"Your time upon this web is about to be rescinded young man," said another wisely. "The power of the serpent elixir has shown you the purpose you have been born unto. I am keeper of the maze to the higher mind; it is the only path upon the Earth that allows understanding and acceptance of self as empath, as a minute light-being delving in this maze, the minuscule grain of sand we are in the cosmic sense," said the Tibetan Master, sentinel of the gateway to the eleventh vortex.

"I have journeyed upon the great cycle of life, returning time and time again to Mt. Kailash. My brother monks sustain the shield to the hidden path and the way to my reincarnation through time. Like your brothers, in your lands, will help retain yours.

"Now let me lead you back through the labyrinth and to your father who prepares the final initiation, for you to become the twelfth keeper of the fifth world that awaits awakening."

Upon the finish of dialogue from the wise ones, the walls of council dissolved. The serpent uncoiled and swallowed the warrior whole, spitting Wahweyho back to the entrance of the Crystal Cave.

The shaman, Red Hand, was dancing and shaking his rattle over the young journeyer's body, drawing his soul forth, into the third dimension. He continued singing in his helpers to assist, through a whistling song, to guide the boy safely back.

Their ritual had just begun, one of death into birth: a linking between worlds, between the two of them. He was to be, as always, the boys mentor on this plane and into the realms beyond, through prayer and a mindlink, until the end count of time into unity.

The young brave's burnished red skin glistened in sweat. His long, ebony hair lay twisted around his midriff in a sheltering cocoon.

The shaman knelt and quickly put down his gourd rattle when he saw the seers' black eyes flutter open. Red Hand began to wipe his son's sinewy limbs with a warm tea of the sacred flower, the young man's body licking up the spirit medicine.

"Here, my son, consume the strength of the great pte, he will lead you back to the depths of the Mother's womb where you will await the calling forth," he spoke in reverence, placing the delicate mushroom tops under the hope of a nation's lip.

"I shall be with you, my son, a beckoning away," he continued in a grave voice as he handed Wahweyho another gulp of the serpent elixir to wash down the bitter flavor of the little ones.

"Awaken to the momen,t my son, and allow me to show

gratitude for your existence and the blessing you have given this old man, as son. I am highly honoured that I was chosen to guide you on the path of your awakening to wisdom. Though we are not of the same blood, we are of the same people. We have the same purpose among our brothers as protectors of Mother Earth. We shall not fail, my son. We journey to the big sleep and pte will guard our safe passage," spoke the elder, growing in the magnificence of being's shining light.

The doors of Wahweyho's mind flew open in a rainbow of cascading knowledge as he watched the great medicine man of the Sioux unveil to the skies the glittering crystallized buffalo skull. It lay nestled in a bleached hide, the twelfth skull the time walker had alluded to. And then he knew what awaited. In silent acceptance he bowed to his tortuous and honoured end.

Red Hand placed the skull at the mouth of the cave, the entrance to the twelfth vortex and the doorway to the people's call to awaken and walk the Red Path Way.

He began to dance around the relic skull in a figure eight, raising the energy to a high, vibrating hum. In each pass through the center of eights' infinity he would swoop down a raven's feathered wing across a glimmering field of vibrancy. On the twelfth pass of the Unity Dance, the healer, the only father the young man had known, pulled out his obsidian blade and slit the warrior's throat where he sat.

Their eyes joined, emitting love and respect of the higher path, one they would journey together.

Red Hand knelt beside the seer and put a gourd cup under his throat to catch the blood, a wailing cry held deep within his mourning heart. He then sat down beside his son and drew the blade across his own wrists. A slow bleed out to allow time for the journey medicine that he had previously consumed to work. When the gourd was full, the weakened healer mixed the dried herb of Jimson weed into life's river. He then applied the deep, dark blood paste to his body in sacred symbols and runes. He embraced his son and awaited the deep sleep to come. "All is as it should be," he thought as a beatific smile befell his face and he jumped upon the serpent's back for the ride to the Underworld.

Present

Willow and Joe arrived at the clearing in front of the cave. The shimmering veil sang a song of greeting as they set down their packs at the side of the entrance.

"Well, I see you have awakened the Way, for the Mother sings her blessing song," said the Native elder as he started to unpack his bag.

He began to whistle a tune that evoked the innocence of childhood in the nervous woman. She felt very unsure of everything that was manifesting. Even though she walked in a trance of prayer, she had a hard time believing that what she had secretly sought was actually manifesting. She had always believed in the mystic, in ancient worlds, aliens and the realms of spirit as a means of escape and an attempt to understand a mad world, but this was a rather unexpected path. Yes, she had been preparing for years to be in service of the higher purpose, but she thought that it would be as a medicine woman.

Willow had studied herbal medicine ever since she was nineteen; the knowledge had fallen onto her lap from her grandmother's diaries and her travels abroad.

Life had once seemed to be a huge vortex pulling her down. This sense of being swallowed by the Earth itself had helped her understanding be born, seeking tendrils that stretched forth toward the light. The older she became, through each lunar cycle, she felt less and less a part of this world. At times, Willow wanted to leave the manifest behind and enter the warm, dark embrace of the beyond. No more pain, no more viewing the atrocities of humankind wrought upon women and children, mother and brother and the Earth herself. The more she learned the more the young woman called out to the gods to show her how to help and now she saw that her pleading soul's cry had been heard.

"Please, powers that be. I am your vessel. Fill me to overflowing with love to help heal this world. Please show me the way," she had asked. It seemed the gods were now calling in their chips and the fulfillment of her request was at hand.

"Watch what you ask for," flitted through Willow's nervous, churning mind.

"Come, stand with me here in front of the cave, my child," said the guardian, drawing Willow out of the trance of her mind.

When she looked up, the old man had transformed into a warrior chief. Joe had applied what appeared to be blood from the crown of his head down the center of his now shirtless torso.

"Do not be afraid, trust in the Way," he said, as his hand motioned her forward. Willow took a deep, grounding breath, walking to the place of his beckoning.

Joe lit the tip of a thick sage bundle and began to

smudge the smoke over her body. The ebony wing of a raven fanning chanted healing words in song through her being. She closed her eyes and was enveloped in the warm embrace of sacredness.

The medicine man called forth his aides and totems to help bring about the awakening in the woman, to help her remember the path that she was destined to walk.

When Willow opened her eyes, the form of a cougar began to appear through the filtered cloud of wispy, blue smoke. On the right side of the great cat stood an elk, and a bear beside him. A great buck and then a female deer walked into the clearing, as did all creatures great and small, one at a time from the forest's realm, slowly forming a circle around the figure of the young woman.

The raven, Hermann, flew in wide circles above the clearing singing out to them: "ka-caw, ka-caw."

The young woman smiled up to the heavens and thanked her grandmother. She looked around in a shocked daze of awe and in her passing gaze upon Earth's creatures an understanding took hold, it was her awakening to purpose.

White Buffalo Calf Woman smiled through the web at the beauty of the young woman and spoke upon a fine thread linked to Willow's mind. "I am honoured that you have opened a place in your heart for my manifestation, my child. The Mother has reached her time of the great cleansing purification. She loves her children and has asked us to unify and become as one. As one, we will help activate the doorway to the last of the twelve energy vortexes. There have been many signs that I know you have become aware of. Many have sought to grasp the multitude of messages the Great Mother has sent forth in preparation: those from the prophecies to mystic crop circles, unexplained phenomena to great quakes and waves and lights opening temples unseen. Creators from many realms beyond our own have gathered for the shift, as well as those from below and within her womb. She has spoken aloud for years, across vast lands with a great echoing moan, and still she goes unheard. The time is now, my warrior princess. It is time to call forth the elements and our tribes that lay in wait. Our brothers await, let us move forward."

Willow collapsed to the ground in exhaustion, all concept of time lost.

Joe came to her side. He smoothed her hair and gently raised her head, putting a vessel of cool water to her lips.

"What happened? The last thing I remember was you smudging me, that must be some powerful sage you have there, Joe," she joked.

"Hmm, she does not remember? Maybe this is a means for her mind to handle the Way?" thought the old Native.

"You will have to think about what befell you, young lady, for only you can be the true interpreter of what has passed before you." Joe waited a moment before continuing, "We best head on down the path back to camp. Your young man will be looking for you soon. You go ahead, and I will follow and cover our path. I'll drop by your fire tonight if possible. I'll need to take council with my tribe to tell of your coming, and the cave's calling."

Willow nodded in agreement. Standing on shaky legs she grabbed her pack and found her way back to the trailhead and followed its windy descent back to camp.

Ranger Bob was sitting at the picnic table, a broken ax handle at his feet, when she arrived. He began telling her, in a frustrated voice, about how the ax was a piece of shit, and how it broke when he was splitting wood for a fire.

"It's all right. We'll replace it the next time we go to town. I already have a box of kindling split under the van. It is easily enough to get us through the weekend, so, don't worry," said Willow.

"It's getting late, where did you wander off to?" Bobby asked.

"Oh, I just double-checked that we got all the garbage off the trail, and that the signs were visible. Maybe we could ask the warden about closing the trail. It might be for the best," she said.

"I want to see a bear, that's why I'm here!" exclaimed Bobby.

"Yeah, well, a grizzly is not anything I would want to run into. They can be very territorial, and they're hungry in the spring. It is rather unusual for them to be so low this early in the year," responded Willow.

"Whatever, I'm not afraid. Maybe I'll hike a bit on the trail tonight to see if I can encounter something. Everything has probably been scared off from the helicopters and wardens running around looking for that woman from last weekend anyway," said Bob.

Willow disliked the cockiness in his voice. Her mind flipped to a sense of all knowing foreboding. She was quite sure nothing had been scared off, just the opposite in fact! The couple had dinner: a luscious meal prepared over dancing blue flames. Shortly after cleaning up, Willow could barely hold her head up and decided to lie down.

Ranger Bob was determined to see some wildlife, so he headed off down the gravel road toward the trail. Willow hoped that Old Joe had covered their path well enough as she watched Bob waltz off into the dark depths of the trail in her mind's eye, as she drifted off into the embrace of deep sleep.

Bob's headlamp bopped along with his self-assured gate. He had walked just beyond where he had seen Willow descend that morning. When he looked in the direction she had come from, up the steep embankment, he thought he could see a shimmering light.

"Well who the hell is out this time of night? Nobody is registered with us but that crazy, old Indian. I better go check it out," he thought.

"Hello, anybody out there?" he shouted, as he tried to ascend through the brush-tangled path. The lilt of his accent sounded meek and shallow in the depth of the forest's echo. All of a sudden, just as he was pushing back a branch, a great crashing mayhem came hurtling toward him. To Bob, the sound came like a violent boom from every direction. A great whoosh of wind swirled through his mind, taking his breath away as his body was powerfully thrown from the trail and down the embankment.

Wahweyho's manifested spirit form stood over the unconscious man's broken body.

The warrior had been observing the white man's antics since his arrival as well as the golden aura of the healer woman.

He had almost touched her when she took the rabbit's foot from his hunt, but he knew she had not embraced the second sight yet. He could not afford her running off, as the rabbit had, through energy's thinning veil for time was paramount, the call to awakening had to begin.

Red Hand's great-great-grandson, Joe, was now in the process of speaking to the Tribal Council and requesting they begin the Circle Dance's calling forth once again.

The warrior, Wahweyho, craved the sensation of warm blood in his veins, he wanted to feel the sinewy strength of muscle, to feel alive. So, he bent over the young man and on the next gasping breath of Bob's frail and weakened body, he entered his form.

Moments passed, and finally the warrior awoke in Bob's body. He stood, rubbing his hands across the bruised forearms. The broken ribs seeming to mend upon contact with the fortitude of the warrior's spirit. The young brave ran down the embankment, laughing aloud, as he spit the metallic taste of blood from Bob's split lips.

"Now, I must go to the woman while my energy retains the vital force of this body. She must awaken to her transcendence and the urgency of our purpose," said the impassioned warrior spirit.

Willow rolled over sleepily as Bob entered the van.

"How was your hike? You weren't gone long. Did you experience a close encounter of the furry kind?" she asked mockingly.

"No, my love, I just slipped upon the trail and decided to return. I missed you today," said Bob in a deep, weary voice.

"Are you all right?" Willow asked with concern.

Bob said nothing, he just sat upon the bed and gently placed Willow's foot in his lap. He began to massage it in small, soothing circles.

"Relax, my goddess, let me share the flames of the desire you awake in me," he spoke in that same mystic voice, before lowering his mouth to taste every ounce of her essence from toe to sacred valley.

Although confused by the romantic poetry of his words, a throbbing erotic desire engulfed her. Willow reached impatiently to unbuckle the belt of his pants. Fire's passionate hunger drew them together. He slowly reached under Willow's shift. Ever so skillfully he caressed the soft, moist and warm flesh of her inviting womanhood.

Wahweyho's mind reeled from the long-forgotten experience. Hearing her gasp of pleasure, he continued to fondle her expertly, flowing with the rhythm of desire. As their throbbing lust peaked, Willow pushed him back upon the bed and rose to mount her man. She could no longer resist the desire to have him deep inside her. Rising slowly above him they joined in the oneness of unity; rolling and swaying as the turbulent seas, penetrating deeply and falling into the tides of ecstasy. Willow moaned aloud as her orgasm approached, searching for the eyes of her lover in the darkness. Never had she felt this intensity of passion. She found his face and stared into the eyes of a warrior god. They became one in an explosion of light and then gently held each other until dawn.

Father Sun spread his golden rays upon the day while Wahweyho's spirit wavered weakly over the sleeping figure of this woman that set his long-dead spirit ablaze. He could no longer retain the strength needed to continue the crossover. He must return to the Crystal Cave for renewal soon.

Willow yawned and stretched while gazing lazily upon her lover, the cool mountain dew gently kissing her awake.

The heady scent of sweetgrass filled the van's small space drawing her mind to rescind the fires of passion the evening's blissful love session had left smoldering. The two of them had not been making love often. The bickering and

fighting that stemmed from job transitions and travel across
continents had taken its toll on their ability to create a
lasting relationship. Willow felt exhausted from the effort it
took to create harmony with Bobby. They were from
different places, and the philosophies they held close to their
hearts varied greatly.

He believed in the glory of instant gratification. His
ego, his looks, his outfits and the pursuit of attaining a mind-
numbing high, at all costs, were first and foremost in his
mind regardless of life's responsibilities. She could lay
hidden alone in the forest, never needing the security of
recognition that he craved. She'd never paid attention to
trends or fashion. Shit, Willow wouldn't even bother to
shave half the time and never wore makeup. The young
woman survived on believing in a dream. Bobby never had
one.

Willow snuggled up to Bobby as he slept deeply. She
felt a little guilty for her mind's eye creating the vision of
another man making love to her—one whose face still
lingered in her mind. Her thoughts began flowing through
the beauty and poetic romance of a Rumi poem:

> The minute I heard my first love story, I started
> looking for you, not knowing how blind that was.
> Lovers don't finally meet somewhere.
> They're in each other all along.

Feeling the satisfaction that only deep, passionate love
can bring, she smiled to herself and prepared to get up and
make some coffee for Bobby. He wouldn't be dragging
his ass out of bed for hours.

Willow reached down to the end of the bed and
grabbed her merino wool long underwear and sweater,

putting them on under the blankets in an effort to retain body heat.

She reached across Bobby to close the curtains on the van window behind his head, and in the feeble light noticed the dark purple bruises upon his face. His breathing was coming in raspy, laboured breaths.

"God, he must have really had quite a bad fall on the trail last night," she thought. She reached out and gently rocked his shoulder, "Are you all right, babe?"

A feeble groan escaped his swollen lips followed by a loud, agonizing scream as he tried to roll onto his back.

Willow jumped out of bed startled, bursting through the lingering mist of her one true love, Wahweyho.

Bobby could not believe the pain that engulfed him. All that he remembered was something attacking him and falling down a ravine off the trail. "What happened, how did I get here?" he croaked.

Willow was in shock. "How did he make love to me last night in the shape he is in? He must have been on some sort of drug again," she thought.

"You came back to the site after being gone only about a half hour. You said you had fallen but seemed just fine, you were making light of it. You were actually quite amorous. We made amazing love and you seemed even more than fine."

"Well I'm not fine. It hurts to even breathe! You must have been dreaming about your fantasy lover because I sure the fuck couldn't have performed. I think I need a doctor," he said through his gasping breath.

"Let me prepare some warm water and clean you up, so we can see what damage you have done to yourself." She exited the van and went to start the fire, feeling confused and a little brokenhearted. The tenderness within her loins was all the proof she needed, she had not imagined anything.

Willow started the Coleman stove and put a pot of water on to warm. And then began to prepare the morning coffee. "Maybe Bobby will feel better when his mind is cleared from a potent java?" she calmly spoke to herself.

When the water was ready, she returned to the van and began to gently swab Bobby's bruised face.

"The blankets feel heavy on my chest. Can you pull them off of me? I can hardly move," Bob said, his voice barely louder than a whisper.

When Willow pulled back the blankets, she let out a gasp. "Oh my God, what did you do? We need to get you to a hospital," she said, as she looked at his concaved chest and the gashes upon his arms and legs. She bolted out of the van and straight to the truck to radio her boss. She needed to tell him about the incident and the need to get Bobby into an emergency room.

From across the way, Old Joe noticed the ruckus and decided to walk over to see if everything was okay, his sixth sense was telling him something. He had just returned from the council meeting with the elders. His people agreed that the time and messages were enough to begin preparation for the cleansing way.

The predictions of their forefathers were soon about to become a reality. The call was being made for all the nations' children to unite across the Mother's vast lands.

"Joe, thank God you are here. Can you please help me get Bobby into the truck? He's had an accident," called the frantic woman as the old man approached.

"What happened?" asked the now worried elder.

Willow began telling him about how Bobby had returned from his hike on the trail, and his story of how he had fallen when he was attacked by something. She told him that Bobby had seemed just fine in the evening (leaving out the details of their intimacy) and then how suddenly beat up and bruised he was upon his attempt to rise out of bed.

"Don't worry, my dear. The universe unfolds as necessary. We will get him in the truck and to the hospital. He'll be just fine," said the guardian.

The calm of his voice was like an elixir on her frayed nerves.

"I'll need the details of what happened and exactly what it was that attacked the young man," thought Joe, as he fingered his medicine pouch that lay deep in his left pant pocket.

The two worked together, teacher and apprentice, to help the young English man into the truck.

He screamed out in pain and fainted when they first tried to lift his battered body. The healer could see the black and blue markings of what appeared to be hand prints on Bob's chest. A deep sense of a foreboding stillness settled into Joe's bones.

"Willow, I am going to give Bobby a little bit of my special medicine to help him with his pain, so he'll be comfortable on the drive, okay?" Reaching into his pocket, Joe extracted the medicine bag of his ancestors.

"Go ahead, Joe, whatever we can do to help him," said a worried Willow.

After Joe had pulled the leather pouch from his pocket, he opened the sinew ties, pulling out what appeared to be a folded leaf from its confines. He then began a chant to the spirits. One to manifest a dark shroud of forgetfulness over the tendrils of the boy's mind.

"Can you get me some water dear? So your young man

can wash down the medicine," said Joe.

Willow quickly ran off toward the outhouse to get some water.

The minute she was gone, Joe blew the fine powder of the little ones' blend in the face of the prone, broken man who sat unconscious and propped up in the passenger seat of the truck. Joe jabbed his fingertips forcefully into each blackened bruise, to help give the appearance of a buck's antlers. The young man did not move. Willow returned with a glass of water and Joe poured a little across the lips of the unconscious man.

"Now you go ahead and get out of here young lady. Take him to the clinic in Bragg Creek. They can shoot him off by ambulance to a hospital, if need be. I'll stay here and check out the trail to see if there are any signs of what happened to him. Hurry up now and don't worry, he'll be fine," said Joe, who was now anxious.

Willow hopped into the driver's seat of the truck and took off flying down the winding gravel road toward town.

Old Joe went back to his site and grabbed his pack. "I must begin the ritual now to protect the thinning veil. Something, or should I say, someone, has entered through the portal! The boy must have crossed the boundaries, the fool," he mumbled to himself in frustration.

Willow screeched into the emergency entrance of the small foothills clinic. An attendant rushed out to help her put Bobby on a stretcher. He had not awoken during the drive, just painful groans and jumbled words had escaped his lips, something about a bright light.

"Hello, are you the one who brought in the young man?" asked the doctor in attendance after Bobby had been wheeled into the trauma center and stabilized.

"Yes, I am his girlfriend. Is he going to be all right?" asked Willow.

"He has had quite a fall. Looks like he may have been attacked by a buck or something? He does not seem to remember anything about the incident. He should have been brought to the hospital last night. I don't know how he endured the pain of five broken ribs and the massive contusions he has all over his body. His nose is broken as well, and his jaw is cracked," he continued. "I see that he is not a Canadian citizen, so we will need any information you have regarding his insurance coverage. He is going to need to stay in the hospital for a few days to make sure there is no internal bleeding. We did not detect any as of yet. You understand that it is still fairly early on in his diagnosis. We need to do a lot more tests, the air ambulance service is on its way now," said the young doctor.

"Oh God," Willow gasped, her mind was reeling. "How the hell did he make it through last night? How did he make love to her? What is going on?" she thought.

"I better call his family. I don't know about any medical insurance coverage. Can I see him?" she asked through falling tears.

"I think you better call his family first. As it stands his medical bill is going to run into the thousands of dollars, and that doesn't include the air ambulance fee. I am going to need some assurance that he can pay his bill. We will need either a credit card or an insurance policy number before we release him or give him anymore care."

Willow felt the heartless bureaucracy of greed spilling forth from the doctor's mouth, as he explained rules he had little choice but to follow.

"I'll need you to fill out an incident report with the police so that they can notify the game wardens as well," he added shamefully. "Where exactly did he get attacked?"

Willow's face paled and she began to shake. "I need to sit down a moment," she said, in a trembling voice. "Okay, think, think," her mind rambled. "What the hell am I going to do? Breathe: one, two, three, four, five, six, seven, eight.... Okay, better," said her focused chant to self. With directed intent she accessed the warrior self to accept life as it presents itself. "We cannot change anything but our perception of the moment."

"Here's my credit card. I'll see him now and call his family once we have a complete diagnosis," said Willow haughtily.

She was led into a sterile room where her lover lay under bright, invasive fluorescent lights. His eyes were black and swollen—sore splits seemingly ready to burst.

"Oh Bobby, what did you do for this to happen?" she thought. "Hi babe, feeling any better?" she queried, as his blood-filled eyes locked with hers.

"I'll live. So much for being a wilderness adventurer," he joked feebly.

Willow smiled at the brave face he tried to put forth. "Do you want me to phone your family?"

"Yeah, you best give my mother a call, she'll be frantic. I need to go home. You know I cannot pay for a hospital stay. My family will help me get home. I need to go home," he said, choking on his words.

"Okay, whatever you want, sweetheart. They'll take you by ambulance to Calgary. I'll do what I can from here. You know I can't leave with you Bobby. I need to stay and finish

the job contract. I'll go get your belongings together," she
responded, the coolness of a mountain-fed stream cascading
over her heart.

Willow felt numb, the usual state of being when love is
lost. But in this case, it was because love was found.

"How could I have been blessed with such an ecstatic
spirit of love last night?" Willow contemplated as she drove
back through the heart of the Kananaskis mountains. "Was
the warrior image that filled the core of my essence to
overflowing just part of my imagination? My true love really
does live within," she surmised, a peaceful euphoria
descending over any sadness in losing the young man whom
she had shared so much. "Everything I need already lies
within," she thought, a beatific smile of acceptance gracing
her mouth.

When Willow pulled into the campground she was met by
the vehicles of her boss and the park warden.

"How is Bob doing?" asked Carlos.

"He is in pretty rough shape and has decided to return
to England," replied Willow.

"Well, I am sorry to hear that. But I did have a feeling
that this job wasn't the right fit for that city slicker of yours.
His accident has now caused the park's campground to be
closed. This incident, as well as the last one, has now caused
an unnecessary concern for public safety," said her frustrated
boss. "Willow, this is Mike, he's a warden with park services,"
he added.

A tall, handsome man reached out his hand, nodding at
her in acknowledgment.

"Mike is here to lock up the access gates to the
campground. You better pack-up and get your van out of here

while you can. I'll have your pay cheque ready at the office. I take it you were going to give your notice anyway, right?" asked Carlos.

"Well, in all honesty, I didn't think I would lose my job over my boyfriend's misfortune. I can still handle the position on my own. I wasn't planning on leaving. I don't really have anywhere to go. I love it here," said Willow with tearing eyes.

"Okay, don't go getting upset. I guess I will need someone to keep watch over the campground while it is closed, to prevent vandalism. If you are willing to take a pay cut, I guess you can stay. That is, if you can handle a security detail? Besides, that old bugger 'Injun Joe' wouldn't pack up his camp citing some sort of righteous spiel about his inherent right to stay on the lands of his ancestors. He will be around to help you if you need anything," he said.

Willow happily jumped back into the truck and quickly headed to her site.

Joe was pacing the grounds when she arrived.

"I guess you heard about the decision to close the campground. I get to stay on as security, so we will be all alone for a while it seems. At least until they determine that it is safe," said an emotionally depleted Willow.

"Sit down, little one, you look exhausted. Let me make you a nice cup of fortifying tea," said the worried healer.

"Thanks" she responded, tiredly.

Father Sun had rounded the mountain peaks' rise, laying warm, healing rays upon her tired eyes while she lay back to rest in a chair.

"Here you go, drink this straight down. It is a little bitter but will allow you access to the understanding you will need to proceed," said Joe, offering the cup of warm tea to Willow.

"I didn't tell you everything, Joe. I was visited last night by a warrior spirit. It could not have been Bobby. He, it, made love to me. Who was he? How could this be? I am so confused."

As the soothing effects of the tea began to weave through her mind she slowly calmed down.

Old Joe, medicine man, seer and guardian of the Crystal Cave, then began to tell the story of the First People. Those from all realms and dimensions, until creation's beginning:

"There was a time long before our own. This time is labeled as a place of myth by many. Society at present cannot seem to fathom, with their limited and veiled thought pattern, that vast and powerful technology once existed that is far beyond our own capabilities now.

"At this time, the first highly conscious people were called forth from galaxies afar to come and live upon the beauty of the Great Mother Ge, for she was lonely. She is better known to you, my dear, as Gaia. This visiting race paid great respect to the Mother. And, in embracing her beauty and abundance, they built a colossal palace. This kingdom of the first ones was surrounded by five concentric rings of land and ribbons of water high upon a mountainous island in the Atlantic.

"The palace design was built to represent the first symbol Gaia had given the new lords. A reminder to the people of the cycle of life and creation's ability to renew herself, for she alone had had the power to form from the fathomless black nothingness of the universal pulse.

"The leader of the star visitors who commanded all became known as Poseidon in the history of our time. His wife was a mortal woman named Cleito. The ruler divided

Gaia into twelve regions for his sons, the children of their union, to rule over. Within these individual regions, portals were created that would serve as doorways allowing the young gods to commune with one another and receive counsel from the all-powerful Mother of this creation.

"The energy vortex that the portals created when activated in unison sustained and balanced Earth's energy while her resources were extracted. Love and gratitude of her existence blessed the whole with a flowing harmony of giving and receiving.

"Over the years, the lust of the visitor's children to become gods, yet remain mortal, grew. What had been consummated in the coalition of mixed blood, those of stardust and Earth, collided morally. When the greed for gold over-shadowed gratitude the place known as Atlantis was punished. The Mother was furious with their lack of respect and buried the nation's founding city under a wall of water through the eruption of a great volcano. She then rolled onto her side, and the Earth's foundations changed the face of her surface. These lands would be lost until creation's wholeness was called upon to be formed once again.

"The great lands of Antarctica, at the South Pole, house this place, which is not one of myth. Atlantis lies buried under a mile of ice, one that is now melting at a shocking rate to expose Gaia's laws of wisdom. This wisdom is one that those of the first visiting race do not want us, her true children, to attain," spoke Joe, his form transcending into the power and luminosity of a formidable wise man.

The passion of his story began forming visual pictures of this lost world in Willow's mind.

"Wow, I have read about Atlantis, and have always believed in my heart that our beginning was much more complex than Christianity's story implied. There are so many wonders of the world that are beyond comprehension, unavailable for even the greatest minds to grasp! We would be fools, and have been, to believe in the lies used to mask the greater consciousness of our existence," said Willow.

"Why do the people of the First Root Race want to deny us our story. Her story, of creation?" questioned Willow.

"Because, those that know the true story of Earth's becoming are still hanging onto the lower vibration of the physical realm. They are consumed with the greed on the material plane. These beings, the descendants of the lizard race from galaxies beyond, still long to be gods as their ancestors once were. They fear evolution, and the awareness that will be attained when Gaia awakens through the re-activation of the twelve energy vortexes, a shift they plan to stop!" said Joe, anger darkening his features.

Willow breathed deeply in a trance the tea held, she followed a path into the images the elder's voice evoked. She saw within her mind's eye, the forms of the once glorious race. They were tall, regal creatures with large slanted eyes of obsidian black. The height of these gods, standing ten feet tall, created a sense of awe. An erect Mohawk fan of dark, leathery skin protruded from the center of their narrow head like a crown. The oblong mouth of the visitors was framed by thin lips and a small tongue flickered in and out constantly tasting the air.

One of the creatures seemed to sense something as he probed the air and began to pace in frantic circles searching the heavens. He stopped abruptly and then pointed with a fearful looking staff into the hovering eye of Willow's mind. She gasped, and flew up and into a pink, mystic cloud. The young woman's spirit body quickly accelerated to a place of safety. And from the heights of Heaven, Atlantis lay at her feet as her history continued to unfold.

The mountain was magnificent. An amazing castle with walls carved out of huge crystal shafts stood atop the sheer, purple walls of the mountain. The five concentric circles shone in the shimmering green of wavering fields that sat within the turquoise of the bluest sea. She could feel the vibrancy, the frequency of love and abundance, overwhelming her senses with joy.

A black cloud of concern overtook her mind. The images flew by like a movie reel in high speed. She saw great mining operations, with a multitude of ancient looking slaves extracting gold, silver, opals and gems of all forms. There were flying saucers that zoomed about. And field upon field of terraced land for farming. There were vast orchards in bloom—their heady scents wafting up to the heavens.

Then she saw war. Greed for the Mother's gifts consumed the visitors, and Gaia, feeling violated, screamed her discontent. Three days of darkness from the volcano's eruption froze the majority of the lizard people. Those who didn't die instantly, drowned from the tsunami that followed and consumed the island.

There were some that escaped, scattering like leaves in the wind and taking their intelligence to many corners of the Earth. But they continued to forget the wisdom in the knowledge of gratitude. The first in the seven lessons of consciousness once taught to them.

The visions swirling past her mind blackened further and a loud hiss erupted, shaking her to the core. Willow jumped into the present and quickly openied her eyes to the concerned, hovering face of Old Joe.

"Daughter, shroud yourself, quickly pull the doors of

your mind closed!" he shouted in a panic, moving around to her side.

He lit a smudge stick and began to frantically whisk the smoke about her seated body. "Repeat: 'I am here now,' three times," and then he began a chant of protection.

She followed his orders.

"I did not expect you to be taken so far in the weaving of story my dear," said her guide. "I should have given you more protection," he admonished himself.

"I'm fine, they have left. I have Grandmother Fading Dawn's protection," said Willow, holding up the small leather amulet she wore around her neck.

They both looked up at the screeching cry of the raven. He was circling around the campsite's perimeter and diving down. It was Hermann the Harbinger and he caught their attention as intended.

Joe tilted his head to the sky, consulting the bird's antics. "Damn, they may have left you, but they have crossed over through the realms. I believe they have followed your trail upon the web.

"We need to work fast to strengthen the veil until my brothers can begin the movement. Time, as we know it, is about to speed up. The Mother's spin will become very erratic. The tilt of her axis is beyond repair. All as we have known it shall change with the upcoming shift into the fifth world if we do not prepare!

"I must go and make preparations, when can you come to the cave? We still have many stories of prophecy to cover. You need to be informed of the worlds beyond our own to comprehend the depths of your calling. The purpose you were born to manifest."

"I need to pack up Bobby's bags first. He has decided

to return back to his family in England," said Willow. "You never told me who it was that I encountered the other night, Joe. Do you know who it could have been?" she asked sheepishly, a deep blush upon her face.

"Yes, I believe I do. He is another verification that the veil is parting. I am sure your visitor is the one whom the ancients had summoned, from a time almost a half-century ago. He has been awaiting your arrival all this time; since the time the red man's loss of heart occurred. He, as you, has been chosen to be a bringer of the awakening and the call to walk the Red Path Way.

"He has been left to roam upon the web of time. And I, as my forefathers before me, have been his guardian, as well as the guardian of the Crystal Cave of Light. It is the access point to where you both must travel for council. Where you both must meet to save us all and end the slavery of the Mother's children.

"We who remember the stories, but have forgotten the path, need the awakening your crossing over shall bring. You have been chosen to incarnate as White Buffalo Calf Woman and I believe the warrior shaman you have encountered across the veil has claimed you as his wife. Together you will birth into consciousness the shining path back to wisdom—the cosmic circle recreated. The Keepers of the Earth will reclaim the throne of council that we were created to sit upon. Now hurry, I will need you at the cave's entrance by dusk. Don't eat anything solid, as you must be pure for the next journey. The lizard people are aware of us now. We must use all our tools at hand to protect the twelfth portal. They will do everything in their power to stop the shift of awareness, turning it instead into one of vast devastation," he shouted over his shoulder, as he hurried back to his site.

"Who was he? What is his name, this man you say is now my husband?" Willow called out after him.

"Wahweyho, the most powerful and acclaimed seer of all our people," he said, chuckling to himself at the impatience of the young warrior to claim his bride.

Willow hurried to the van and grabbed Bobby's backpack, throwing his poetry book, toiletries and clothes in to it haphazardly. She would have to radio Carlos to reopen the entrance gate. She had just enough time to drive back to the hospital, say her last goodbye and give her well wishes to Bobby before dusk.

She threw the bag in the back of the truck and took off down the road. She was just about to radio her boss when she noticed that the park ranger was still at the gate.

"Hi, Mike, right?" she asked, rolling down the window as she pulled up. "I was wondering if you could let me through, so I can go back to the hospital to say goodbye to my friend. I shouldn't be more than a couple of hours. You could even just leave it dummy locked until I get a key. I'm going to get a key, right?"

The strikingly handsome official seemed to be in a daze. Slowly, he turned in acknowledgment and removed his sunglasses. "I don't think you are going anywhere" he said, with a lewd smile. His yellow eyes blinked rapidly, as a long, black tongue flicked across his lips.

Willow screamed and slammed the truck into reverse, spewing gravel over the inhuman thing.

"Oh great beings that reside across all realms, protect me!" she cried to the universe. The truck was swerving side to side, in the speed she deemed necessary to escape what, surely, she could not have imagined.

Willow lost control as she tried to maneuver the first loop of the campground. The truck went flying, headlong off the road and into a cedar tree.

She came back to consciousness moments after the jarring impact. The possessed park ranger was attempting to pry open the passenger door. The driver's door was jammed against a tree. Willow tried desperately to remove the locked seatbelt that held her firmly in place. The reach of the beast's slimy hand was leaving searing burns upon her flesh.

She pulled the Buck Knife she kept on her belt forth and used it to slash frantically at the creature to try and keep him at bay. His putrid, rank breath spewed acid spittle in recourse.

Willow recoiled. She grabbed a thermos she had on the seat and smashed out the driver's window. She cut the seatbelt with her knife and leapt through the broken shards of jagged glass.

The screaming hiss emitted from the mouth of the lizard man deafened her senses as he quickly ran around the vehicle.

She found the warrior within and stood her ground upon the high road of righteousness. "Stay back, you fucking abomination!" she yelled, grasping firmly onto the small knife she held in her trembling hand.

She could see what appeared to be gills, opening and closing rapidly along his collar line.

"Dear God, what are you?" she asked in trepidation.

A horrid chuckle escaped his awkward mouth. "I am your end," he said, as he reached for the courageous young woman.

A loud sound of smashing tree limbs exploded from the forest as a stampede of hooves came crashing through the trees. With a leap a great buck appeared, with his body blocking the lizard's grasping reach its antlers thrashed wildly at the man-thing.

The lizard recoiled for a brief moment. Recovering quickly, it fell upon the back of the beautiful animal, sinking its small, fine teeth into the glorious creature's neck.

Willow ran as the two fought the good fight—one for light, the other for oppressive darkness. She heard the raven's call in the distance and prayed to all that is sacred for a path of escape from this living nightmare that pursued her wakened state.

Hermann appeared, flying down from the heights of the gods. His talons were spread wide as he sunk them deep into the gills of the ravenous beast that bathed in the blood of his brother guardian.

All animals, those great and small, were fighting in unity for the awakening that would bring respect and consciousness for the only hope of survival left. The first and the most important lesson had been lost and forgotten: that all creatures and all elements are one, and within one, in the living Mother. The place where we were breathed into existence the same as where we shall all return to. The place we move within and without. The one great universal breath shared by all, well, almost all, creatures.

Willow turned toward the screeching bird's bravado, and in a flash of fury she ran and leapt on the wings of faith. A warrior's scream cried forth to the heavens as she landed on the back of the beast and slit its lizard throat from gill to gill.

Hermann cocked his head while perched upon Park Ranger Mike's head. He looked directly at her, cawed, and then reached his beak inside the dead thing's oversized socket and plucked its eye out.

Willow fell back on her haunches exhausted and stared down at the freakish entity that lay before her. She shuffled nervously backwards, peering side to side. Her survival instinct was in control.

"Well, Hermann, I sure the hell hope I never see anything like that again. Let's get the hell out of here and find Joe. He will want to know the details of what has just transpired." Willow fearfully looked around the area. All seemed calm and quiet until her gaze fell upon the tragedy of her first defender.

"Oh, sweet beauty, thank you for your sacrifice," she said to the magnificent animal that lay on the bloodied dirt road. She knelt at the buck's side, smoothing his chestnut fur and closed the long-lashed lids over his soft brown eyes.

"You shall hold a place of honour upon my altar brother," she said. Standing on shaky legs she went to the truck, reached into the back and finding a hatchet, returned and chopped one of the five-pointed antlers off.

Old Joe was frantically running around the clearing before the cave's entrance searching for branches to begin building the sacred fire: one stick at a time, each blessed upon its placement. When he finished, he could sense in his bones that something was wrong. Stopping what he was doing, he began to pray.

"Tunkasila, hear my call. Come to me, great-grandfather Red Hand, for I seek your counsel."

The wind picked up force, while the trees began to sway and bend in the billowing gusts. White clouds appeared, rolling into the form of pte, the sacred buffalo.

He also spoke to his lineage: "I will need the spirit force of all those who have come before. The wise ones need to awaken and jointly instill strength to my essence to help me fly beyond this shell I wear. Allow my spirit to be all seeing, for they come in legions across the realms to destroy the Mother and make her barren. I fear, my elders, that they have come to stop the birthing of the fifth world. Our brothers, the Keepers of the Earth, are presently gathering for the movement. The Circle Dance has begun and will soon reach all nations. The 'Idle No More' movement is calling forth all those that have been in the big sleep on these lands. The people of Turtle Island rise now to defend the protection of our life blood and that of our Mother's.

"I need the sight to help see the reptilians' plans. They slither upon the web now, allowing the ethereal force of the first lost ones of their race to return. I'm afraid I cannot fight them. We are alone in this moment, and they are many," cried the weary medicine man.

"You are never alone," responded an inner voice of wisdom to the shaman's prayers. "This is part of the cycle we have chosen. It can only be changed by the unity of all our relations upon the physical realm. White Buffalo Calf Woman has chosen to arrive because she has seen the time to rise is now. She is much more powerful than you know, our brother. Do not fear. She will reign with force and great fury if need be.

"She is here to help all peoples reclaim their right, as Keepers of the Earth. Or the race of man can choose to bow to the greed of the lizard mind for another millennium. All is up to the awakening of those on your plane. You are all being called forth to be idle no more, to protect what is your sustenance.

"The slaves of all nations upon Gaia need to dance in her reverence to find and claim their power as co-creators within their universe. Within the Omnipresence.

"We cannot help you beyond the calling forth of the elements and animals from your plane to assist. Not until all twelve portals are open. Then the two leggeds will walk in reverence upon the Mother's glory or be buried in her wrath. The wheels in the circle of life turn. The serpent eats her tail: life, death, rebirth. All is as it should be; the power of choice is each one's own."

Gatekeepers of Time

Willow began to recite the prayer that sustained her in
times of fear and doubt. One that brought faith and courage
to face the challenges that haunted her walk back to camp:

"O' Great Spirit,
whose voice I hear in the winds,
and whose breath gives life to all the world.

"Hear me! I am small and weak;
I need your strength and wisdom.

"Let me walk in beauty and make my eyes
ever behold the red and purple sunset.

"Make my hands respect the things you have
made and my ears sharp to hear your voice.

"Make me wise so that I may understand the
things you have taught my people.

"Let me learn the lessons you have hidden
in every leaf and rock.

"I seek strength, not to be greater than my brother,
but to fight my greatest enemy—myself.

"Make me always ready to come to you with
clean hands and straight eyes.

"So, when life fades, as the fading sunset, my spirit
may come to you without shame."

These words of prayer cloaked her in a field of vibrancy that
emanated from all. Her eyes fell upon the shimmering
spectrum that surrounded her physical body. All that had
been named seemed aglow in the fluctuating, pulsing ether of
life's creation.

Willow carried the long antler of her protector like a
weapon, grasping it firmly midway down its length. The veins
of her forearm popping with a white-knuckled, death-grip
clutch of her left hand. Her small hunting knife's blade
dripped thick, black blood in her right hand.

Each step taken was a step closer to the Creator. Her
strength in purpose was renewed.

Hermann the raven sat perched upon her shoulder
whispering knowledge to sustain the warrior that stood
awakened in the young woman. "What am I going to do about
the truck? How the hell will I explain what happened to the
police? Nobody will believe it," thought Willow.

The cooing of raven's wisdom began to infiltrate past the doors of the physical realm and she saw the solution laid out in simplicity.

"Yes, go, my friend. Call our brothers to help," said Willow.

The raven spread his midnight wings and took to the air with his mission at heart.

The Goddess walked the illuminated path back to Old Joe's campsite.

Hermann rallied a cougar to action, one that rested on a nearby mountain top.

The mindlink all four leggeds share with the Mother was sent forth with the vision to drag the body of the park ranger out of sight and into the brush.

The raven swiftly flew back to the site of challenge. Landing on the lizard man's chest, Hermann began nuzzling his beak into his breast pocket. He grasped firmly upon the keys hidden there, and with his mission accomplished he flew back to his charge.

Old Joe awoke from his vision quest with the knowledge of danger heavy upon his shoulders. The dread of mankind's fate, a swallowed acceptance, was a leaden knot in the pit of his stomach. A great silence filled the forest and put the medicine man's senses on high alert.

He looked to the heavens at the parting clouds. "And so it shall be," he said, as he turned his attention to the making of a sweat lodge for the purification necessary before the naming ceremony.

Joe began by bending the supple green willow limbs that he had gathered in prayer from the healing tree, binding them with sinew. He then draped the freshly scraped buffalo hide over the rounded womb of journey's gate, leaving the entrance open and facing East. All was prepared for the becoming of the woman.

The cave glowed with luminous anticipation among the red hues of Father Sun's setting—Gaia calling forth her request to manifest.

"Where is she? Tell me brothers," muttered the gatekeeper, Joe, as he waited in trepidation.

Joe now wore the regalia of his standing: the red of his family's shamanic, guardian bloodline laid in a stripe from his crown down his weathered body's core symbolic of man's dualistic nature. Eagle feathers were woven through his hair. His body was nude to the elements, as in birth, except for a deerskin loincloth and the long-bladed knife that lay tucked at his waistline.

The howling of a pack of wolves erupted from the surrounding woods. The message sent through sound's inflection sent a chill through his very being and set his legs moving with the speed of an antelope down the ravine and back into camp.

Old Joe came flying through the woods, appearing from the brush with a loud thrashing onto the site. He startled Willow who stood on guard: her weapons held at the ready with a deadly ferocity upon her face.

"Jesus, you scared the hell out of me, Joe," she said when she finally found the strength to find her voice. "I have been tested on the foundations of my faith, and I believe that I have crossed into the realm of insanity," she continued numbly.

"What have you seen my daughter? What happened that has brought about such fear?" asked the winded shaman. "I am here, and as your protector we will walk hand in hand through all the doors of perception, strengthening the weakened pillars to become that of the great oak. The awakening to the Red Path Way depends on you lighting the fire in the hearts of the brotherhood of men but first you must instill it deep within the depths of your own being. Come, sit down at my hearth's fire and let me bring you the broth of pte to strengthen you." Joe put his hands gently upon her raised weapons and lowered them to her side. "Here, drink," he said, putting an ancient clay vessel to her mouth.

The warm buffalo broth soothed her spirit as she drank.

"Now, tell me through your vision what has happened," He looked into her eyes and placed his hands upon her shoulders. When he saw all that was passing through the reels of their mindlink, he harrumphed and walked to his old Jeep. Joe radioed his brethren, brothers of his people's tribe, to help guard the campground gates and clear up any of the evidence not already been tended to.

"We must go. The Sun is touching the breasts of the Mother, the time is now to enter the womb for your naming to become fully human, just as the first ones birthed by the Mother were named. Come quickly and bring your weapons," Joe said, before he retreated back into the brush along a path only he could see.

After a short time, the two reached the cave's clearing. They walked the transformed grounds clockwise before entering the ring of four ages, the home of White Buffalo Calf Woman and the gated pathway to the opening of the fifth world.

Willow stood in reverence as the cleansing fire of

purification was lit and the flickering flames began to heat the twenty-eight rocks that lay within the sacred wood bundle's heart.

"Prepare to enter the womb of the Mother as she bore you," said Joe, who stood stoically in front of the sweat lodge.

Willow's exhausted mind slowly grasped the threads of his words and finally understanding, she began to remove her clothes. Standing naked as a babe in front of the medicine man, he approached her and began to rub an ocher-tinted bear fat upon her skin. One like Red Hand's, although Joe's was already infused with Jimson weed, the "loco" herb, for it could drive you mad, or drive you home to see the face you wore before you were born.

The two seekers began to dance in a circle. Willow followed the elder's movements, raising her arms to the heavens on each pass, turning inward toward the sacred fire. The hungry flames lowered slowly, dying down as the blessed fuel was consumed. Finally, the rocks glowed red in a bed of coals.

The woman's mind was swirling, each passing in the Circle Dance drawing her deeper toward the passage to the womb.

Joe confirmed the salves effectiveness with a glance: expanding pupils darkening the eyes of the initiate was a sure sign. He stopped at the entrance to the sweat lodge, opened the flap and motioned for the young woman to enter. Willow lowered her glistening, sweat-covered body to crawl through the small opening allowing the blackness of the dark interior to engulf her mind and swallow her whole.

The shaman began to carry one rock at a time into the lodge's womb, cradling each one lovingly in the embrace of two small deer horns. As he placed each stone he chanted a prayer to the corresponding direction and element. To the North, love, respect and gratitude of Earth was honoured. To the East, blessings for wind with which the wings of prayer are carried upon were given. Fire was revered to the South, for the searing purification of one's heart. And to the West, the cooling, birthing waters that bore the matrix of creation were praised.

On the placement of the fourth stone, the fire keeper poured from a hollowed buffalo horn the steeped waters of sage tea, whisking the steam about the darkened confines with a cedar branch.

The fifth stone was placed to represent the heavens and all that resides above. The sixth laid to honour all that comes from below, from the place of emergence and rebirth. Lastly, the seventh was set to represent the ethers where the Mother herself was born.

At the end of the first round the flap was closed, and the old man began the story of man's emergence from the Mother's womb:

"When the first people, those of Atlantis, broke the chain of gratitude in honouring the Mother's gift, long after her rumbling settled she became lonely. The longing for the love and respect she once had encouraged her to create her own children that she formed from clay to become Keepers of the Earth. They were the red of ocher—the blood of Earth upon their skin.

"She told her children of creation's purpose. She told them that as gatekeepers of the twelve portals and energy vortexes, they sustained the Mother's ability to grace those who fed upon her great abundance. These children, after their teachings were instilled, crawled forth from the womb at two places, only one of which would remain open after the birthing.

"In the North, those of Middle Earth emerged from the opening but then chose to return remaining hidden deep within the loving folds of the womb, only appearing when called forth. They have now been awakened to the call, as all creatures great and small have. The sound of the Earth's mournful groan is being heard over vast continents.

"The second place of emergence is at the door to the ninth gateway in Sedona, Arizona. The home of the Hopi and ancient Anasazi. The name Anasazi was given to the ancient ones, but sadly became synonymous with 'the enemies.' They were only truly feared as enemy by those of the lizard race that continued to multiply on Earth.

"The Hopi have held fast to their stories and sacred teachings, burying the wisdom deep in the wombs of kivas. The prophecies have been fulfilled and time now calls forth the Four Races from the four directions to join the four stone tablets that portray wisdom's story of emergence.

"Knowing will be remembered, and in the linking of the pieces of evolution's puzzle, humankind will become whole once again, causing the Mother to shiver with delight.

"Go back to the place of your beginning, daughter; rediscover the expressions of the great mystery, as you are sculpted from the very blood of the Mother herself.

"When you become the pulse that beats as one, suckling her breast, it is then that the Mother will name her child and you will emerge anew and reborn into your purpose," spoke the wise man.

His voicing of the remembering was the gatekeeper of

time; his words wove the web of existence's story back into being, his words reclaimed what was lost and buried deep in the dark recesses of Mother Earth.

The words of the medicine man drew Willow down a spiraling path that led to the bowels of the Earth. With each of the four rounds, in the placement of seven stones, the continuous chant retained a constant prayer of blessing to the elements and directions. She spun, her skin on fire, burning away the masks she wore: the martyr, the victim, the whore, Chiron no more. Her consciousness lay exposed, a liquid pool at the feet of the Mother—within the Mother. The whispering of awakening poured upon her spirit and drew her forth and into the arms of the Creator. She listened and became heart, her tears a river whose trickling track led her up the trunk of the tree of life; her name was blazoned upon the scorched purity of mind.

As the birds sang in the dawn, Joe slowly rolled back the flap of the sweat lodge letting fingers of light caress in a new day, blessing the birth of a human being.

He was also purified, although his seeking was different. For now, he was cleansed of doubt, with renewal etched upon his flesh his purpose reigned forth with clarity.

Joe walked around the fire's smoldering embers to exit the circle of life, the cool breath of the mountain wind refreshing and invigorating his senses.

He walked to the bank of the stream that quietly gurgled beyond the mouth of the cave and filled a clay vessel with its cool, crisp waters. He drank deeply. Then he refilled the cup to carry it back to the woman that now stood outside of the womb, cloaked in a misty shroud as steam poured off her sweat-drenched skin.

"Welcome, daughter, embrace this day. Do you know your first given name?" queried Joe.

"Yes, Tunkasila, I am, as all women, the embodiment of Gaia. I have awakened to embrace the Wiyan Wakan that I am.

"I evoke Kali, Venus, Madonna, and all the names of all that is of the same energy: the Goddess that bore forth creation. Her river—my blood, her mountains—my breasts, her valleys—the crevices of life's longing.

"I am White Buffalo Calf Woman and I am fully awake!" spoke Willow, transformed in the glory of knowing.

"Come, my daughter, we will rest, for your journey was long. We must return to our place and path upon this realm until all preparations are secured." With that he draped an embroidered white hide of pte upon Willow's shoulders, the people's history stitched in a cascade of silken colour now her shroud.

Old Joe had been keeper of the maiden's cloak since the time of the Crystal Cave's closing. His relations assumed the guardianship of the shroud upon the death of Red Hand. The Holy man's instructions passed from generation to generation until the end of the fourth age and the return of White Buffalo Calf Woman.

The crystal skull that had once been wrapped in the buffalo hide cloak still sat buried at the entrance to the Cave of Journey; protected until the matrix of the web of life's vibration sang forth.

The two followed the Powder-Face Trail down to the camp, where brothers of the People's Nation Tribe awaited.

The small group of warrior men and women broke

their circle around the small camp fire with the approach of Willow and Joe.

They looked upon the eyes of the glowing woman and a unified chant rose to the heavens in gratitude for the call to action that her appearance brought.

"We remember the Mother, we shall dance in the awakening of the uniting of all nations across all realms; we shall walk upon your beauty in reverence. We, the Keepers of the Earth, will not be destroyed again. We have waited, as instructed, for your arrival to be idle no more, an honour. Now let us begin!" said one large Native stepping forward, long braids swaying with his movement.

Every man and woman in the circle came forward and grasped the transformed woman's hand. They bowed and spoke in reverence, "A'ho."

Tears fell from the eyes of the humble woman; the young lady who no longer walked alone through the realms of time, for now she was seen and her glory was blinding.

Old Joe led Willow by the elbow into the tipi that had been erected on his site and laid her down to rest upon the pelts of all her relations.

In the late afternoon, Willow awoke with a start unsure where she was for a moment. A hazy fog of disorientation lay upon her sleepy mind as she removed the bear hide blanket that weighed heavily upon her body.

When she looked about the tipi, the warm familiarity of coming home suffused her heart and invigorated her spirit. A dream catcher hung above her head, crystals woven into the sinew web with an obsidian center to absorb negativity. At the entrance to the tipi, bundles of dried mugwort hung from the structure's long poles for protection from the evils that are known and those which are not.

Her eyes lazily searched about for the source of the sound of rustling feathers that distracted her from her reverie, they fell upon the sight of Hermann who fluttered his wings in greeting.

"Good day my friend, what a joy to see you under better circumstances," she said in a raspy, parched voice.

The raven nodded with a "caw" of acknowledgment.

"Let us go and see what the day has in store for us," she said, pulling herself from the bed of pelts. "Oh," she stammered, "I suppose I better return to my camp and grab some clothing," looking down and noticing her naked, red-tinted skin. "God, I smell like a dead animal." She grabbed a long, oilskin slicker that lay at the end of the fur and pallet bed and parted the flap of the tipi, leaving its security behind.

The Native giant that had first spoken to her in the morning smiled a toothy grin from the fire's edge at the appearance of the bedraggled woman drowning in the over-sized jacket.

Willow smiled in return, "It is so nice to see you again. I'm sorry I do not know your name?" she said reaching her hand forward.

"I am Black Bear, Wiyan Wakan. I am blessed with the honour to be your guardian, my sister," said the mountain of a man.

He stood just above six-foot-five, weighing at least two-eighty. Deeply etched, parallel claw marks ran down the right side of his face. He appeared to be in his early 30s, strong and fit, in black jeans and shirt. The man stood tall and proud, fingering the Buck knife at his belt, an amulet and bear claw necklace graced his thick neck.

"Oh, please call me Willow," she said blushing. "I thank you for your offer, but I will be fine. I do not need a guardian. I am just going to run over to my site, grab some clothes and clean up. Do you know where I can find Joe?" she asked.

"Joe has gone back to the reserve to raise our brothers and sisters into action. They are going to form the procession for the long walk; one to reclaim our lands and form a circle of protection over the Way and you." Black Bear motioned with a sweep of his strong arm, "This park was part of our original hunting grounds and a place where our sacred relations were honoured, that was until the government betrayed our treaty back in the late eighteenth century. You must not be alone, little one, as there is a great enemy at hand. The man you encountered yesterday was the first of many."

"My brothers and I have removed the body from the brush where the four leggeds hid it, and we have taken the ranger's truck across the mountains to the next valley over. We disguised his death with the help of brother bear," he smiled, rubbing his hand fondly over his scar. "Joe has left his old Jeep for you to go and finish your errands. We must not raise any suspicion. You must go say goodbye to your young man and take him his belongings. Then you must radio your boss and tell him that you cannot cross the barrier that will be set up by the peoples' march, and the Idle No More movement that has now formed. Then we will set the official camp vehicle on fire at the gates, in a ritual of purification and a show of our stand. The coiling, coal-black smoke of the fire will represent the true result of the greed of oil and the snake that is destroying our lands," with a twinkle in his eyes, he chuckled heartily.

Willow's heart beat quickly, pounding with Earth's oneness from the image that appeared flowing before her eyes. She knew that the vision was of the universal heart; this was not just a Native movement, it was one for all races and desperately needed to unite all as a humane, empowered people. The poor and the oppressed that have been disallowed their birthright to live in harmony with nature shall awaken to the truth. Those that have been denied the right to use the plants that grow freely from the windblown seeds, those denied the right to clean water and the right to embrace the responsibility to love the land as sacred will revolt. The masses that are entrenched in poverty, subjected to mass-produced, genetically-altered food and enslaved by a society built to control their every movement would unite as one people and rise up to the all-pervasive evil eye of the corrupt, hedonistic elite.

"Well it seems that you have thought of everything," she said in shock and wonder, and a little fear and trepidation.

"Not I, sister. We, the Tribal Nations, have been preparing for a very long time. We have awoken from the deep sleep. Our purpose has been written before both our times," said Black Bear.

"Yes, and it feels great!" Willow said smiling and raising her arm in a cheer.

"I must go clean up and grab some clothes, so I can head to town before dark. I am starving, do you know if I am allowed to eat?" she asked.

"Yes, here, I will get you some broth," he said, walking back to a pot that hung on a tripod over the small camp fire.

"I put a nice hunk of the meat of pte in your bowl to

fortify you," the warrior brave said when he returned with the soup and a piece of bannock bread.

Graciously accepting the bowl, she dipped the bread in the hearty broth of buffalo and headed back toward her camp, shouting over her shoulder that she'd be back in an hour or so.

When Willow arrived at the site, she set the near empty bowl down, noticing Bobby's backpack. "Great this should be fun," she thought, thinking of how much she hated goodbyes. She threw open the door of the old van and reached in to find her toiletry bag among the disarray. She quickly threw on a light cotton shift and fresh underwear and headed to the gurgling river on a path that wound down the hill from her camp.

The afternoon sunrays were as glorious as the morning beams had been, but now it was warm enough to bathe.

It seemed to Willow as if the very essence surrounding her, from the rushing flow of the river to the rustling of the trees, was beseeching her to remove her clothing. Lazily, she shrugged off the silky summer dress and shed her cotton panties.

Laying back and resting her head upon a rock, Willow pulled out her bag of heady medicine and proceeded to spark the joint that was conveniently rolled in the pouch. She inhaled deeply to bring in a sense of calm acceptance and to help her process all that had passed. Casually hauling on the sweet herb, the dance of its effect swam through her senses. A nice mellow buzz swarmed her brain as she contemplated life through the tidbits of history she now retained.

The trickling stream and the flow of its whispering

song encouraged her mind to drift into the realms of unconsciousness, delving into the seat of the soul. "Oh, how the sweetness of nature imbues one's essence," she thought.

As she drifted into the ecstasy of being, something stirred the air around her accompanied by the strong scent of sweetgrass.

Willow sat up alert, searching for any signs of disturbance in her blissed-out state.

The wind picked up prickling her nipples into erect pink nodes. She relaxed, thinking maybe the scent was coming in on the breeze and proceeded to lay back down.

The wind still whistled around her head whipping her long hair across her face as it began to caress her. Willow relaxed into its soothing whisper. With a life of its own, the gentle breeze whipped up her legs, lingering on her breasts; it's subtle swirling felt like cool lips upon her. She became aroused and slowly began to touch herself. Her long slender fingers stroked her tanned and glistening body. As she began to reach down to her sacred valley, it felt as though there was another entity there. Her hands seemed to be held back and the previous sensation of cool lips upon her breast increased to the reality of a powerful, tugging and suckling sensation. She didn't quite understand what was happening but was too caught up in the joy of touch to not respond with passion to the mystery that was upon her. The moment of fleeting panic subsided to want.

Wahweyho sensed her relaxation and acceptance of his presence. The longing of a hundred years poured into every tantalizing nibble, every flicker of tongue. And in every whispering, ghostly touch he chanted ancient songs of love's longing and yearning into her ears.

Willow moved and responded to his words. She was in another realm, ecstasy encompassing her on the journey to another world, one filled with purity and the romantics of love. She felt as if she was riding a wild pony bareback across the plains down into grassy meadows: the stallion's backbone rubbing against her buttocks and mound.

Willow tried to rise out of the sensation for she felt as if she was galloping into a realm too deep to get out of—the physical into the spiritual.

Wahweyho sensed the mysticism he weaved was breaking apart. It was difficult for him to participate in the physical reality and retain his cloak of power in material form.

Yet he needed to enter her, his desire was too strong, his longing an eternity.

As Willow tried to gain control of her feelings and pull herself up, she was pressed down; there was a mouth upon her, the probing of a sweet tongue inside.

The scent in the air was dizzying and in the electric field's mist, he entered her, thrusting deep into the only flesh he longed for in a thousand moons.

Willow gasped and moaned. Her eyes were wide and fearful, not fully understanding what was happening. Her arms were raised and held gently above her head and then she knew who was upon her and gladly joined her warrior lover's passion in their union. His mouth ravaged her hungrily as the thrusting of hips rolled on the waves of ecstasy.

Wahweyho grabbed her buttocks and raised it toward himself. He slowed his motion to calm her desire, suckling her fingers as they came to search out his manhood. He pulled out of the entrance of her sacred cave. Emotions of confusion, ecstasy, fear and passion cascaded through her mind. She reached down to touch the fullness she sensed and drew it back deep inside her

Oh, heaven on Earth, she never felt such oneness—a chanting harmony that drowned her senses, releasing all of her inhibitions. She felt the goddess within rise up from oppressed millennia and scream out her glory upon release.

Wahweyho, as well, cried out upon his release. His power spent, he caressed her one more time while whispering his love to her, his Mother Earth, the sacred Creator.

She shone as the brightest star on the darkest night, her joy rolling forth in glistening tears. Her glowing spirit poured into the Great Mother, pleasing the forgotten Goddess for it had been a very long time since she had been blessed with love's recognition, the woman and her now one.

Red Hand's spectrum lingered among the trees above Wahweyho and the sacred woman.

He saw how much energy the young warrior spent in staying in the lower realms of physicality.

"Youthful spirits, whether in or out of body, are troublesome and headstrong at best," muttered the shaman.

"It takes many journeys to the nine levels of essence before a spirit rises above the longings of the lower energy centers. He himself still had the odd drawing to this form of spiritual release. It provided a great sense of oneness with creation, although only fleeting, to all entities, even the trees he rested among now felt ecstasy at their union.

Red Hand flew down to the young, drained, pulsating spirit concerned that the warrior had forgotten the way to the realm that was their home. Wisps of Wahweyho's ethereal body were still entwined with the woman's. He must draw them apart. Their spirits had a strong longing for one another and it would be difficult to bring the warrior back. He hoped the sacred drum would help his journey back to their home.

"The young fool should have waited until the bringing forth of the crystal skull of pte, then the young woman could come across to their side easily and without forsaking the warrior's spirit. Wahweyho knew this encounter was dangerous without the aid of a physical body to possess," thought the old seer.

The shaman was determined as he beat upon the drum of his ancestors from across the realms. The vibrating sound created the thrumming of the eternal pulse. Red Hand, with the aid of prayer and chant, drew his son back into the realm of the old ones: the realm of the first people, the first tree, the first flower, the first blade of grass.

Black Bear stood on the hilltop watching the young woman, having been drawn to the river by her ecstatic scream. He smiled at the shadow of spirit play and the knowing that the thinning veil displayed.

Willow was spent; her senses held a lingering euphoria. She lay back and watched as her warrior lover's spirit dissolved, returning to the essence of where it was formed. Aural waves tuned to the rhythmic beating that called him home.

Her desire to rise and follow what had filled her cup with overflowing completeness was overwhelming. She lay still in awe, held back only by the excitement in knowing her place in the upcoming unfolding.

She smiled in contentment and with a fleeting wave and a nod blew a kiss to the magnetism that hung in the air.

"Goodbye, my love, 'til next time," she said happily, then jumping up she dove into the icy, glacier-fed waters.

"Whoa, that is cold!" she yelled, raising her goose-pimpled body out of the freezing river. Quickly, she grabbed the bottle of natural soap she had brought and slathered its fresh scent all over her rather odoriferous body. The sweat lodge had done what its word implied: cleansed accumulated toxins. It refreshed the body like nothing else, especially after when life's blood was awakened with cool, clear waters.

"Hello Bear," said Willow waving up at the giant who stood watching from the hilltop above.

Black Bear turned around quickly, "Umm, I'm sorry. I was just making sure you're all right."

"It's fine, I'm fine," she chuckled, diving back into the river to rinse the suds out of her hair and off her soapy body.

"I'll be right up and then we can leave," she said when she emerged from the water.

When Willow returned to camp a few moments later, Bear was waiting beside the Jeep.

"I'll be just a sec'," she said, running to the van. She threw her bath bag into the back of the van and grabbed Bobby's pack.

She jumped in the passenger seat of the Jeep next to Bear, "Okay let's go, we need to head to the Rockies Hospital."

They arrived at the hospital about an hour later. Black Bear dropped Willow off at the entrance and then went to find a parking spot.

Willow had asked him to wait in the Jeep, frustrating

Black Bear, as he was supposed to be with her at all times, especially in the city with so many people around.

Willow found her way to the front desk and asked what room she could find Bob in. After getting directions, she went to the cafeteria and grabbed him some food and a men's fashion magazine. "He'll love this," she mused to herself.

The room was on the seventh floor and she didn't see any stairwell entrance, so she'd have to take the elevator. "God, I hate elevators," she thought finding the corridor with a bank of four doors to enter, two per side. "Which to choose?" she asked herself. "I'll push both buttons and hope for the best."

The doors to her left opened immediately and a gentleman in a dark blue pin-striped suit and a red tie appeared inside.

"Going up?" he asked.

"Only one way to go and it isn't down," she said smiling. She entered the compartment and pushed the necessary button. The elevator took her directly to the seventh floor with no other stops, so the nausea she commonly experienced was thankfully avoided.

"This is me," she said, stepping out of the stuffy, melodic steel box.

The man remained still as a pillar, his eyes staring blankly at hers as the doors closed behind her.

Willow found room 712 and with a quiet knock she entered, Bob's bag slung over her shoulder.

"Hi, how are you feeling?" She asked with heartfelt empathy when she saw him. "Have you spoken with your family yet?"

"Yeah, they have arranged a flight for me tomorrow. You know it is costing us almost $1000 a day to be here!" he mumbled through cracked, puffy lips. His eyes were not as swollen as when she had seen him the night before, but his blue irises were now lost in a sea of red that was somewhat worse to look at. He had black bruising, as if someone had attacked him with a poking stick, all over his arms and his ribs were bound in gauze.

"You look great, Willow. Shit, you're almost glowing. Thanks a lot for your apparent joy. I didn't expect you to be so happy!" Bob pouted.

"Oh sweetheart, I am not happy about how this is ending, nor about the pain and suffering you are in. I wanted more for us it just wasn't meant to be. You know that as well as I do. I do love you, you are a great guy, but it is apparent we are destined to move on," she said, kissing his cheek as he stared up at her in a daze.

A couple of minutes later he slipped into a light sleep, dozing from the effect of the pain medication. She exited the room, wiping tears of mournful sadness from her eyes.

The Sun's hues of warm pink and soothing orange splayed across the pale white walls of the hospital halls. Willow felt peace in the comfort of sunset. She was still wiping her eyes and trying to stop crying as she arrived at the corridor's bank of elevators. Through her cloudy vision, just as she was reaching her hand across to push the down button the elevator doors slid open and there stood the same solemn man in the blue suit. Willow surmised that the poor man must be in shock and pain over a loved one.

"Oh, are you going back down as well?" she asked a little startled by his presence.

He did not respond, he just continued to stare off into space.

"Umm, you go ahead, okay? I'll catch the next elevator," she said, turning away.

His hand quickly grabbed her arm and he tried to pull her in through the closing doors.

"Ahh, don't!" she yelled, pulling her arm back quickly and causing him to stumble forward. Turning, she took off in a run heading for the door to the stairwell she suddenly spotted. Willow ran like the wind, flying down the stairs two at a time, round and round spiraling down with the crashing, stumbling sound of the zombie dude close on her trail.

She searched frantically for her knife as she ran and then remembered it was still on her belt at camp. She didn't put it back on with her dress, "damn fashion etiquette!" she cursed internally.

As she rounded the third-floor landing, the doors crashed open and she almost ran into the bulking mass of her guardian warrior.

The fear in her eyes and the quick look behind her shoulder was the only message Bear needed. He threw her behind his tree of a body and in the flash of a moment had his Buck knife in one hand and a tomahawk in the other.

Willow's attacker, only seconds behind her, jumped down upon the landing.

The flying tomahawk smashing into the center of his unexpecting deadpan face.

"You get out of here now, Willow. The Jeep is running out front in the drop-off zone, take it and head back to camp. I'll stay and deal with the body. Go, go!" he yelled at the frozen woman.

"I'm not going to leave you Bear. Now, hold him up. I'll go and get a wheelchair, there has to be one close," she said while running through the door, shock buried deep inside for the moment. She returned in seconds with a chair and a sheet to cover the body, there was not much blood as the small embedded ax held the flow in check.

They fled the hospital in a flurry, throwing the sheathed body in the backseat of the running Jeep. They flew out of the hospital parking lot like bats out of hell and took off down the road and back to the safety of the camp's forest.

When Willow and Black Bear reached the outer limits of Bragg Creek, they pulled over at the entrance to an off-road trail and dumped the body deep in the bush.

"I will have Old Joe conjure up a request to have our sister, mountain lion, deal with this atrocity. She will gladly comply," said the stoic warrior as he pried the hatchet from the dead man's head.

Willow began to shake uncontrollably, shock numbing her senses and taking over her body.

The mountain of a man gathered her up in his arms and carried her back to the Jeep. Reaching into the medicine bag all warriors wore around their neck, he grabbed a pinch of the little ones and placed the bittersweet healing plant under her lip.

"Rest without fear, for we are almost under the watchful eyes of the tribe of our brothers and sisters. We will raise the field of protection tonight with dance. There is no time to waste!" he said, wheeling the old Jeep onto the road, gears grinding in screeching protest, as he sped into what he hoped was the greatest movement to wash across the lands since the great deluge.

When the two arrived at the camp, a throng of gathered people parted to let them enter, all wore the face of joy of the awakened soul.

Willow had calmed with the psychotropic effects of the little ones and smiled with calm fortitude at the glowing mass of light emanating from every living, shining being.

The trees shimmered in dusk's delight and birds chirped in orchestrated harmony as animals of all sorts began to appear from the depths of the forest.

Black Bear shut the Jeep off and the two stepped down from the vehicle's confines at the gate to the park as it was locked shut. People of all races had gathered to form a wall of solidarity along the road, all one through the beating drum's heart song, awakened to their becoming as Keepers of the Earth. All of them were chanting their readiness for action in unison, "A'ho."

And so the Circle Dance began in glory and oneness. Willow's company vehicle now the blazing fire they danced around.

The great and foreboding mountain of a man, Bear, led Willow through the throng of people, deftly guiding her to where the Tribal Council of the People's Tribe sat. The elders had gathered in a large tipi that had been setup on a rise to the East to determine the movement's path. The young woman entered the tunnel of rainbow light that poured forth from the tipi's parted flap. As the white buffalo pelt was laid upon her shoulders by Black Bear, a halo formed around her body.

She could hear in the whispering of mind's knowing, the path her brothers and sisters had chosen to take, for all has been written. She knew that their fortitude and their belief in the path of the peaceful warrior would inspire the masses across all lands that existed within the womb's waters.

Many people would relate in remembering their own struggle and displacement for every nation upon the Sacred Mother had its story.

Willow addressed the elders with the wise words of Black Elk, an Oglala Sioux, for they encompassed the truth of the Red Path Way, the path the movement would follow: "The first peace, which is the most important, is that which grows within the soul of all people when they realize their relationship, their oneness, with the universe and all its powers. And when they realize that at the center of the universe dwells the Great Spirit, and that its center is really everywhere, it is within each of us."

The elders nodded in acknowledgment of their wise brother's words that flowed with grace from the mouth of the Goddess incarnate.

"It is time for the making of relations daughter," spoke the elder, Chief Luther Standing Bear. "Our words of purpose must touch the hearts of all across the lands for the awakening to commence. This is the force necessary to overthrow the power of unconscious thought that suppresses all.

"The long walk of the Tibetan people has begun; their oppressors that had hidden the pyramid's power link of brothers under the guise of a mountain stronghold have been discovered." Their journey of peace upon the wheel of time has reached its zenith, and the shimmering clouds of illusion will now part, exposing the doorway to Shangri-La.

"The monks' chant has opened other portal links. The

constant burning of incense by a multitude of Earth's people on shrines upon the web has increased the vibration of the Mother's resonance and triggered a mindlink that unites.

"Those in the East have awakened and see that they are slaves only to the big sleep, they fight for the waters of life, each step taken as one of holy peace.

"The time walkers of Australia have crossed over, holding a door open since they presented the crystallized skulls of Uluru to the masses.

"Shamans from the heights of the great Andes have been practicing the rituals to reopen the doorway of Aramu Muru. The stone animals that have protected its realm will shift and come alive when our universal brothers from the Pleiades come forth through the portal creating a great shift.

"Our alien brothers will pour forth upon our request from all regions to the South to help in the understanding of relations in the fine weave of creation's story. The grid of Earth energies that have sat dormant in the homes of the Mayan brotherhood will be activated. Their ships will rise from the burial grounds and awe will shake the foundations of mind allowing great energy to pour forth like a tidal wave.

"At that time, the movement will become unstoppable, but until then, we will need to walk gently. As you have seen, daughter, not all people are ready for awakening. Most walk in fear and live with the need of conquest and dominance over nature. They do not see the scheme of existence: equal importance of all, reverence for all of life."

The hypnotizing dialogue of Chief Luther Standing Bear, continued to pour forth: "It will be a long time until other men are able to divine and ride the rhythm of creation. Men must be born and reborn to belong; their bodies must be formed of the dust of their forefathers' bones," finished the wise and ancient man.

The young woman smiled, nodding in acknowledgment to the divine presence of her people. She knew it was time to begin her reappearance to the children across the lands, for those who could still see with their heart.

The Goddess spoke, "Since the beginning of recorded time and beyond, our Mother has appeared in her cloak of stars riding upon a crescent moon. Her blinding glory—the blessed energy of transformation. I have been beckoned forth and shall appear in the divine form recognized by each culture and each religion across all lands, just as I have before. I am known throughout the world under many names, but we are all the same.

"On the hills of Tepeyac, in Mexico, I was called Virgin de Guadalupe. Although previously I had been known and worshiped as Tonantzin, the Aztec Goddess of Corn, and Coatlique, the Snake Goddess. My children at this time, in this region, fell victim to the lizard men's ways. The time was one of great evil, one that strangles the true heart until this day.

"We, the seers and I, have hidden my true name slyly under the guise of the many labels of conform. But at times I still appear, if only for the remembering of the feminine.

"I am Kali throughout India, in the Hindu tradition.

"I am Our Lady of Rosary in Prouville, France.

"The Virgin Mary in Lourdes and LaSalette, France, as well as in Fatima, Portugal," the Goddess continued naming the forms of manifestation she had taken.

"I became the lady of Knock to those in Ireland and Mary Queen of Peace in Medjugorje, Yugoslavia.

"I rose and danced above a house of worship in

Zeitun, Egypt for many years, showering rose petals upon all religions even though they worshiped me not.

"I have appeared as the loving mermaid, the Goddess Atargatis to the Assyrian people and Pele on the summit of the caldera of Kilauea, Hawaii, when fear turned my children to pray for protection.

"All have seen me as a loving Mother, but this time I shall appear as I have become, through the disrespect for this gift of life. My wrath will be awesome, and men and women will fall on their knees in fear. My children seek to be taught the hard lesson of respect. One that will bring about the remembering of all the elements that they are comprised of, and what they survive and reside on," said the Goddess incarnate, with rising anger.

"A great fire will scorch the Earth; your skin shall be seared as mine has been. My waters will dry up in places from the trapping of my blood's path and will flood in others. A great wave of despair will wash over all from the deluge of my falling tears. The winds of my breath will blow with devastating force, crumbling and shattering humankind's pillars to their own self-imposed status as gods. My body, the Earth, will rumble, buck and heave, screaming as I give birth to myself once again.

"I have returned in this form to save those of my children who will dance in the new dawn of the Keepers of the Earth. The secret knowledge that lies buried deep within your heart's realm shall not be contained any longer. I cannot stop this path of destruction my children have wrought upon the sacred. Wisdom cries forth rebirth, and so it shall be," finished the all-powerful spirit.

Willow's mind whirled in lost realms, as the words of

White Buffalo Calf Woman poured from her mouth. Her body becoming a temporary vessel, her physical shell, the awakener's home for the moment.

The Goddess, still emanating brightly through her charge's temple of being, turned from the council of elders, stepping forth from the tipi to address her children. "Every dawn, as it comes, is a holy event. And every day is holy, for the light comes from Wakan Tanka. You must remember that the two leggeds and all other beings who stand upon this Earth are sacred and should be treated as such. When you begin the big talk with the pale ones you must remember these words," spoke White Buffalo Calf Woman to the enraptured crowd gathered around her.

"All my children are sacred, even those who have forsaken me. Walk in peace, even when they come with arms, which they will! You must retain your connection to the Great Spirit, Wakan Tanka, the unifying force that flows in and through all things. In spirit, be humble and meek, for you have the force of the Mother's wrath to address those who have forgotten how to walk in peace upon my sacredness," she vowed.

"The cosmic circle shall be recreated in dance, so our people, you, my children, will no longer live in ignorance. Your revelation of purpose to live in a holy manner will become your shining shroud. The great mystery shall be revealed," finished the Goddess passionately.

Willow felt the calming elixir of the Goddess' wisdom leave her body, but the all-encompassing love of life's gifts still flowed through her pulsing veins. She turned to her left where the hulking guardian stood by her side and spoke her need to lie down.

The stars twinkled brightly in black skies; the seven sisters' brilliant starlight poured upon her tired shoulders, as she walked back to her camp.

The four colours of the Earth's tribe danced, cheering the young woman on as she proceeded to sleep's renewal leaving a shimmering trail of glowing effervescence in her wake.

"Oh lord, I am so tired," she said, as Black Bear opened the sliding side door to her van.

"Lie down, little one, you will feel revised by the rising of the Mother's gift of light in the morn'," he said. "I will be right outside if you are in need of anything."

The moment Willow's head hit the pillow she fell into the void of a deep sleep, one of no dreams, enveloped in the peace of nothingness.

The warmth of the day, and the song of the birds' call to awaken stirred the still woman's form. She raised her arms above her head, the twinge of aching muscles causing a moan to escape her lips.

"Well, I best stretch this stiffened, tired body," she said, rubbing her arms.

"Morning, Black Bear, I hope you got some rest last night," she said, greeting her protector upon exiting the van.

"Let me prepare some coffee. Would you like some breakfast?" she asked.

"Coffee would be fine, sister, then we must go and see Joe, when you are ready."

"I really need to do some yoga and stretch first. There is a clearing just to the south of here where I practice the salutation to the Sun. Please, just help yourself to a coffee when it is ready, there is cream in the cooler and honey on the table, if the ants have not consumed it all. I should only be about 20 minutes," she said, heading off with her yoga mat under her arm.

Black Bear nodded to his charge, then called to raven with his heart emanation to rise to the skies and keep watch.

Willow felt the presence of the bird's watchful gaze, it provided her with a sense of ease as she bowed in ritual gratitude for Father Sun's blessed warmth.

When she returned to camp, she quickly coffee'd up and then headed off to see her mentor, Old Joe, with her brother and guardian, Bear, and feathered friend in tow.

"Good morning, Tunkasila," she said, with a small bow of respect.

Black Bear nodded to the honoured medicine man of his tribe. The sound of drumming could be heard reverberating off the foothills of the Rockies. The people's dance had continued through the night, the background noise becoming one with heartbeat's thrum.

"Good morning, daughter, how did you sleep?" the old man asked.

"Like the dead," Willow replied with a smile.

"The dead do not rest, my child, they sit in wait of our awakening and reside just beyond the threshold of our mind's eye," said Old Joe.

"I am sorry, I meant no disrespect Joe," she said.

"Oh, don't mind me, daughter. I am just tired from the preparations. It appears we will soon be visited by the big arm of the law for our rightful occupation of the lands of our ancestors," he huffed.

"I am a little worried, for in this time we have the media's lies to attend with as well as the political aspects. There is so much to organize and such little time."

The seer began to work himself into a frenzy. "We must prepare to present the Seven Holy Rites in a way that all the Mother's children can understand, the way to allow all to see with the heart.

"We are in a time of great crisis and upheaval, one predicted by the Goddess to come before the cleansing and purification.

"Our enemies are very strong and hold the key of control over the many forms and sources of our present communication. They have held the power to put the people asleep: from fluoride in treated water, to the genetic manipulation of corn that is many of the world's peoples' main staple.

"This select elite, that care not for our awakening, bombard the skies with chemical trails at an unholy frequency that suppresses our inherent knowledge," he ranted on.

Old Joe heaved a great sigh and seemed to wither with despair. "We have the drum, and the brotherhood of nations. If we cannot open the last door in the grid of portals our Mother may not survive, and all will be lost."

As the old man had predicted, the sound of sirens filled the air.

The three: seeker, seer and guardian, held hands and with a smile and a nod of fortitude walked together toward the sound of drumming.

When the small group rounded the loop that led to the gate's entrance, they stopped in awe at the size of the gathering that had tripled overnight. There was a tipi upon every clear rise of the land; vehicles, R.V.s and vans blocked the roadways as far as the eye could see. The sight of the gathering of like minds eased the old man's fear a little. But, it was still a long and winding road uphill to erase the fear and judgment held in the heart of people who had embraced and conformed to society.

People parted like a wave upon a rocky shore as the three walked together toward the movement's center and their destiny.

The basis of the Idle No More movement had started in protest to the Canadian government's proposed change and implementation of the Navigable Waters Protection Act (NWPA) under Omnibus Bill C45.

The league of Prime Minister Harper's corporate minions decided the best way to move forward on the Enbridge Northern Gateway Pipeline Project was to rescind the right for Canadians to protect the numerous small waterways that sat upon Turtle Island.

Many of these waterways passed through the lands of the Keepers of the Earth. Grave illness was already rampant among the reserves that bordered the Athabasca tar sands and wildlife irreparably damaged.

The movement was Canada-wide and would soon grow to an international level. Environmentalists and the Indigenous peoples of the world were awakening to Gaia's call to rise and unite. The gathering of brothers and sisters, "the protectors of the water," was coming full circle now. People were standing up for the Mother.

In the South, people had gathered where the black snake—once foretold in ancient stories made not of myth—was held at bay by those of fortitude and soul. The vile, oily serpent sought to slither across all lands to pollute all waters in its hungry search for control and the power to feed on the fear of the dependence of nations.

A world government of elite and exploitative rapists had the use of an endless source of greed as their fortitude, an army of sheep at their feet and the all-pervasive eye of big brother to intercept the people's message.

The people had the passion of the one heart and the dance that would open the doors of perception; and with that, a league of brothers and sisters would pour forth in love and protection of the Mother—their home across the gateways of time.

A great ruckus arose from the crowd as a troop of soldiers marched forth, their billy clubs swinging in front of their shields. Those who did not move out of the way were beaten with the righteous anger of the children taught to follow the conformists' ways.

"You fuckin' damn Indians. You filthy, dirty, hippy, eco-terrorist shits. Go back to your reserves and your shelters and collect your welfare checks!" was yelled from the mouths of the brain-washed babes as they bashed their way forward to the center of the people where the council awaited.

"Mother help us all," Willow numbly mumbled in prayer.

A reply came in song. It was a song that had awakened her soul from the first moment she heard it on

Robbie Robertson's tribute album to his Native heritage; it
was the one song Willow knew from her heart, the
"Cherokee Morning song," a chant that spoke words of
wisdom's truth. And so, they sang in unison the words of
empowerment:

> "We n' de ya ho, we n' de ya ho".
> (I am of the Great Spirit, it is so.)

> "We n' de ya, we n' de ya, ho, ho, ho, ho."
> (I am of the Great Spirit, it is so, it is so, it is so, it is
> so.)

> "Hey ya ho, hey ya ho, ya, ya, ya."

Joy poured forth in the singing of the ethereal emanation of
one heart. One voice in unity sang out the universal truth of
one people, one land, one Mother—the awakening to her
embrace.

The small army of men stopped as the song carried
through the hills and up the mountain banks, the beating of
the drum drowned out their threats with the joy of universal
oneness.

Black Bear stood among the band of warriors Willow
had met at Old Joe's fireside the previous day. She could place
the names to faces with ease. There was Red Hawk with his
long, curved nose. Blue Moon, a bodacious full woman with a
round cherub face standing beside Star, a gloriously beautiful,
petite woman.

As the song carried forth, Willow entered the circle of
her protectors, for she could feel a dark presence lurking in

the midst of her attuned senses.

She grabbed the hand of Winona, whose name meant firstborn daughter, another woman warrior within the band. She was a large, strong woman with a beaming smile that embodied the warmth of a summer day. Standing at Winona's side was Shadow who was as dark and mysterious as his name portrayed. The eldest brother, rightly named Chaska in the Sioux tradition, stood as tall as a pillar beside Black Bear and on his other side stood another massive hulk of a man known as Mahka, whose name meant that of the Earth. It was obvious the three were brothers of the same mother. The last in the band of nine warriors was Little Bull, his name very appropriate for the stance he held: his eyes alert, his body seemingly at the ready to charge in a moment's notice.

The group sensed the holy woman's unease, forming a ring of protection around her.

"What is it you perceive, Wiyan Wakan?" asked Little Bull, his eyes searching the approaching militants.

The song's transforming beauty rang forth causing some of the army throng to hesitate and lower their arms, as a lulling peace eased and awakened their sleeping consciousness.

There was a small group with the markings of an elite force that continued to move forward, their eyes of black focused on Willow and her protectors.

The three brothers, Black Bear, Mahka and Chaska formed a wall, as the rest of the band whisked their charge through the group of elders that awaited the negotiator, the leader of the invading army.

"Come quickly, sister," said Winona. "I fear there are

some in this army that are of the breed of lost souls, the race of the cold-hearted lizard men that you are familiar with from your past encounters. Fear not, for we will protect you with our lives," she said.

Little Bull charged ahead, mumbling to himself angrily for not spotting the dark emanating cloud of the fast-approaching group of elite soldiers.

The small band of warriors circled around the tipi of council then headed up a rise behind the structure and into the cover of the surrounding forest.

Old Joe stepped forward from the group of elders to address the representative sent to try and talk the people into dispersing.

The man approached, dressed in his army fatigues, with the insignia of high rank upon his shoulder. "Are you the one in charge of this group of protesters?" asked the man.

"No, brother, I am not. It is the Mother who calls forth her children to action," replied Joe.

"Well, you need to disperse, or we will be forced to arrest all of you. This park is government land, and it is illegal to block the gates. You are trespassing, as this park has officially been closed!" said the commander with an arrogant bravado of authority.

"I am sorry, brother, that you have been so misinformed. This is the sacred land of my nation, and we are the guardians of the Great Mother whom we all walk upon. We will not leave what we have been created to protect and honour. There is no trespassing as there is no ownership of the land, or of the creatures that walk upon her surface."

Joe continued after a short pause, "Go, and talk to your father, for it is the source of corporate greed whose orders you follow. The ones that seek to destroy what has blessed us all with life! We will not disperse until we have council with those who have dishonoured the signed treaties of our ancestors.

"Our movement has just begun, my son, and the world is watching as you and your throng of thugs try to beat us into submission. We shall not raise a hand in defense, for we are warriors of peace.

"Our time to awaken is now, brother. Put down your arms and release your fear, join us in dance and song and be saved to see the birth of a new dawn," said the shaman, his aura growing in brilliance in the light of the emanating truth.

The army commander shook his lowered head in shame. "I am sorry for the actions of some of my men, I am only following orders," he said with remorse.

"We will pull back and allow you to continue your demonstration, as long as it remains peaceful. Although, I must say that the burning of that truck was a bad idea," he said with a grimace. "I will relay your message, but I cannot guarantee that my superiors will meet with your people."

"Yes, the burning of the truck was a mistake, one meant to represent the evil of man's excessive consumption of oil and the dramatic impact of those actions," replied Joe. "See how black the smoke is that rises from that burning hulk of metal? That is but a small sample of what the oil sands to the North create. They are choking us all with the black heart of greed, polluting our waters and bringing disease to man and animal alike! It was lit only to block the park's entrance and to protect ourselves from your destined army of violence. Just look what you have done on foot alone!"

The man looked around at the hurt and bludgeoned. His group of men stood dumbfounded as the people still danced and sang, blood pouring down their smiling faces.

The commander called out an order for his men to stand down, and they turned to leave in remorseful disgrace. All, that is, except for the small band of elite men in black. Instead they hunkered down low and moved together swiftly over the rise of the foothills, in the direction Willow and her guardians had run.

Black Bear and his brothers stood and watched as the band of soldiers slinked into the woods. They waited a few moments then followed, silent as a cougar on the prowl. Pulling forth their weapons from worn leather sheaths the brothers dispersed, one to either side of Bear, spreading out in a fan formation.

Mahka prayed to his element of Earth to cushion his footfall as he approached two of the group of twelve that took up the back ranks position of the squad that moved forward in pursuit of his family clan.

The brave crouched down to half the size of his lanky six-foot-five-inch frame, his Mohawk adding another three inches. The warrior leapt into action, his piercing war cry screaming forth as his tomahawk fell upon the skull of one of the cold-hearted men, a being intent on the destruction of Earth's rise in energy. Mahka gracefully rolled in a tight ball as bullets whizzed by his head from the other soldier. Then, coming up with the speed of lightning, he slit his rival's throat ear to ear. He did not break a beat in the pace of his low-squatted run, nor turn to hear the floundering death squeal as the lizard man drowned in his own blood. Black Bear flew up the center of the dispersing team running headlong into four turning soldiers that fell behind in response to their teammate's cry. He saw that two of the SWAT team had stopped suddenly to dive and take cover behind a tree trunk on either side of his fast approach. The other two men fell on their knees to the ground in the center, their machine guns aimed at the heart of his bulking mass.

Black Bear roared as he dove to the ground in cover, a rapid succession of piercing metal tore the Earth around him. Both his brothers came to his aid, each sliding up in silent stealth, one to the left and one to the right, their blades griped in their mouths to attack the two that hid behind the tree's cover.

The warrior, still trapped under the spray of gun fire, rose to all fours and dug in his hands running headlong in a crab crawl into the screaming metal flurry. A bullet tore into his shoulder not slowing the momentum of his ferocious attack. He plowed into the two men with such force they fell off to the side like pins in a bowling alley. Bear then hammered the might of his massive fist down upon the Adam's apple of the soldier who lay dazed to his right, and turning quickly, he met the other man in black while leaping halfway through the slash of an upraised Bowie knife.

The warrior gasped in pain as the blade was buried to the hilt in his left thigh while his hands grasped the throat of the man quickly squeezing the life out of him. Before the knife could be removed and brought forward for a second attack, the slit of the militant creature's yellow eyes dimmed,

nd. His strong body winding stealthily through the forest's
er as the mourning song rang eerily through the
kening afternoon sky.

Willow and the group of fleeing warriors slowed their
ape as the haunting sound of their brother's grief
ached their ears.

"Winona and Shadow, stay with the Wiyan Wakan.
st keep moving, your path shall be well-lit, as our
other's spirit now resides on the other side to raise alert
r our need of assistance. Keep going and stop for nothing!"
ied Little Bull, as he and the other guardians, Star, Red
awk and Blue Moon, turned and ran back along the Red
th Way.

Red Hawk lagged behind the group, slowing to call
rth the sight of his friend and totem, the hawk, his screech
erfectly mimicked the call of his power animal. A flock of
awks appeared within moments of the great warrior's
quest. A large, glorious male swooped down to land upon
e girth of his forearm, nuzzling his beak to the ear of his
vo-legged brother.

In a slow trot Red Hawk caught up with the others
nd relayed in quick, shortened syllables what his feathered
rethren had warned awaited them on the road ahead. The
roup divided in two; a man and woman on each side of the
ath their pursuers were on. Little Bull stopped and
eckoned Blue Moon into the step of his clasped hands,
oosting her in a flying leap into the branches of a massive
edar. Red Hawk followed suit with Star on the other side of
the well-used animal trail that their prey ran upon in pursuit
of the holy woman and her protectors.

Little Bull continued to run ahead with Red Hawk at

rolling back to death's door.

The eldest of the brothers, Chaska's, ha
around his sweating face as he was met mid-s
soldier in black, the shroud of his soul as dark
The man had stepped from behind bark's flesh
profound horror befell the eyes of the firstbor
stopping him in his tracks. Before his eyes, the
transformed into the true form of his race's hid
putrid acid flew forth from the lizard man's mo
Chaska as he sang out his warrior cry: the cry o
acceptance. Still he continued blindly in a forwa
momentum shouldering his wall of mass into the
reaching up to remove the blade from his clench

The two enemies rolled on the ground, ea
struggling desperately for an advantage. The atro
man, part cold-hearted lizard, bit into the neck of
warrior, ripping his jugular vein. Death drained li
from the eldest brother, but not before his knife h
the liver's black blood from the inhuman creature

Mahka had just finished the breaking of hi
spine and ran to assist his big brother but was too
horror he fell to his knees, the lizard man lay by C
side, hissing angrily as life left him. The younger b
loss' fury, stomped his foot down upon the blade th
deeply embedded in the monster. Then, falling to h
he bent to the prostrate form of his warrior brothe

Black Bear staggered over and leaned in pair
exhaustion against the tree his eldest brother lay be

"Go, find the others, I will stay with our broth
sing his spirit forth," said the forlorn, injured warric

Mahka obediently stood and turned to run w

rolling back to death's door.

The eldest of the brothers, Chaska's, hair flew loosely around his sweating face as he was met mid-stride by a soldier in black, the shroud of his soul as dark as his clothes. The man had stepped from behind bark's fleshy cover. A profound horror befell the eyes of the firstborn son stopping him in his tracks. Before his eyes, the man had transformed into the true form of his race's hidden being. A putrid acid flew forth from the lizard man's mouth, blinding Chaska as he sang out his warrior cry: the cry of death's acceptance. Still he continued blindly in a forward momentum shouldering his wall of mass into the man, reaching up to remove the blade from his clenched teeth.

The two enemies rolled on the ground, each struggling desperately for an advantage. The atrocity, part man, part cold-hearted lizard, bit into the neck of the warrior, ripping his jugular vein. Death drained life's light from the eldest brother, but not before his knife had poured the liver's black blood from the inhuman creature.

Mahka had just finished the breaking of his enemy's spine and ran to assist his big brother but was too late. In horror he fell to his knees, the lizard man lay by Chaska's side, hissing angrily as life left him. The younger brother, in loss' fury, stomped his foot down upon the blade that lay deeply embedded in the monster. Then, falling to his knees, he bent to the prostrate form of his warrior brother.

Black Bear staggered over and leaned in pained exhaustion against the tree his eldest brother lay beneath.

"Go, find the others, I will stay with our brother and sing his spirit forth," said the forlorn, injured warrior.

Mahka obediently stood and turned to run with the

wind. His strong body winding stealthily through the forest's cover as the mourning song rang eerily through the darkening afternoon sky.

Willow and the group of fleeing warriors slowed their escape as the haunting sound of their brother's grief reached their ears.

"Winona and Shadow, stay with the Wiyan Wakan. Just keep moving, your path shall be well-lit, as our brother's spirit now resides on the other side to raise alert for our need of assistance. Keep going and stop for nothing!" cried Little Bull, as he and the other guardians, Star, Red Hawk and Blue Moon, turned and ran back along the Red Path Way.

Red Hawk lagged behind the group, slowing to call forth the sight of his friend and totem, the hawk, his screech perfectly mimicked the call of his power animal. A flock of hawks appeared within moments of the great warrior's request. A large, glorious male swooped down to land upon the girth of his forearm, nuzzling his beak to the ear of his two-legged brother.

In a slow trot Red Hawk caught up with the others and relayed in quick, shortened syllables what his feathered brethren had warned awaited them on the road ahead. The group divided in two; a man and woman on each side of the path their pursuers were on. Little Bull stopped and beckoned Blue Moon into the step of his clasped hands, boosting her in a flying leap into the branches of a massive cedar. Red Hawk followed suit with Star on the other side of the well-used animal trail that their prey ran upon in pursuit of the holy woman and her protectors.

Little Bull continued to run ahead with Red Hawk at

his side. A sudden signal from the flock of circling hawks above warned of the impending approach of the seven remaining cold-blooded creatures, the warriors slowed and slipped into the cover of brush readied for the ambush at hand.

The group of men in black ran with great speed upon the trail, sensing the escape of the woman they were hell-bent on stopping from opening the gate of the vortex they had mistakenly lowered their awareness.

The warrior brothers in arms held their breath and crouched, waiting silently until the small troop passed. Once the remaining SWAT team was a few feet ahead, they jumped from the brush in full force primal attack, one for life over death.

Little Bull led the charge, his head low, the tomahawks clasped in both his hands swinging wildly.   The group of soldiers broke in two under the surprise attack; four fell behind and the other three ran forward maintaining their pursuit of the young channel of the Goddess.

The charging warrior maimed two of the creatures in a moment's flurry. They floundered on the ground trying to grasp their guns with severed, flopping limbs. Red Hawk quickly finished the job with a deft swipe of his razor-sharp blade, running forward behind the swath of Bull's destruction.

Mahka could hear the fight on the trail ahead. Picking up his pace, he ran with speed and stealth over the forest floor; fury fueling his quest for revenge and retribution in honour of his fallen brother. He raised his eyes to the sky and the dance of hawks and quickly veered off the trail to attack from the front, where the birds signaled in their circling, dipping flight.

Blue Moon stood in the branches waiting for the precise moment when her leap would land her on the back of one of the approaching evil ones. Star, on the opposite side, led the attack. She expertly sent her arrows flying into the group of black beasts as they came headlong into the ambush. With a scream in flight, Blue Moon landed upon an unsuspecting lizard man then twisted his head to the side with such force that his head flopped forward, and his limbs collapsed like a puppet whose strings had been cut. She rolled off his back quickly and just as a soldier raised his gun. Her quick but large form provided an easy target for the elite fighter. A bullet grazed the warrior woman's cheek. The shooter's aim was off as he fell to the ground, an arrow shot perfectly through his eye and into the depth of the gray matter of his brain. Star reloaded her bow, turning on a thin branch in the heights of her lair. The enemy soon discovered the source of the flying arrows and shot an array of bullets into the tree's branches. The woman fell as the falling star does, her light diminishing as she reached the ground.

Blue Moon cried out for her heavenly sister and threw herself at the man that had taken Star's light from the skies. She tore and bit and slashed her small blade until there was nothing recognizable left of the animal, only a dark mass and blood upon the soft, green moss.

The last three soldiers formed a back-to-back circle with their massive semi-automatics raised and shooting madly in all directions. But it was of no use. It was as if the small band of warriors were cloaked in a forcefield of protection for the bullets rained harmless upon the ground.

Mahka held the honour of burying his tomahawk in

the skulls of the last standing beasts.

The warriors stood in a circle covered in sweat and blood, the stench of death was thick in the air. Together, they picked up the body of their fallen sister. The long guttural moaning of a primal scream escaped their collective lips as they carried her body back to join their other fallen brother.

Black Bear, numbed by the pain of his injuries and the grief in his heart, held the head of his brother in his lap. He heard the approach of his clan before he saw them, the compassionate pain in their eyes reaching out to touch his soul as they lay his friend and lover beside his brother. The tears fell from his eyes in a cascade as he smoothed the hair of his woman, her tiny form seeming like that of a child in death's embrace. He raised her hands to his mouth and gently kissed her fingers, she had the kind, peaceful smile he loved still upon her lips.

"You, my goddess, will ride in the heavens, the brightest star in the dark skies. I will love you until the end of time, your sacrifice is the greatest honour," Bear spoke through thick tears. He tore the shirt from his back and laid her head upon its warmth.

Blue Moon fell heavily upon the ground and started to tend to the wounds of her warrior friend. She quickly grabbed some plantain that lay close at hand and chewed it into a thick paste that she shoved into the bullet wound on his shoulder. Then she covered the would with a layer of moss and secured it with a strip of leather that would hold until it could be properly dealt with at a later time. Black Bear had already tied off the wound from the knife at his thigh.

As the woman tended to Black Bear's wounds, Little Bull searched the grounds for the makings of a travois to haul the bodies of their dead back home. When completed, Bear was assisted into the bed, his lover's body placed in his arms and his older brother at his side.

Little Bull grabbed the poles as handles and the small band of brothers and sister proceeded in the long walk back to their home on the reserve, where they hoped and prayed the others had made it safely.

Winona led Willow, Shadow following close behind to cover their back, onto the boundaries of the People's Reserve. The exhausted trio, stopped to rest and set up camp until the others could catch up, settling on the outskirts of a roaming buffalo herd.

The women built a small fire as Shadow went to beseech the heavens for one of his brothers for the blessing of its sacrifice. A small rabbit complied and was roasted on a stick within the fires licking flames as Father Sun painted the sky a deep, dark red.

Dusk had long past fallen into the depths of dark night before the small band of warriors arrived hauling a grief-stricken Black Bear and the two dead warriors into camp.

Willow jumped up, her two guardians at her side supporting her in her weakened state, at the sight of the bodies of those who sacrificed their life for her protection.

Little Bull set his burden down and Mahka and Red Hawk helped Black Bear to the warmth of the fire after he gently laid his lady's head to rest on branches of the travois.

Willow eased the great man down with assistance and stroked his forlorn face in love's caring caress of sisterhood.

The clan huddled around the fire as the weaving of the story of bravery unfolded, tears forming rivers upon their tired faces. When the story was finished, they all laid down to rest in a circle of unity upon the loving embrace of the Mother's bosom. No one bothered to stand watch, as the safety net within the boundaries of the people's sacred land was well intact.

At dawn, they awoke just as the day's light touched the horizon's line and birds began chirping the song of a new day. They immediately noticed the cloud of smoke and dust clinging close to the ground, its billowing trail heading in a line away from their camp and possibly leading their enemies directly to them.

An old and battered green Ford truck pulled up to the guardians' camp. The engine rattled to a halt and an ancient man from the Council of Elders stepped down from its interior.

Old Joe followed in the Jeep joined by a procession of honouring for the great warriors.

As Father Sun's warmth kissed the day, two pillars of wood were built for the fallen. Winona washed Star and Chaska's bodies in warm water steeped with fragrant herbs before the two were placed upon the mountain's stairway to the heavens and the fire was lit.

Wailing cries filled the skies as prayers flew on the wings of angels carried on to death's realm.

Wahweyho, Red Hand, Star and Chaska looked down, from the heights of the gods; a league of thousands of awakened ancestors stood behind them at the ready, they

were those that had been beyond, long dead. Those who had
been strengthened to attain spirit now manifested in the call
of the Ghost Dance and were singing in their welcoming,
with joy and honour. Pride shone forth like a beacon for the
fight of the two great warriors in the Mother's shift to
freedom. Her rebirth was also their rebirth.

Later, as the sacred bonfire of death began to dwindle,
a thunderous war cry rose from the heavens, the faces of a
lost nation's people shone through the clouds of wispy grey
smoke.

Black Bear was taken to the reserve's healing lodge, to
have the bullet that lay embedded in his shoulder removed.
The other group of warriors jumped in the Jeep with Old Joe
and Willow to return along a winding back road that led to
the campground. No one spoke as they bumped and slid
upon the overgrown tracks of the old dirt road.

When they
arrived back to the Elbow Valley Campground, it was dark.
The pitch black of night enhanced the stars' bright light that
illuminated the surroundings.

Willow was accompanied to her camp to grab her van
and move it over to Joe's site. It was much wiser for them to
stay together.

The buffalo broth of fortitude had been watched over
and added to by a fire attendant. The group sat with bowls in
hand around the fire's embers in silence. In the automatic
slowness of shock, they ate their fill before retiring to the
bedroll of the hardened Earth in utter exhaustion. Old Joe sat
in silent meditation calling forth the protection of a wolf
pack. When he heard their howl in acceptance of the watch,

he fell into the depths of deep sleep as well.

Willow awakened to the security of chirping birdsong. The little winged friends flitted about bringing in the new day as always—dawn's innocence of light cleansing the wrongs of yesterday.

She eased herself up and moved to add wood to the smoldering embers of the previous evening's fire before greeting each warrior with a gentle smile, that of strength and the warmth of fortitude.

They savored the strength of the hot aromatic coffee that Willow had prepared while sharpening their weapons of war.

Old Joe had previously arranged all the necessary tools for the ritual that he and Willow would need to perform.

The web's tentacle threads needed reinforcement after the weakening caused by Willow's last journey upon them and the first seeing that had allowed the crossing over of the small force of lizard men they had just contended with.

Willow noticed the circling pack of timber wolves that guarded the camp's perimeter. The leader, a large black male with circles of brown surrounding its eyes, became her companion as she walked to the bathroom. When she returned freshened for the day, she and Joe gathered their provisions of ritual. They headed off to the magic and empowerment of the Crystal Cave with the wolf pack accompanying them along the trail.

The remaining tribe of warriors headed back deep into the forest's depths, to gather the bones of their enemies. The cougar and bear had gladly devoured the putrid shell of flesh from the alien forms as requested.

The band of six guardians stood adorned in full regalia, their faces smeared in war paint and hair shorn in honour of the fallen.

The honoured brave, Shadow, broke their silence: "We must bury the bones of those creatures, for Wiyan Wakan has asked us to remember her words: that all creatures are sacred, even those that have forgotten to honour the home of their Mother. They will remember the great teachings one day, when the bones of their ancestors turn to dust and the need for the shedding of our brother's blood has passed."

The wolves ran the trail ahead in silence upon the morning mists, Old Joe and Willow quickly following behind. When they reached the clearing, an ease and comfort nourished the fretting of their war-weary minds. The weave of vibrant energy that surrounded the sacred site renewed their senses.

Joe was fully awakened to the medicine man's way now; every moment, every step taken, was one of conscious prayer.

The old man laid his tools upon the fragile, ancient hide of ritual: buffalo-horn, flask, peace pipe and rattle, all placed gently alongside the serpent elixir and ointment of travel.

Willow stepped out of her clothing, calmly standing as the shaman rubbed the psychotropic bear-fat ointment over her flesh. He then spoke to the woman, as there was an intent in this vision quest.

"Daughter, when the doors of perception are opened,

and you travel through the tunnel of light, you must seek the counsel of my ancestor, Red Hand. I need you to ask him where the crystal skull of pte resides. In the oral stories of my grandfathers, when the sacred trust held in the lineage of guardians became necessary, it was our duty to retain the gateway's seal.

"This time, long ago, coincided with the sacrificial death of a great seer, and a keeper of the Red Path Way, Wahweyho. His adopted father and teacher, Red Hand, took his own life to accompany the young seer to the great beyond. Red Hand's son, when of age, returned to bury the bodies of these honoured heroes of my people, but the ritual crystal skull of pte was nowhere to be found, it was no longer buried at the gate as prophesied. We cannot fully reopen and activate the twelve portals without its assistance," he finished.

Willow nodded her understanding. Joe poured the serpent vine elixir, ayahuasca, blended with the leaves of chacruna into the buffalo horn and handed it to her.

"You must drink this aid, daughter. It will help transport you to the doors of death's realm."

Willow recalled reading about this sacred plant from South America that had been shared among shamans. The plant was a gift from the Mother for the learning of communion with plants, one to absorb their powers and understand their curative, medicinal properties. The plant had been traditionally traded, a shared path of knowledge, long before written history. Its secrets were protected and held close to the hearts of the wise ones. She was afraid to see the faces of death and the snakes that would rise to consume her perception. She knew the effect of the plant's vision were reputed to be similar, equal in all people across all lands; the serpent appeared to all.

The thick, bitter, black elixir caused Willow to gag, before it slid down her throat. Time passed slowly as Joe danced around her seated form whistling the song of his helpers to her aid. Her stomach began to heave, and her bowels loosened. She got up and purged, then sat down again. The serpent coiled its body around her form, raising its head in a hypnotizing stare just before swallowing her mind whole.

Wiyan Wakan lay exposed on the floor of a great crystal hall, her lover stepped forward and covered her body in a glimmering white shawl of pte. Standing behind him, the hunched form of a wizened old man leaned upon a staff. Stepping forward, he introduced himself, "I am Red Hand."

"I honour the sacrifice of your awakening, daughter. I am sorry to say you are too late to meet the members of the Council of Twelve. Our tribal brothers have been called forth to aid their people across the physical realm. Their combined strength is necessary in order to open the portals. I believe you have already met my son, Wahweyho," he smirked, the blue-grey of his blind eyes twinkling in mirth.

Willow could barely move her eyes from the beauty of the man whose love had renewed her faith in the ability to find her true heart and the purity and wholeness of unity in the matching of soul upon soul.

Her heart swelled at the sight of her warrior god. His hair cascaded down his well-muscled back and deep, dark, intelligent eyes were held in his stoic face regally painted in streaks of white upon black.

Willow pulled her awe away. "Yes, Tunkasila, I have

had the honour of meeting the one I was born to embrace," she said, shyly.

"I have come to ask for assistance, at the request of your ancestral grandson. A great medicine man of your lineage, honoured father. He, and those before him, seek the hidden home of the crystal skull of pte. It was not guarding the Cave of Light's entrance like your son was told it would be when he was summoned to honour your burial requests," spoke the glimmering essence of the holy woman.

"Yes, there had to be a change in plans." spoke Red Hand. "On the journey of my last vision quest, I was shown that the portal's seal would be safer if under the guard of our great brother grizzly bear. He removed the skull from its resting place and took it to his den high among the Three Sisters mountain range close to where your camp is made. That is where the key is buried, guarded fiercely from generation to generation, just as the wise brotherhood of man has guarded the portals of time, through all of time, since creation first blew her breath into our becoming. The man that wears the mark of brother bear upon his face has been the one chosen to lead you to the skull," said Red Hand.

"As we speak, the others that await the rise of Earth's energy vortexes are placing their skulls upon entrances across the lands of the Great Mother. Go with this man chosen in prophecy, my daughter, and find the skull, for time is of the essence. Now, I will leave you two alone to say your goodbyes," finished the old seer before hobbling off.

Willow smiled and bowed to the wizened old soul. She could see the resemblance in his character with Joe, traits passed on through roots within the family tree.

She turned and looked into the eyes of her lover, the

one she thought she would never meet, in this lifetime, or next. The two lovers embraced, hearts beating as one, his lips smothering hers, as her legs weakened.

Wahweyho held her close in his arms, the scent of sweetgrass on him was dizzying to Willow's senses. Neither spoke as they merged within one another: their tongues probing gently, sucking sweet lips. Passion's addictive taste was overwhelming. His erect penis pressed against her stomach as his hands fondled her breasts. The shawl fell from her shoulders onto the floor. He lowered his head licking her nipples teasingly as his hand cupped her breast. Willow moaned and reached her hands to roam down his muscular back and over his buttocks, grinding her body against his hardened shaft in longing.

"Oh, my love, how I long to be held in your strong embrace," she spoke in a whispered gasp.

"Soon we will be together, my sweet. Our time is not now, for I can no longer cross the realm to be with you. Our last encounter cost my spirit force too much. I need to conserve all, for the upcoming shift," spoke Wahweyho.

"I must be ready to lead those that have raised to the call of our ancestors. Come and see, my love," he said, as he reached down and grabbed the hide shawl, placing it back upon her shoulders.

"You must spread the word to our families and all Keepers of the Earth, what the power of the Circle Dance has started," he said.

And, moving his hand across her eyes, there suddenly appeared through mists of vision a league of thousands of warriors, all at the ready for the entrance of the fifth world. Star and Chaska smiled, waving from the front ranks, a shroud of silvery-gray glory enveloping their auras.

Wahweyho stood proudly behind her, his manhood pressing against the small of her back—creation's drive never slowing throughout realm upon realm.

Willow leaned into the pillar of her man's body. Warmth, gratitude and a great pride infused her with unwavering strength. She waved to the two warriors that had sacrificed their lives for her protection and the guardianship of a nation's freedom, all through their knowledge of purpose.

Willow heard a whistling, a chirping bird call, that began to draw her away from the shimmering scene to a fading mist in her mind. Her body seemed to be held within the arms of the other world, she did not want to leave. She wanted to stay and fight from this side, to be with her lover, for with him she felt complete. Her fears and insecurities dissolved with his touch. She stared into the deep, caring eyes of her spirit lover; his face forever etched upon her heart.

"I am being called back! I don't want to go, Wahweyho!" she cried.

"You must return, my love. You need to relay the message of the vortex key's location. To tell the others where the sacred skull of the great buffalo is secretly guarded under the protection of our fiercest of brothers," he said with encouragement in his eyes.

"We will meet again, when time allows. We must honour our path and what is woven within the great web of time. A weave of gleaming energy shall be upon the Mother in love's warm embrace once again. As shall we." She savored Wahweyho's passionate words of wisdom along the wave of melodic song that accompanied her home to the waiting shaman.

Three Sisters

"Welcome home, Wiyan Wakan, my daughter. Tell me of your vision and the words of stories past and future. Those that my grandfather has spoken," Joe said with a smiling heart.

Willow let her mind process the visions, all she'd seen and heard from the land of the ancestors and the interpretation of her remembering began: "Red Hand spoke of the Three Sister mountains as the place we must search to seek the crystal skull of pte. It lies hidden within the den of the great grizzly. He directed us to pursue this quest with the aid of the one who wears the mark of the bear upon his face. He alone will know the way. I was given no further directions as to where we must journey beyond that. I have been given the gift of seeing the magnitude of the song's awakening upon the other realm; many ancestors await their call forth.

"Star and Chaska were there. They live, they are

strong and intact! They stand at the ready to lead the upcoming shift into consciousness alongside Wahweyho, my heart and Red Hand's apprentice," she continued with pride.

"When those of this realm see that we are of the all-powerful eternal light, fear will melt and run like water upon the lines of the ancient river's path and we will all walk hand in hand unified within the manifestation of creation's song," said Willow in a subdued and fatigued joy.

"Well, no wonder we could not find the skull," said Old Joe, his face alight in the vision's story being told. His wise eyes chuckled, as he rubbed his chin in understanding wonder. "The mountain range of the sisters lies an hour by truck from here, just on the outskirts of Canmore. I know this range well as my ancestors used these mountains for hunting and gathering. The area has long been known as a place of foreboding power."

"I hope Black Bear is capable of the long drive and hike to the heights of his totem brother's home," said a worried Willow.

"He is of a strong will and constitution. He will be overjoyed his ancestors have blessed him with the honour to lead our quest. This is a great recognition of respect in the way of the warrior for one such as he that follows the Red Path Way," said Joe, quickly gathering his spiritual tools and placing them lovingly in their leather roll.

Willow got dressed slowly, wobbling slightly from the effects of the elixir and ointment that lingered upon her numb flesh. She still felt disoriented. The world seemed painted with hints of rose—all seemed ethereal—wavering in streaks upon a flimsy canvas.

She reached her hands out, pushing her fingers through the veils of time, as Father Sun set behind the mountain's rise.

The two seekers came through the bushes at the back of Joe's campsite. The sound of song hung in the air from those that continued the Circle Dance at the park's gateway.

At the healer's site, half of the guardian warriors sat waiting. When they heard Old Joe's approach they turned in unison. Joe was feebly supporting the weakened body of the holy woman at his side. Shadow jumped up to assist, and together they led her to a chair to rest.

Willow smiled in gratitude. After a light meal of smoked fish, Willow went to lay down in the comfort of her old, green van as Joe radioed a message to the reserve to make sure Bear would be ready for the upcoming journey.

After the ritual burial of the lizard men was complete, the remaining clan of warriors united, gathering around the sacred fire's light. Joe spoke and began to lay out what was to come of the days ahead.

"Ancestor's Song," a favorite chant among the young warriors from Robbie Robertson and the Red Road Ensemble, was sung among the group:

> "To our elders, who teach us of our creation and our past, so we may preserve Mother Earth for our ancestors yet to come, we are the land.

> "To our brothers and sisters and all living things across Mother Earth.

> "Her beauty we've destroyed and denied the honour the Creator has given each individual.

> "The truth lies in our hands.

"All my relations."

The power of the words instilled strength and renewed belief in the quest for the small band of remaining righteous fighters.

Willow tossed and turned through the night with lingering visions. A serpent-shaped heavenly body slithered its way in an obscure orbital path between Saturn and Uranus sharing its knowledge of origin and of the wounded healer, Chiron, that lay within all: "The entity's physical location and orbit leads us from the known to the unknown, from the seen to the unseen. She is the trance-dancing, shamanic harbinger of mystery." Where these words of telling fell from Willow did not know, for its wisdom lay in the mystic.

In the morning, Willow felt rejuvenated from her rest, rising to Hermann's greeting to the day's light, "ka-caw, ka-caw."

The churning of her queasy stomach from the journey's little helpers had finally eased, releasing her from the clenching grip of nausea. Today was going to be a good day.

"Good morning, everyone. What are our plans for the retrieval of the buffalo skull? When shall we head out?" she asked excitedly, thrilled with the thought of seeing Black Bear.

Little Bull was seated, his muscular shoulders being rubbed by the strong hands of Winona.

Mahkah and Blue Moon were gathering water containers, dried pemmican and nuts for their sojourn. Red Hawk and Shadow were busy overseeing the weapons when Joe wheeled the old Jeep onto the site.

Black Bear sat up front looking fierce, a stoic depth of intent etched upon his face. The slashing scar of his spirit brother's claws more pronounced in streaks of black coal.

Willow ran over to the Jeep and gave a small bow and nod to reflect the great honour she felt at the sight of the man. She then addressed the warrior whose path they would all follow.

"Do you know the way to where the totem of your animal spirit calls, Bear?" she queried.

"Yes, Wiyan Wakan, I have seen the signs our great warrior brother has left upon the web's filament. He waits with welcoming arms," the massive man said, breathing in deeply—the embodiment of his totem—a playful smile gently rising to his lips. The powerful man stood, stretching his arms up and then out to his sides, growing in magnitude even further; he was a fearsome warrior shining with his purpose.

Little Bull jumped in the back of Joe's Jeep with Willow, as the rest of the group threw the supplies for the journey in the back of an old, beaten, red pick-up truck. The truck had seen better days and dents and rusty fenders scarred its features. Winona pulled her bulk up behind the wheel of the beast as Blue Moon and Shadow slid in alongside one another. Red Hawk and Mahkah jumped in the back, with a loud warrior's "whoop."

The group headed to the front gates where the throng of people in support of the Idle No More movement and Circle Dance continued to grow.

The media had been in attendance for the last two days, trying every angle they could to falsify the truth behind the awakening and empowerment of the people, just as it always had in the years leading up to this awakening.

The Natives of North America, as all of Earth's people

that embraced consciousness, had been suppressed for a millennium. The disempowerment and genocide of a people's beliefs created a nation of lost souls living in a heartless society. The fall of the Keepers of the Earth had been a great loss for all of humankind.

Yet, the Circle Dance continued to build momentum, as had been foretold.

Social media links were joining the Indigenous from all directions and from all lands across the vast surface of the Mother; her energy was rising in the joy of recognition.

Governments across the planet that were secretly led by the lizard men's minions began their attack years ago understanding that their old tactics would no longer suffice.

Corporate entitlement hid behind capitalism's greed and abuse affording themselves unjust rights: the right to protect their non-living corporate entities, the right to instate martial law, the right to provoke and continue war.

These beasts controlled society and trained the people like sheep to slept through the universal call to awakening, as fear governed their veiled vision.

Governments had labeled and categorized environmental movements as acts of terrorism. They monitored all forms of personal communication by invading privacy and entrapping those who defied laws that allowed for the rape of nations and resources to continue.

These corporations were desperately trying to stop any movement that parted the veil by poisoning foods, spraying the skies and depositing poison in drinking water.

The world was in upheaval; people heard the call but were afraid to progress because years of conditioning led them to reject the truth. The people enmeshed in the consequences of fear-based training began to use armaments

that were easily obtained, killing and injuring those of
wondering innocence with pepper spray, smoke bombs and
endless showering bullets.

The brainwashing was complete, but the vibration of
dance upon the web's threads was dissolving all illusion of
dependence on a system that failed its people and served only
the rich.

People were beginning to claim the right to the lands
they were born upon: the right to clean air and water. They
could not stop the Mother from reclaiming her freedom from
abuse, although the corporate elite were trying; however, the
futility of their quest to continue with a world of oppression
would soon be realized. Freedom would reign when the
vortex energy grid was activated.

The group of warriors would not fail. The crowd
cheered and sang, waving the banners of Earth's four
colours, as they guided the convoy through the throng to the
old gravel road that led to the Three Sisters range. They sang
in unison of heart, showering glory and blessings upon their
quest.

Willow was in ecstasy as they flew along the back
road. The fragrant scent of forest pine and cool water
whipping across her face was exhilarating.

Black Bear sat in a regal repose like a warrior king.

Little Bull was chanting, as he mixed a red ocher paste
in a little bowl on his lap. Joe appeared lost in the focus of
intent; the Jeep was seemingly guided through the rutted
dirt track by spirit and faith alone.

Willow glanced over her shoulder and smiled at the
crew that followed behind. Winona bore the same stern face
of intent that Joe carried.

They all knew that the quest was a dangerous one, for

once they found the skull of pte, there would be no stopping
the joining of realms. The Ghost Dance had truly only just
begun. The rhythmic shuffling of feet had followed the path
of the Sun for two days now. The Circle was growing daily
with the joining of brother and sister alike, each
participating by gently grasping one another's shoulder as
links in a chain.

The leaders of the dance, those that were of the pure
blood of the First People, wore shirts and robes of
protection: white with blue collars, adorned with feathers
and claws, images of moons and stars and the remnants of
sacred animals woven within. The men wore leggings of red
and the women wore decorated sashes upon white, fringed
robes—all designed under a chant of power.

The drums no longer beat as the masses danced
around a great pine in a trance of religious ecstasy. In three
more days the prophecy would be fulfilled, and ancestors
long-departed would join their relations in protecting all
creatures great and small.

The shift would commence when the Mother knew
her children were safe within her bosom. The Earth would
soon be covered in a crust of new soil that would bury the
lizard people and their followers and return the Mother to
the primordial state of her beginnings.

All Indigenous and all the oppressed and
disillusioned across all lands were dancing in their own
prophecies and calling forth the images that sang to their
own beliefs—none right and none wrong—all one in the
love of Gaia.

That is, if the group of warriors could discover the
hidden location of the crystal skull. If the twelve vortex
doorways were not all opened the imbalance would cause a

planetary tilt that would stop the renewal of the Earth and her children. Everything would pass into the nether world. Only the cold, dead-eyed lizards and the cockroaches would be left to feed upon the carcasses of the masses.

Black Bear was silent when Old Joe pulled up an hour later to the South-West access to the Three Sisters range. Each peak stood veiled in a shroud of ice, the snow of white depicting a habit's wimple: the origin of their name.

Winona wheeled the beaten truck in behind the Jeep, the two anxious braves leaping out of the back before she reached a full stop.

Joe stood solemnly alongside Willow as the small band of warriors gathered together discussing the strategy that would take them up the near 10,000 foot ascent of Faith, the tallest of the Three Sisters.

Black Bear had known through a vision in dream, that she was the mountain that held the sacred power object, the crystallized buffalo skull, buried deep in the den of a great grizzly.

Little Bull passed a jar of red ocher paste, the warrior's paint, around the group. It was applied to represent the blood of those fallen and to provide a joining of spirits long gone.

The group looked fierce in the full regalia of their tribe and each held their weapon of choice in hand. Little Bull gripped his war club, Winona an atlatl (spear thrower), Shadow, Blue Moon and Red Hawk each held lances, while Mahkah and Black Bear had tomahawks. They all had quivers strapped across their backs and Bowie knives tucked in their waist bands as well.

Willow had never seen such an array in the tools of

war. She was not going to let her brothers and sisters sacrifice their lives for her this time, not without fighting alongside them. She chose a simple slingshot device and a tomahawk along with her own knife. Righteous anger would guide her hand if necessary not the skill that would guide the others.

Joe would be staying behind to call forth the elements and his totem animal's spirit to accompany the warriors on their quest. He was too old to keep up and could better serve in the realm of spirit.

The band embraced in a circle, each with hand upon one another's shoulder, while standing around the fire Joe had built for a base camp. They bowed their heads asking the Mother for guidance and protection. They gave a war "whoop" in unity and headed out and up to the heights of the clouds to find the home of great brother bear.

Black Bear took the lead as only he knew the way of his totem's calling.

His brother, Mahkah, walked alongside him with the three women nestled securely in the middle. Shadow and Red Hawk followed behind and Little Bull took up the rear.

The sounds of life surrounded the band with the glory in purity of creation: birds chirped, wind's gentle breeze filled the air with the scent of pine while waving grasses in the field of a passing alpine meadow calmed their minds. The trickling of cool waters soothed their senses as the soft Earth cushioned their footfalls. Hermann, their raven friend, circled, ka-cawing from the heights of the vast blue skies above.

The terrain soon became more challenging just as the protection of forest's cover diminished into that of small shrubs. The mountain's sisters, Charity and Hope, stood majestically alongside the awe-inspiring view invigorating the group. The traverse would take them no longer than seven hours round trip. If all went well they would be returning just as Father Sun laid his head to rest upon the breast of Mother Earth.

Bear stopped alongside a small trickling stream to refill the water bottles as the next part of the journey was a challenging scramble across sedimentary rock layers of limestone, dolomite, sandstone and shale. He needed to rest as his injuries still throbbed and slowed him down a little. A small reprieve from the challenge did not bother the rest of the group, some being fitter than others.

"I know from my dreams, that the den of the silver-tipped brother lies at a height where there is no longer any trees or brush, somewhere on the North side of big sister Faith's mountainous terrain," said a fatigued Black Bear.

"We should sit and rest for a while. We can ask Hermann to fly ahead to guide us to the den. The markings of his home must be fairly obvious from the raven's height," said a concerned Willow. She was not accustomed to seeing her guardian in such a weakened state.

Willow called out to her feathered friend. He swooped down upon her beckoning and landed on her shoulder. She spoke to the bird in thought, projecting their need to the intelligent raven's inquisitive mind. Hermann cawed in acknowledgment and took flight, his black wings swooshing past her ears.

As all rested, Winona began handing out pemmican to give strength for their last push forward. They sat quietly in contemplation of the day's events, each in a world of their own, some miles away in thought.

Willow stood up from the huddled squat the group

was in, stretching her calves. "I think I will go and find a place to relieve myself. I'll be right back," she said.

"I'll go with you," said Blue Moon, jumping up.

The two women headed toward a small patch of bushes, chitchatting as they walked over the rocky terrain. They stopped abruptly when they heard the sound of falling rocks. Blue Moon quickly stood, at the ready with her lance up front, she deftly pushed Willow to the side. A blood curdling scream erupted on their right as the vision of a banshee appeared. She was covered in a dark, red blood that pooled around the apparition's feet: a forewarning of death.

Willow stood with her knife drawn and tomahawk at the ready as something sprang with great speed from the bushes and flew straight through the ghostly image. All was a blur, the women found themselves being circled by a large cat that seemed to have appeared out of nowhere. Blue Moon swept her lance in an arch over her head while shouting at the massive, lithe cougar. It hissed and mewled in defiance. Its yellow eyes starred deep into the depths of Willow's soul as it paced in its hunter's pose in front of the women.

The other warriors heard the howl of the banshee's warning and leapt to their feet running with weapons drawn. The cougar would never attack such a large group of people, especially not in daylight, something was terribly wrong with this situation.

The band formed a semicircle around the large cougar allowing it an escape route. The massive cat, seemingly weighing two hundred and fifty pounds, did not seem to notice them as it stared directly through the group of warriors and straight into the heart of Willow. Winona placed a spear in her atlatl as the tawny, formidable cougar swiped at the air in an angry and aggressive stance.

"Go, brother, we do not want to hurt you," she spoke in quiet reverence, her eyes locked on the cat as she prepared the spear throwing device.

The cat, sensing the impossibility of the situation, casually turned and disappeared behind an outcrop of rocks.

The group gathered, lowering their weapons in relief.

"Shit, I always wanted to see the great cat, but that was a little too close for comfort," said Willow in a jittery laugh. "Now, I really need to go to the bathroom!"

"That was not the behavior of any mountain cat I've ever seen or heard of!" said Black Bear. "We must keep our senses in tune and stay on our toes, for I fear the enemy is at hand," he continued in warning. "The banshee spirit does not appear screaming her warning without cause; that alone makes my skin crawl and my senses tingle."

As the group continued to discuss the freakish incident, Willow wandered off to the side to relieve herself before they continued up the mountain. She stayed close to the group, squatting behind the first shrub that would offer enough coverage. As she stood sighing with relief the hairs stood up at the back of her neck. She slowly reached to pick up the tomahawk propped at her feet and turned around expecting to meet the fearsome yellow eyes of the predator that seemed only interested in stalking her. There was only a large boulder about 40 feet away on a rise directly behind her, nothing seemed out of place.

"Oh God, my nerves sure are getting the best of me," she thought aloud, blaming her prickling senses on nervous tension. She chuckled and shrugged, a sense of relief washing over her just as the cat appeared from behind the rock.

She had no time to think as the cat gracefully catapulted itself into the air crossing the 40 feet that divided them with ease. Flying in a smooth arch the cat's massive body easily reached a height of 20 feet. Willow was awestruck at the agility of the great cat. She stared numbly upwards, her mouth agape, while a wailing howl escaped the cat's ferocious mouth as it flew across an expanse of pale blue sky.

A spear pierced the tawny hide of the beast's chest mid-flight and the cat landed on Willow with the force of a train. She could hardly breathe with the dead weight heavy upon her chest. The stench of the predator's breath caused her to breathe in small gasps through clenched teeth. She had smashed her head hard on the fall and lay dazed as Little Bull rushed over and hauled the cat's carcass off her body.

Winona had a blank look of great sadness upon her face, she held the empty atlatl limply by her side. "I had no choice my friend," she mumbled sadly. To take the life of such a grand creature, any creature for that matter, without the ritual of prayer was devastating to them all.

Willow sat up slowly, her wide eyes entranced by the faint mewling of the cat's last labored breath. "Oh, sweet beauty, why?" she spoke through choked tears.

The feline stared at her, the strange oblong slit of pupil transforming to its natural shape within dimming yellow eyes as the shapeshifting entity that possessed the cougar left its body.

Willow stroked the matted fur while whispering prayers and blessings for the sacrifice the animal had no choice in making. "You are a beautiful and noble creature. I shall honour you and all the relations of your species for the great bravery you have shown us all." She spoke with reverence, slowly closing the cat's eyes as it passed on and into the next realm.

The warriors stood around the great animal, its body almost nine feet in length, and all bent to gather a whisker from its muzzle to be carried in the amulet that each wore around their neck. Then they gathered rocks and buried the beautiful, agile creature swearing their vengeance for the invasion of her noble spirit.

Hermann the Harbinger arrived, circling in great arches around the new grave, drawing the group out of their reverie and back to the quest at hand.

He had found the den of the silver-tip grizzly at unexpected heights: a mere two hundred feet below the mountain's highest precipice.

The clan of warriors headed out with a furious awareness stoking the fire of the impending battle. They divided into two smaller groups as Willow was slow and felt feeble due to the expanding goose egg at the back of her skull.

Black Bear plowed ahead with his brother, Mahkah, in the lead, with Shadow and Blue Moon following a few steps behind.

Little Bull walked alongside Winona, followed by Red Hawk and Willow a couple hundred feet back taking up the rear knowing that an oppressive darkness lay ahead. Aware of the fact that they had not seen the last of the evil, cold-hearted beings that were asleep to all but Earth's betrayal.

They had lost hours in the honouring of their animal friend and were now quickly losing the safety of daylight. The cool mountain air was thinning, making it harder to breathe with every step. They decided to drop their bags and proceed forward with only their weapons to help ease the difficulty of the incline. The group proceeded warily through the eerie silence of the rocky terrain.

The raven led them to the den that was excavated into the side of a slope of sheer rock. He hopped up and down on top of a grey slate boulder above what appeared to be the entrance when the group appeared.

Black Bear cautiously approached along the West side, angling along a piled stretch of broken rock. His brother, Mahkah, crept a short distance away to the left of him, while Shadow and Blue Moon continued to approach from above.

The other group of warriors stayed a good distance behind watching for signs of movement from below.

A grey-blue alpine vista of rock, boulders and scree runs now surrounded them. The trees and shrubbery that lay further below appeared as tiny, green specks from the perch of their lofty height.

Black Bear put down his weapons and removed the arrow quiver from his back, placing it neatly on the ground. He knew that they were not sneaking up on brother bear, he would be expecting them. The bear could smell most everything within a 30 km radius depending on wind direction. The group was not trying to disguise their approach in any way whatsoever. Their brother knew the time would come for releasing the sacred treasure that he and his kin before him had fiercely guarded.

The warrior knelt in prayer—a chant sent to the spirit of his guardian totem. Black Bear slowly removed the amulet he wore around his neck pulling two sets of bear claws from its confines they were the remains of a brother's front paws.

The claws were rare as they were white in colour, curved and 10 cm in length. Each claw of the padded paw was threaded with a leather thong. He wrapped each set around his hands and began to grunt and scratch at the ground throwing the strewn pebbles and rocks about to call forth his brother from his lair where they believed he lay in wait.

Just as the warrior approached the den's entrance, a horrifying roar erupted. It was one that loosened the bowels and it seemed to be coming from beyond the mountain ridge.

Hermann flew to the skies in a squawk, while the other warriors raised their weapons to the greatest fear known to man: being torn limb from limb and eaten alive.

Black Bear turned to his band motioning for them to lower their weapons as the figure of a massive bruin came charging over the rise. The intimidating grizzly screamed down upon the warrior running toward him at full speed. Drool spewed from the mouth of the raging beast. His teeth shone as daggers behind curled lips as he came to a halt a few feet in front of the brave, unmoving warrior. The bear stood on his hind legs, towering over 14 feet tall and dwarfing his massive guardian brother. His weight must have exceeded a thousand pounds, yet still, Black Bear stood stoically proud in confidence and bravery. The silver-tip approached even closer while releasing a deafening, mind-numbing warning. Finally, the bruin stopped and swiped at the air with massive paws that could easily rip the head off a deer.

Still the warrior stood as a statuesque pillar of strength, his hands clenched in fists, with the white claws of his spirit brother gleaming at his sides.

The bear lowered his powerful front legs to the ground and began sniffing the air with his lengthy muzzle and lolling his head side to side as he swaggered forward.

Black Bear lowered himself to his knees and bent his upper body into a prostate salutation.

The grizzly continued his approach. The hot stench of its breath fell upon the warrior's neck as the bear's face hovered above his head. The grizzly suddenly lowered his mass dropping to lie at the brave's side. The two embraced like the long-lost brothers they were; the great beast of an animal playfully grasping Bear's head in his powerful jaws.

The band kept their distance, laughter relieving their furrowed lines of stress.

The two brothers were united in spirit by the scar Black Bear wore upon his face—a badge of honour the warrior wore with pride.

The grizzly raised himself to stand on all fours and ambled over to the entrance of his cave. He seemed almost to speak to the warrior as he motioned with the swaying of his massive neck for the brave, young man to enter the depths of his den.

Black Bear nodded and dropped to all fours crawling into the heart of the bear's lair while the grizzly sat like a tame circus bear at the side of the entrance.

The den was dank and dark and there were tufts of molted hair lying about. As Black Bear crawled further into the confines of the den it began to widen and open up allowing the man to walk stooped over. His eyes soon adjusted to the blackness as he inched deeper into the recesses of the mountain. The narrow space soon opened into the roundness of a cave. The alcove of the bear's den of hibernation.

Black Bear began scanning his surroundings searching the grounds of his brother's home for the sacred treasure, the buried skull of pte. In a far corner, the warrior noticed a rise in the ground and falling to his knees he began to dig. Soon he came upon bones. Layers and layers of bones. A rising sense of urgency fueled his drive to unearth the treasured skull.

Outside, the grizzly rose to stand on his hind legs sniffing the air. Sensing his forewarning the warriors looked intently about the rock-strewn terrain, eyes peeled to find what the bear's keen sense was smelling. The massive bruin dropped to all fours and ran down the hill veering off to the right of where the lowest band of guardian warriors waited.

Blue Moon stayed to stand guard at the den's entrance, as Shadow and Mahkah flew after the grizzly, shouting a warning to Little Bull and the others to be at the ready. None of them knew what was approaching but they knew a great challenge would be at hand: the war of good versus evil.

Little Bull heard the call of his brother and told Winona to take Willow off to the side of a scree run that offered protection behind a tall rocky crag. On the opposite side of the natural barrier was a sheer drop off.

The women quickly scrambled over gashing bits of slippery shale and hid. Each deftly using their spear as support while crossing to avoid slipping uncontrollably down the natural slide and falling into the abyss that lay thousands of feet below.

Shadow and Mahkah nodded as Red Hawk came up from behind, neither wanting to move his eyes from the rising cloud of dust the charging grizzly had raised.

The massive animal had reached the tree line and disappeared into a stand of pine and fir. The reverberating siren scream of a howling attack echoed through the still mountain air.

The men drew their weapons and spread out, anxiously waiting to see what great brother bear had scented in the winds.

"Over there, do you see that form slithering behind the rocks?" Red Hawk said, pointing to where a line of brush joined the scrabble of rock.

"Yeah, I see it," said Little Bull, impatiently tapping his war club in the palm of his hand.

They continued to keep their eyes peeled and soon noticed what appeared to be at least four more figures moving low to the ground, slinking forward with an inhuman motion of a rippling wave.

Suddenly the air was filled with the sound of crashing timber as the silvertip came charging from the brush, right behind the approaching lizards. Four were running for their lives in futility and the bear tore into their flesh downing two in his swiping run. Blue blood sprayed from their wounds mixing as in an artist's palette with the stone-grey terrain.

A war "whoop" erupted from the three warriors as they charged the remaining team of seven invaders. Those that slithered along the ground rose to meet the band of brothers since their cover was already blown. The others turned to face down the grizzly knowing they could never outrun the incredible speed of the ferocious animal.

The grizzly swiped madly at the ones that stood and faced him. The other two he had already downed lay behind, hissing and withering while their torn limbs spurted life's blood onto the ground.

One of the lizard men leapt into the air, landing on the great hump of the silvertip's back. The bear raised himself to his hind legs with a roar as the other creature charged into the suicide of his swinging reach. The unspeakable thing that

rode upon his massive shoulders stabbed a long, serrated
blade repeatedly into the depths of his furry hide which only
infuriated the grizzly more and compounded his drive to kill.
In a rage, the bear crushed the other creature that fell into
the grasp of his mauling arms, the spewing acid causing his
fur to smolder and painfully eating away at his flesh. The
slimy creature freed his arm and shoved a 9mm handgun up
into the pit of the grizzly's embrace, providing him with the
contact shot that would kill the magnificent defender of the
Red Path Way.

The grizzly clamped his teeth upon the neck of the
creature ripping its throat out while keeping it held within
the grasp of his powerful, crushing arms. The bruin fell,
rolling as he collapsed; his thousand-pound body crushing
the thing that rode upon his back killing the enemy of his
terrestrial home in his last act of defiance.

Little Bull, running in the center, plowed headlong into
the first lizard man he saw, swinging his war club and
crushing its skull. One yellow eye popped out of its socket
from the explosive force and dangled in the air, swinging on a
purply-blue tendon. Moments later, the misshapen form fell
to the ground with a thump.

Mahkah arrived at the same time, coming in from the
left to meet two of the creatures: spearing one as he flew
through the air while hammering and felling the other with
his tomahawk. The warrior continued running straight
toward the two enemy forms that still withered upon the
ground, their arms laying somewhere behind them after the
bear's attack and severed their heads with ease in
retribution for the horror that befell his brother, the great
and noble grizzly bear.

Shadow was in combat with the last two invading

squad members. He danced around them with ease, just over a rise and out of the sight of his brothers. His lance was keeping the two at bay, neither having a chance to reach the guns strapped and holstered at their hips.

They aimed their acid spittle toward him, but the warrior eluded their projectiles and aptly jumped out of the way. He parried in a twirl, spearing one lizard man through the shoulder while mistakenly embedding his lance among the rocks. The other saw its opportunity and quickly whipped his gun forward taking aim with precision. A spear penetrated the creature's spine and in an instant all his focus was gone. The screaming hiss of death's surprise filled the air. The shot rang out, luckily ricocheting off the left shoulder of the warrior brave instead of penetrating his heart as intended.

Winona stood along the outcropping of rock where she and Willow had lain hidden below, the atlatl dangling empty at her side. She screamed out with fear, as she watched Shadow fall. Both women ran as fast as their legs would carry them safely down to their fallen brother. When they arrived, Little Bull and Red Hawk had already started the nurturing. Little Bull holding Shadow's head upon his lap.

Willow fell to her knees to assist, as Winona absorbed the nod of gratitude and proud words of acknowledgment for her skilled precision—twice today she had held the honour of protection. The bullet had passed through the shoulder, so Shadow would be fine once the bleeding was staunched. Willow found some clean moss, stuffing it around the wound before binding it tightly with a piece of cotton torn from the hem of her shirt.

They lifted the man to his feet as he shook off the encounter with bravado. Everyone joyously slapped one another's back, laughing in congratulations.

The band of warriors then walked over to the corpse of the fallen grizzly, seeing the death of such a beautiful and magnificent beast was heartbreaking.

"My brother will not allow the sacrifice of this noble guardian to be left without being honoured. We must bury the foul dead bodies of our enemies as the spirit of Wiyan Wakan has asked of us previously. And somehow, we must return the great mass of our spirit brother to be embraced in the comfort of his home, for the long journey back to the spirit realm," spoke a solemn Mahkah.

Little Bull responded as a leading soldier, "I will drag all the lizard scum into a pile and cover their bodies in a rock cairn, so our feathered friends will not sicken if they come looking for the source of the stench. Red Hawk, you and Winona can gather some strong branches to make a travois to move our brother back to the heights of his home. Shadow, why don't you head back up the face of Big Sister and see to your woman, she will be worried. Mahkah can help you up the embankment. I sure hope Black Bear has discovered the resting place of the wicapasaca hidden within the grizzly's den. I fear this is just the first wave of these unspeakable atrocities that we shall encounter. Willow you can help me by removing their weapons. We may need them, and maybe somehow they will help us discover where these creatures are coming from."

Willow accompanied Little Bull to the area where most of the lizard people lay fallen. She bent down over the two that were beheaded and gagged at the sight of the deadpan, yellow alien eyes and the drying pools of blue blood. The gills that were hidden behind the ears particularly disturbed Willow.

She turned her focus to the task at hand and quickly rifled through the clothing of the dead for any identification, removing the holstered guns and ammo. She wondered why more of the enemy had not used their weapons, maybe the bear's attack had rendered a nerve-shattering shock.

The weather was cooler atop the mountain making it harder for the lizards to respond with speed she surmised, still trying to understand their haphazard assault. The two headless bodies held wallets that Willow flipped open, discovering the inhuman things were the members of an elite government team.

"Now, let's see whose identity you are hiding under. Lieutenant George Bushmill and Sergeant Powell Collins. I wonder where your orders come from?" she spoke to herself. "How the hell did they find us? And why the hell are they so intent on stopping Earth's children from finding, peace and happiness through equality? This sick enslavement of humanity needs to end! The raping of Mother Earth is the path to all our destruction. How can they not see this?" she choked, as tears rolled down her cheeks in frustration.

Little Bull grabbed the dead bodies of the two creatures Shadow had fought, removing the spears embedded in the slimy, misshapen forms. He easily dragged one in each hand over to the pile of corpses.

Willow probed the newly added bodies, recovering their wallets and once again their IDs connected them to the same Black Operatives Force. Montie Santos and Charlie King were mere soldiers within the league of minions it seemed. The other corpses did not have IDs on them, but one did have a GPS tracker.

"Shit, these bastards have been following us. Probably through a cell phone or a bug on one of our vehicles," Willow said to an exhausted Little Bull.

He flopped down in a heap, winded after hauling the last five corpses to the death pyre. "There is no way any of any of us would be stupid enough to use a cell phone. Those mind-numbing, cancer-causing devices have been invading our freedom and privacy since they hit the market!" said the warrior. "Damn smart, multi-level marketing media bastards make it impossible for the children of this nation to have even one independent thought anymore, between phones and gaming," he said, clearly infuriated.

"Well, they must have found a way to use some sort of tracking device. How else would they be able to find us so soon? We'd better check the vehicles when we get back to base camp. God, I hope Joe is all right. I have a sick feeling. I am so worried, we need to head back as soon as possible!" said Willow.

With impeccable timing, Red Hawk and Winona approached with a travois.

"Okay, let's give Mahkah a shout and get Black Bear here as well. There is no way we can lift the thousand-pound mass of our brother's carcass without their help," said Red Hawk.

"I'll run ahead and ask them to come help," said Willow despite her continued weakness.

When she reached the bear den, Black Bear was still inside.

"Has anyone heard from Bear?" she asked. "I really hope we can get going soon. I am worried that those things have been in contact with Joe."

Black Bear was still digging furiously, through the mound of bones, when finally, his hands hit the protective barrier of a rib cage. He pried a lighter out of the back pocket of his jeans and flicked the flame into being.

"Wow, would you look at that. You are very smart, my brother. I could not have hidden it better myself!" he said in awe and respect.

Within the heart of a buffalo ribcage lay the gleaming crystal skull of pte. The shards of light were blinding as he brushed loose dirt away with his free hand.

"I found it!" he shouted over his shoulder in jubilation.

"Did you hear that? It sounds like he found it, that's Great!" said Mahkah.

When Black Bear emerged from the den, he held the skull up for the others to see. The amazement in their bewildered eyes was enough to make him laugh aloud.

"Here you go, Wiyan Wakan, I gift you with the tool of our awakening," he said, smiling and holding the skull toward Willow.

She took a deep breath before slipping her backpack off. She unzipped the pouch and placed the sacred skull safely inside her bag. Her heart was beating out of her chest with energy that sang with the clarity of a rising dawn.

"I must go and thank my brother, my honoured totem and spirit guide, for safeguarding the skull for all these years," said Black Bear.

Mahkah stepped forward and slipped his arm around his brother's shoulder whispering words of condolence as he pointed down to the corpse of brother bear. The grizzly's huge body sat atop his quarry, the stench of lizard flesh flattened beneath his mass, blue blood glowing in the red of his blood-soaked fur.

Black Bear fell to his knees as a primal scream tore from his mouth shattering the silent mountain with grief's song.

Little Bull turned to Red Hawk and they continued to pile rocks for the cairn upon the bodies of their enemies. Their morose eyes met in understanding of their warrior brother's heartache in losing such a great beast connected by a shared spirit.

The entire band soon gathered around the grizzly and they stood together in a deeply shared forlorn reverence.

Black Bear knelt by the animal's side whispering praise in the ear of the great warrior beast and gently stroking the grizzly's muzzle before he was rolled onto the woven branch bed of the travois.

Little Bull quickly grabbed the legs of the two crushed bodies that had been trapped under the bear, adding their carcasses to the nearly completed cairn. While he was dragging the corpses to their final resting place, Willow noticed a leaf of paper stuffed in the breast pocket of one of the fallen.

She ran over and pulled the paper out. "Well, look at this, it seems these evil creatures have been given orders by someone named Steve Brandon, and the employer's logo is part of the Bilderberg Group. I should have known those elitist bastards would be behind any attempt at equality and empowerment. How could they join with the lizard race to suppress their own people? All this suffering for money and control, for greed. It is sad how little it seems we've evolved!" said Willow.

"At least we now know the face of our enemy. When the time is right we must share our knowledge. Come, let's finish up here and take our brother to his final resting place within the Mother's embrace before it gets much darker," said Mahkah.

The men took up the poles, two warriors per side. They struggled with determined pride to haul the beast's one thousand pounds of dead weight up the mountain rise to his home, his den. They did the best they could to ease his body within the narrow space and then covered the entrance with stones. To an observer, it was just another rise of craggy rock lying along the mountain's peak.

The blaze of Father Sun was setting upon the peaks, as the last prayers and wishes were sent to the heavens. The sacred animal's spirit joined his ancestors on their heavenly journey across the realms.

The group—guardian, warriors and incarnation of the Sacred Mother—walked down from the resting place of yet another brother slowly and methodically; the loss was great, yet fortitude rang clear.

Willow could feel the weight of the skull upon her back. The force in the light of the gatekeeper's manifestation gave her the sense of having the weight of the world upon her shoulders, which she did.

When the terrain changed from slippery shards of rock to sparse forest the group picked up their pace to a quick jog, silently weaving their way down the steep slope. The last tendrils of dim light from Father Sun splayed upon the forest floor. The light formed an intricately etched path that accompanied the band back to base camp.

They all sighed with relief when Old Joe appeared from behind a stand of trees, taking turns embracing the shaman in an outpouring of love. They released the fear they had held for the medicine man since discovering that they had been tracked into the mountains.

"We have found what we sought, Tunkasila. But we have lost our honoured four-legged guardian brother in

battle. We must leave this evening as our safety is at risk,"
said Black Bear.

"I know, my son. I have watched all that has
transpired from beyond the veil. We must stay here and rest.
We are safe, as I have cast a web of illusion around our
camp. You must eat and replenish your bodies, for the forces
of evil will soon fall upon us as the greatest of storms. The
Dance continues as the unity of universal awareness sings
forth. The continued attempts of her lost children to stop the
circle's renewal anger the Mother. Her wrath will be
awesome, and many shall fall and quiver in fear. Yet we will
rise to dance in the dawn. A'ho."

The weary band sat down upon the ground and ate
some stew that Joe had prepared from dried pemmican and
a variety of wild-harvested herbs.

Willow choose to fast, drinking only a broth for
fortitude, as was expected in the preparation before a
journey quest. Her intent was bound solidly within the
web's strong weave. The crystal skull of pte talked to her in
the form of gentle clouds of wispy vision. The beauty of the
play—a magnificent drama—orchestrated magically within
the dance of each nation's birthing song. She would be
playing the lead role. A spectacular ending culminating in a
glorious beginning of empowerment for all who waited. The
painter's brush held as a wand firmly grasped in the people's
belief of manifestation: each becoming a god unto oneself,
each the creator embracing the consciousness of love and
the beauty of rebirth. Like the snake shedding its skin, the
renewal of Earth's children would spill forth in the spectrum
of an expanding existence.

The group of friends, bound in the common quest for
awakening, lay around the embers of the smokeless fire.

Little Bull had found the tracking device under the fender of Joe's Jeep. They speculated that the lizard men must have attached it when Willow and Black Bear had been at the hospital, as that was the only time the Jeep had been left unattended.

Black Bear took the tracking device on a long hike away from their camp after they had finished eating; one he also took to clear his mind and say more prayers of gratitude to his power animal.

Later, as the group slept, Joe looked upon the bodies of the resting warriors, the pride of his nation, and began to pour love's protective shield upon their shoulders. He had been in a trance of prayer for almost 24 hours now. He could feel the force of the source's web of power entwined in the braves' auras.

He could perceive many faint images from across the spirit realm: all animals great and small spread out across the lands, warrior braves from times past were dancing the Circle Dance, women and children working together across sprawling teepee villages, all of this smiled gloriously down upon the small band.

He could see the beautiful and delicate form of Star, Black Bear's heart-song, lie down along his side to embrace his massive sleeping body.

Chaska's ethereal body knelt beside his brother, Mahkah, lovingly stroking his third eye in honour and love.

The great spirit of the grizzly paced around the bag that held the crystal skull at Willow's side. While her spirit lover, Wahweyho, stroked her hair, sitting in the attentive squat of the warrior.

In trance, Red Hand had already come to Joe to tell

him of the ritual duties that would be required in order to hold the gateway to the twelfth vortex open. He listened intently to the directions as he mixed the red ochre paste with the strong elixir of datura. He added some sweetgrass to the mixture to help the journeyer, Willow, find the spirit of her lover with ease and to prevent her from being dragged down into the lower realms.

Earlier in the day, while the group was on the quest for the sacred skull, Joe had gathered the fresh little red flowers of the psychotropic fungi from the dung of pte. He had to sneak among the herd that roamed protected within the gates of Banff National Park.

The Keepers of the Earth knew the buffalo herds had been intentionally wiped out to try to destroy the sacred tool that empowered the people in opening the doors of perception. The decimation of the buffalo also served to starve the last resisters and to force them onto reservations where they would live and die. The great herds were simply slaughtered at times for game from rail cars upon the winding steel snake that divided their lands. The herd of pte remembered and gave way to the shaman, for he, too, was to be their retribution.

Fading Dawn, Willow's grandmother, stood at Joe's side chattering away. Giving him direction on how to make the salve more potent by adding the crushed blossoms of St. John's Wort to quell the nervous system.

He impatiently tried to shoo her away, swatting at the wispy silhouette while still following her advice.

Willow's grandmother's eyes shone with overwhelming pride at the granddaughter she never knew, the girl she'd only connected with through the whisperings of love and from the shared stories of her diaries. Soon they would embrace across the realms and she could look into the eyes of her Wiyan Wakan.

Joe turned his attention to the variety of dried herbs he had lain upon the red felt cloth. Singing in his spirit guides in the quiet chirping of a bird's waking song, he slowly began to add varied portions of each sacred plant into the stone mortar.

The shaman could feel the power his song evoked, as he sang in the elements of each plant's teachings. A small offering of the seed of the thornapple (Datura) was ground with pestle, blended with a few peyote buttons and a generous pinch of tobacco. When he completed the little smoke, he took the gourd that held the serpent vine mixture and continued to sing his songs as he swirled the thick concoction over the warm embers of the dying fire. He continued his ritual and prayers until the red of dawn's early rise took the sky.

The group awoke slowly, each warrior shaking off the lingering realm of dream that still hovered in their minds.

All seemed larger in stature, the smile that played upon their lips brighter, all feeling the unity of all their relations imbued within their essence.

The lines of stress and the frown of pain and grief on Black Bear's face had smoothed as he stroked a long strand of Star's hair. Intertwining it in his fingers, lost in thought, he knew she had blessed him with her presence; her sweet scent still lingered in his mind.

Willow felt joy rising in her chest as the scent of sweetgrass filled the air. Her breath was coming in small gasps, her body left quivering in the longing of her lover.

Blue Moon stood nurturing Shadow, changing the

dressing on his shoulder wound.

Little Bull sat behind Winona, holding her in his powerful arms. Whispering the sweetness of undying love in her ear while she blushed like a schoolgirl.

Mahkah and Red Hawk talked strategy, as they paced through the throng of ghostly warriors that stood nodding their approval from the other side.

Finally, Joe spoke, "Okay, let's load up and head back to Little Elbow Campground where our family awaits. The yellowing of the sky speaks of an incoming storm. The web is thinning, and the parting of the veil is almost upon us. I must prepare the people for what shall be and what their minds may perceive. The shroud of protection we must create to strengthen the web again is in the hands of those that are able to follow the procession of the Circle Dance into creation. If their belief is weak it shall diminish all that we are trying to create.

"There must be those that stay here: people from every nation across the vast lands to carry on and preserve the teachings of the awakened, to stop them from being buried again behind the dense, foul conscience of greed. And there will be those that leave to join their ancestors, here and on other realms in other dimensions and across the vast universes in order to allow the healing necessary for the Mother's abused system.

"Only those that embrace the ancient teachings of the Keepers of the Earth, the Red Path Way, shall be saved," said the medicine man through his channeled vision.

The warriors stared at one another in the great sadness of knowing that the journey that they were about to embark on would be difficult, yet beyond necessary, and there was no turning back. They knew that much would change upon the plains of the great surface of their sacred home. The mountains would fall, and the oceans would rise. The Mother would yawn awakened from her troubled sleep to swallow cities whole. The Earth would spin into herself with a shudder as the axis mundi would tilt to end the warbled rotation.

Together they walked slowly toward the parked Jeep and battered reserve truck stopping to embrace one another before climbing into their separate vehicles.

The dirt forestry road still lay in the shadow of the Three Sisters range, helping to cover their stealthy retreat.

Joe, Black Bear and Willow followed behind the truck in the Jeep. The crystal skull of pte bounced along, secured in the pack upon the lap of the Wiyan Wakan.

Willow sat lovingly stroking the outer mesh of the bag that held the skull so many had died for. She remembered reading about the discovery in Australia of crystal buffalo skulls years ago, but they were much smaller than the one she held now.

The Pre-Colombian, Mesoamerican, crystal human skulls that were found throughout history supposedly held mystical and prophetic abilities. There were stories of people being drawn deep into a vision of the Earth's history after looking into the crystal-lined eye sockets. This seemed unlikely to many in the past, but now as the vibrations from pte were overpowering her senses with apocalyptic visions interspersed with the glorious greens of a vibrant, abundant Earth, a rainbow spectrum of profound renewal in the spirit of awakened souls, Willow knew these stories to be true.

They had been driving for just over 20 minutes in a grey haze. The soupy skies triggered a foreboding tension in the stomachs of all.

Winona was driving with Blue Moon and Shadow up front, while the other three warriors sat in the back griping at the dreariness the weather imparted on their spirits.

"It is a sign of things to come. See those clouds, they do not look right!" said Little Bull. He was always gazing at the clouds, forever in a righteous anger of conspiracy theory regarding chemtrails.

The truck was just rounding a corner when Winona slowed and then braked to a stop. Up ahead, along both sides of the road, was a huge murder of crows mingling with a conspiracy of ravens. They flew up in a swarm and out in the lead appeared Hermann the Harbinger of Woe.

"Well, here we go," said the clan of leery warriors in unison.

The flock of birds continued their flight, circling above the truck in a swirling black cloud.

The Jeep pulled to a stop behind the truck and Willow gently placed the skull down before leaping out of her seat as Hermann swooped down to land upon her outstretched arm.

"What have we here, my friend?" she asked in apprehension.

The raven stared deep into her eyes then nuzzled her ear and flew off. His message was spoken on a wavelength of telepathic sight.

"It seems there is a roadblock up ahead waiting for us," said Willow.

"Yeah, I didn't think these foreboding skies and this sick feeling of apprehension was coming out of nowhere. A warrior knows when the enemy lies ahead in wait," said Little Bull. Mahkah and Red Hawk laughed, shaking their heads at their brother's self-assured gloomy prediction.

"The Mother is on our side," said Black Bear.

"And, so are our fine-feathered friends," said Old Joe.

Willow and Joe exchanged a knowing glance and told the others to lay low. The entourage of warriors began to drive again and picked up their speed on the approach to their destiny.

A smile spread across Winona's face as she gave a nod and the gas pedal hit the floor causing the old Ford's tires to spin erratically down the road. Old Joe followed laughing with glee, a bandanna pulled up over his face to help combat the cloud of dust.

Willow lay low on the floor in front of her seat with the backpack beside her, while Black Bear stood to his full height of six feet four inches bracing himself on the Jeep's frame and releasing a war cry to shake the nations.

The warriors in the back of the truck also ducked down, as they would be the ones to be hit first with what was sure to be a barrage of flying bullets.

They grasped their tomahawks and spears at the ready to leap from the flying truck as they plowed through the roadblock that lay just ahead.

On the straightaway, after they screeched around the final corner, two black SUVs sat facing nose to nose. Deep ditches were dug on either side of the vehicles to try to stop their passage.

Four men with Uzis in hand fired madly from behind the cover of the vehicles.

Winona was bent low, her eyes barely peeking over the dash to see the road as the others up front lay across the seats. The woman directed the truck with accuracy and speed toward the narrow gap between the two vehicles.

The sound of the bullets ricocheting off the vehicles was deafening. But not as nerve-racking a sound as the cacophony of hundreds upon hundreds of ravens and crows, jays, sparrows, eagles and hawks who had joined the murder and conspiracy screaming out their call of defiance. The lizard men had no chance as the birds tore into their eyes and shredded their faces with their strong talons.

The old truck hit the blockade with a shattering force, smashing through the barricade with ease—just one more war wound on the Ford's battered body.

Winona slowed the old truck slightly, as the warriors in the back warbled with laughter at their attempts to stand. Little Bull pounded the roof, showing his pride for his woman's impressive driving skills. Shadow and Blue Moon pulled themselves upright in the front with a cheer.

Willow pulled herself up from the floor and laughed with joy, waving to the others in front as they flew down the road through the opening Winona's driving had provided.

"Well that was easy," she said to Black Bear and Joe, giving them a rub on their shoulders.

"I am so grateful to Hermann for his assistance, what a powerful sight that was!" she said, glancing back at the circling flock of their feathered friends.

The vehicles kept up their quick flight down the gravel road toward the campground. The skies now a sickly yellow-grey there was a heavy oppressive sensation building in the thickening air.

The group drove on for another fifteen minutes before they could see the rising dust cloud formed from a thousand feet shuffling in the Circle Dance.

The manifestation of the electrical field was ominous, as were the flashes of lightening that ricocheted off the mountain heights embracing the people's movement in a violent force field.

When the two vehicles wheeled into the campground the sense of welcoming was overwhelming. The crowd parted like the Red Sea in the biblical telling. The source was on their side and love's manifestation was at hand.

The resounding cheers sent chills through the warriors' very beings as they parked alongside the central circle of teepees.

Old Joe led the group through the throngs of people while they continued to dance, never losing a step, always in beat in the procession of Father Sun's path. The re-linking of hand upon shoulder after their passing through the circle's core the only break in form.

The medicine man greeted the elders and entered the sacred lodging of the Tribal Council. He held the flap open for Willow to follow while the remaining warriors encircled the teepee to stand guard in the stance of the noble guardians they were.

"My brothers, I have been in council across the realms and am called forth to prepare those that are united in the circle for what is to come," said Joe.

"Some will be tempted by the old fears of their upbringing to break the chain. This must not happen. When the elusive dream of this reality dissolves and the veil parts, the Circle Dance must continue to its completion two days from now. We must embrace what our eyes, through heart's longing, will finally reveal. The reuniting across realms of all our ancestors will be a great shock to many, but still we must dance in and embrace the shift into universal consciousness. For only in embracing the unknown will we be able to find our lost virtue and strengthen the web once again—becoming one heart instead of two in the divided man," Joe finished. His magnificent aura had filled the tent with an iridescent golden light that spilled out of the teepee's walls and cast radiant beams across the valley.

Willow stood in awe at the beauty emanating from the seer. She knew in her heart that the warrior's path—the path of the hero—existed within all.

The Red Path Way was the gleaming light within every strand of DNA: truth, friendship, respect, spirituality, humanitarianism. All part of the teachings and the last metaphor were these virtues, and the responsibility they required was the path to walk to live within Creator's rule.

White Buffalo Calf Woman's words rang throughout Willow's essence and the spirit of the woman sang through her veins: the two becoming one as the prophecies had predicted. The light being could only fully return when the human race had learned and embraced their lessons enough to bring in a shift of consciousness and a new way of being, the Fifth Root Race, into the fifth world.

The shaman exited the council of elders, followed by the shimmering-white ethereal woman; the crystal skull shone blinding rays of magnificent light in Buffalo Calf Woman's upheld arms.

Gasps of awe came from the crowd. Their hands slipped off shoulders to open a path as the two wove their way back to the center where the sacred tree stood. Tears of joy fell upon the ground in a cascade of rain as the dancers looked on.

Members of the Tribal Council and the band of warriors followed the procession of the sacred relic, the circle reforming tightly behind them.

The vibration from thousands of shuffling feet sent shock waves through the Earth; the Mother was ecstatic at the reawakening of her children. And with this great show of respect upon her skin, she peeled forth with laughter that echoed and boomed throughout the skies and across all lands.

The people almost fell to their knees in fear, but the shaman raised his voice in reassurance above the shaking and rolling tremor of the skies: "The Mother sings forth her glory, my children. Do not be afraid. She lies awake with trembling joy at the dancing in of awareness and the intention we have set forth with our dance. It is of the utmost importance that we continue the Circle Dance so that all our relations may cross into this realm."

Joe paused for a moment and then continued, "There is a great shift that we must go through as part of our awakening. For we have forgotten how to manifest from within this elusive dream in which we reside. When your vision is tested and what you see causes fear and incredulity embrace belief! Do not fall to your knees in ignorance!

"Dance instead to the one true eye being opened. You will never be shown what the mind of your heart and soul cannot fathom. The trees may sway, and mountains may fall, but your intent must remain clear to shatter the illusion and recreate the dream.

"All the peace and joy you have ever felt, all you have ever dreamed of being, let it shine forth. All the hurt and fear and pain, let it fall on the ground with the ashes of these false walls built up around your essence.

"When the sky falls and the heavens tilt, dance the dance across the universe. For you shall be here to bring forth the new dawn of a new world cleansed clear of illusion: an empowered creator, one with the breath and breadth of all that ever was or will be.

"When the procession of the Circle Dance is complete

you will see from the light of your inner being. At that time, you will be able to perceive all your relations.

"The veil will have parted enough for unity in consciousness to exist as finally the webs of time have grown thin enough for this to happen. The Earth's energy grid has been dormant for far too long. There is a path we have been requested to light, as Keepers of the Earth, this is the Red Path Way.

"Our very souls have called forth White Buffalo Calf Woman for the cleansing her prophetic appearance foretold in the stories of old. The purification that is about to be unleashed is an integral part of the circle of life. Our duty is to survive and be present as creators for the Mother's next incarnation. This will depend on our ability to strengthen the web through the reactivation of the twelve energy vortexes that exist upon this vast planet we call home.

"When we, all Earth's children, across all the lands, embrace the truth that the unity of all, as one, is one. That every hateful thought, every border and line drawn through our hearts has caused this great division—the lowest of vibrations and one we have grown accustomed to and have been trained to depend on to sustain us for the last millennium. Only then with awareness will this reality shift into the beating of one heart.

"Right now, as I speak, there are forces working with all their might to prevent us from surviving this shift, the lowly ones that prefer a lower vibration are stuck. They prefer to exist on the material plane where the few have much, and many have nothing, instead of elevating to the higher vibrations of co-manifestation, equality and love.

"We have been given the honour, here on these sacred lands, to open the last of the twelve energy vortexes.

And we shall be challenged the most! The world shall dance together in this one vision, one that we must all hold strong.

"When you see your ancestors reach out and grasp their hands as all other people, at all the other sacred sites, will be doing as well, all of us together at the same time. It is then that we must activate the energy grid to cast a dome of protection across every piece of this amazing planet that you call home.

"Hold true to your thought's projection and stand tall in loving gratitude for what you shall behold is what is in your heart," Joe finished with reverence.

The crowd continued to dance and, while listening to Joe's impassioned words, grew in the magnificence of their being; all were shining in the brilliance of thought's creation as hail began to pelt down upon their forms and gales of wind blew forth torrents of harmful debris. Still their smiles did not fade, and their ancestors waited proudly with the longing of a thousand years beyond the veil.

The shaman seemed to wither from the exertion of projecting his voice over the people's shuffling dance, the vibration it created and the coming storm. He bent and whispered to Willow, White Buffalo Calf Woman: "Come, daughter, we must leave and find our way to the Crystal Cave of Journey. I have cast a glamour for us to use to leave in peace. The Mother's children have fully embodied the teachings of the Red Path Way. The rest is up to us!"

The wizened old man grabbed Willow firmly by her arm and the two passed through the crowd of dancers with ease, the link in arms breaking in raised salutation as they magically slipped through the people. It seemed as if they were wrapped in a shroud walking upon a different unseen plane, traversing quietly along a fragile thread in the web of life. The two walked gently arm in arm upon the Earth, their heartbeats reverberating as one with every step taken as they left the thrumming Circle Dance.

Willow and Joe headed directly to the camp using the shortcut to the back of his site. They did not expect to see the warriors milling around the cold fire pit.

"A'ho, Wakan Tanka," said Black Bear as he bowed in honour of the approaching pair.

Old Joe laughed, his smiling face tearing in long-awaited recognition and gratitude for being seen in this incarnation before leaving.

"A'ho, Wiyan Wakan," spoke the great bear of a man. He truly embodied who he was, on all levels and elements one with his animal spirit guide; a holy man himself who would be called to task in the new world.

"I am honoured to behold your presence again, Black Bear. You are a great man, my brother. I am forever grateful for your sacrifices. All is written, and you shall always be remembered," said Willow, choking up while embracing his strong, broad shoulders.

Each member of the warrior clan, Winona, Little Bull, Blue Moon, Shadow, Mahkah and Red Hawk, walked up to place honour at the feet of the holy ones through their spoken word. Their prayers of love and gratitude cloaked the very souls of the incarnate spirits, giving Willow and Joe the strength to stay present in their bodily forms to complete the task at hand.

Eventually, the pair left the group and wove along the forest trail to the sheathed veil of protection that hovered in guardianship over the cave's entrance.

All the animals of the forest were present, and Hermann sat in the branches of a tall fir ka-cawing his welcome.

The sky over the cave shone the clearest of turquoise blue; the only patch of gleaming daylight in the surrounding torrential rains. The winds were calm in the circle and the silent peace of the forest was awakened with the whispering of a beautiful orchestration. Every blade of grass, every plant and flower, along with all creatures great and small and every universal entity sung out in harmony telepathically along the humming tentacles of light:

> "Hanta Yo, Hanta Yo, Hanta Yo. We are clearing the Way. We are clearing the Way. We are clearing the Way."

The Wiyan Wakan's and Wakan Tanka's hearts swelled as they laid the crystal skull of pte upon the trembling Mother's breast before the opening of the Crystal Cave of Light.

The Web's Weave

Members of the Bilderberg Group and the Bavarian Illuminati sat anxiously awaiting the most recent news from the self-proclaimed leaders of the group, the Babylonian Brotherhood.

A representative of the Talisman Corporation, Buff Warren, sat with his head in his hands, visibly infuriated by the images displayed across the large plasma screen that played above their meeting table.

The head hybrid alien of the Babylonian Brotherhood, the king of the Annunaki, Marduk, addressed the elitist members of the Club of Rome: "They have succeeded in finding the twelfth skull! These base creatures of terrestrial origins! How can it be? I believe," he continued sarcastically, "that the idea was to stop the Rainbow Serpent's energetic path with the construction of the Belo Monte Dam in Brazil and the North Dakota Pipeline that is now well underway. The plan was to stop its winding along the grid of Earth's vortex points and to stop the steady eco-movement from moving North. Yet, Earth's children are still awakening! How can this be happening?"

A major general of the Non-Terrestrial Special Forces Unit stood and began to address his peers in defense: "It began when our station at Pine Gap was breached, an act that culminated in the discovery of the 11 crystal skull artifacts at Uluru. Those damn Aboriginals have become more empowered since the reclaiming of their rights! Their children have been awakened with stories of the sacred era. Now they walk in Dreamtime, creating and naming as they go!" he screeched, briefly losing his composure.

Another member of the Non-Terrestrial Special Forces Unit who stood alongside the general added, "They followed the melodic contours of the song lines that allowed them access to the remembering."

"They remembered how to climb down the great red rocks of Uluru instead of up. That is how they found the totemic spirit of the buffalo," hissed the creature that led the colonial lizard militia and oversaw all the functions of the top-secret station buried deep in the Australian Outback.

The Pine Gap facility was built in 1966 under the guise of a satellite relay station. The investors burrowed over eight and a half kilometers deep within the Earth's core and that is where their true works of evil began, hidden from prying eyes.

It was, in truth, a joint military and alien research center; in exchange for advances in technology, the extra-terrestrial aliens could continue to research methods of genetic testing and mental manipulation on human subjects. The research center was established as one of many means of heralding in the new world order. It became the leading implementation station of the world wide web surveillance network: the giant eye in the sky. For their plan to work, they needed to establish an above ground network, a terrestrial honeycomb of sorts.

One network facility stood in Dulce, New Mexico, where the council was currently meeting. Another lay in Montauk, New York, another in New Swabia, Antarctica, among many others intricately placed upon the cosmic grid. This network of facilities spread across all the vast lands of Earth and even upon her surrounding cosmic bodies.

Attempts to hide their electron propulsion relay system had proven difficult and glimpses of strange blue light rays had alerted the first freedom thinkers to the Brotherhood's activities. It had been increasingly difficult for the Brotherhood to hide their actions and intentions of the surveillance network over the years.

Shamans and seers, medicine men and medicine women, healers, hackers and whistle-blowers had all been accessing and utilizing the very web that was designed to weaken them.

Their intent and desire for the constant evolution of Earth consciousness was unstoppable. Their ability to avoid being controlled by the governing council and their fortitude to face the oppressor produced a movement that was gaining momentum and becoming a war cry that was getting louder every day.

They knew the alien beings had held the knowledge of free energy, and flight without the use of fossil fuels, since their appearance on the planet. There had never been a need for oil extraction or the constant depletion of Earth's minerals. All of this was being done in the attempt to weaken the web's weave from the heavens above. And below as well, for their caves were spread like giant anthills throughout the many lands, just as they were spread like an infectious disease above ground.

Of course, greed and the lust for power played an immense role in the fight for control of Earth's domain; in order to control the masses, the aim was to dumb down the people and to keep them hungry, wanting and desperate.

All documented knowledge of Earth's magnetic biosphere was suppressed and contorted. Human history was falsified and manipulated just as the historical record of archaeology and the impressive technology of the Egyptian, Tibetan, Incan and Mayan cultures had been.

People were so easily destroyed by government manipulation: geniuses were made out to be mad men and fools and their gifts of wisdom accessed through the universal mind was sought out and powerfully suppressed.

This innate need and ability to govern and control became a sociopathic genetic trait that was purposely breed into the hybrid beings through incestuous union. This brotherhood of blissfully unconscious entities developed technology such as the High Frequency Active Auroral Research Program (HAARP) and other massive so called "radio towers" to deflect impulses of cosmic energy. This was all done in an attempt to shield the Earth from the flux of universal consciousness each planetary precession and passing of the equinoxes created.

The alien lizard race from the Draco Constellation had been residing upon and within the planet for almost 12,500 years. The introduction of religion from the Annunaki Brotherhood of fallen gods and angels was the first mechanism of suppression employed by the hybrids long ago.

It was a system of oppression kept in place until the Brotherhood could set up the technology necessary to disrupt the energetic flow of the web's source. With this first introduction of religion, the world's people had foolishly become hypnotized by fear, the very sustenance the Brotherhood craved and fed upon.

Fear grew into the fear of death, fear of difference and fear of independent thought. The rising dominance of this fear created fear for the Earth herself—the very foundation and source of existence.

The rejection and disempowerment of the innate and natural oneness made it easy to control Earth's children. Hell became the Underworld of Zibalba controlled by the devil: a reflection of the cold alienation of the true entity from the self that took on its own living form. The people's detachment soon thrived on the lower base instincts of hedonistic and ego-driven impulses, all wrapped nicely in an envelope of endless fears that led to the fall.

The fallen Annunaki that survived the first deluge had chosen to reside in an interlaced maze of underground networks. A labyrinth of evil intention bore forth to create and maintain a grid of relay stations on the Earth's surface that would support phase two of the suppression.   These underground stations that formed the grid's matrix could be accessed through many different sites including the Urstall, Staffordshire and Freiburg tunnels in Europe, as well as others in Siberia. The lizard hybrids built and hid in underground stations at Mount Mashu in Greece, Azerbaijan, and Mongolia as well as on the Trobriand Islands. Their tunnels interlaced beneath Ojinaga, Mexico, Hnagchow, China and Montreal, Canada, as well as the Grand Canyon and numerous places throughout the Amazon.

All were connected; some were explicitly hidden under the protection of the Smithsonian Institute and Governmental Laws (lies) of Protection and others controlled by corporate rights and development.

The complex network was designed to stop the awakening of the Keepers of the Earth and all her children to the beginning of another great cycle.

The distortion of the pulsating cosmic wave's flow along the web combined with the religious suppression of Gaia consciousness was meant to stop the prayers of gratitude upon the Mother and stamp out the old ways of the Indigenous people.

All of this was being done in a desperate attempt to try and offset the dodecahedron (12-faced polyhedron, a geometric compilation of 12-faced pyramid-like structures) makeup of the crystalline inner structure of the web.

But, try as they may, it was not working as planned. The people had touched the Earth and heard her song and secret societies had moved to her dance for millennia. Her being was alive, awake and eager to absorb the universal pulse.

The alignment of the planets along with the earthlings who remembered the rituals of old empowered the web. The outer icosahedrons (20-faced polyhedron, a geometric compilation of 20-faced pyramid-like structures) of the planet would once again become sufficiently charged to usher in a powerful shift of awareness; an evolutionary impact that would change the very DNA of a now enslaved people into which would soon become the Fifth Root Race.

This story slid through the universal mind and that of the leader of the Babylonian Brotherhood as he processed their recent failures. "Why we ever shared knowledge with the high priests of the ancient ones is beyond me," frothed the tall lizard king of the Annunaki who stood at the head of the table pointing his scaly finger at the fidgeting government men. "And now here we are sharing knowledge again! I suppose our plans would not be manifesting without your corporate government by our side. Although you are halfbreeds and of the mixed race of lizard and primal man, you at least still carry the same lower vibrations of the amphibian mind that feed our base instincts of greed and understand our desire and our right to be gods!"

He paused and looked around the room before continuing. "The intended suppression within the Amazon Basin with the Belo Monte Dam has not had sufficient time to corrupt the lands and kill off the tribes that still sing to the Earth and raise her vibration. This is the fault of organized religion's fall from grace in the eyes of your flock! A careless fall brought on by a failure to correct continual sexual abuse cases brought against you and monetary misconduct. You group of fools! You should have been able to suppress all Indigenous cultures by now. You have had thousands of years of practice. You've sufficiently wiped out North American First Nations and others with ease!" The gill atop the lizard king's head now flaming red.   "Now, due to you fools, it seems that our technology upon the matrix has backfired on us. The power of knowledge in the oneness of being, as true conductor, has been accessed," finished Marduk, directing his wrath at the Pope who sat sheepishly near the end of the table.   The board continued with the pointing of fingers of blame. Issues ranged from the current and past economic collapses of Wall Street and bank fraud to overzealous resource extraction that foolishly led to wars of greed that drew unwanted attention their way.

The fallen gods could not afford the awakening, for then all Earth's children would be equal creators and fear would be replaced with glory, which was something they could not feed upon. The Babylonian Brotherhood and their league of minions would be left alone to walk only in the realm of the Underworld. Left with nothing to feed upon but their own fear—the fear of having no underlings, no slaves. Becoming slaves to the illusive material world the select few enjoyed was a reality beyond terrifying.

All Earth's children would embrace the web's flow of consciousness behind thought's intention and create an abundant green world, singing upon this vibrancy with love and gratitude deep in their hearts. That is, all except those who would choose to remain under the governance of greed's pulsation, a distorted energy that is not sufficient to bring about a shift in DNA. To choose the path of greed would sentence those of the disconnected essence of being to the purgatory of the Underworld.

Valiant Thor sat quietly in tranquil observation among the bickering fools of the perverse round table. The Venusian was an extremely handsome man that had not aged a day since his arrival on Earth some 58 years earlier.

Valiant, the tall, dark man, had landed his spaceship in Alexandria, Virginia, on March 16, 1957, just 22.5 kilometers South of the Pentagon. Valiant was molecularly configured into a form that would allow ease of recognition for the earthlings, a configuration that provided a safety net the human race still needed. He was sent as a messenger on behalf of Universal Central Control to convey a cautionary warning against the use of atomic weaponry. Nuclear arms were considered the most heinous of weapons in all universes. The violent wave patterns they emitted impacted all realms across all parallel worlds.

When Valiant first arrived, he had to use thought transference techniques to calm the frightened military regime. Telepathy allowed him the opportunity to communicate to officials the ethical laws that were to be adhered to upon the universal web.

The governing representatives at the time, Eisenhower and Nixon, agreed to sign a contract called the Open Skies Agreement with Universal Central Control. They did not have much choice as the Venusian was sent from the godhead of the Ascended Masters, an entity that had been in existence before the biblical times of Adam and Eve to observe the planet and its creatures.

The agreement would allow all beings of the universe free, uninterrupted access to Earth's portals as well as guarantee the cessation of unwarranted attacks upon UFO fleets. A further agreement was made for the creation of the Human Freedom Act that would prevent any attempts to interfere with future evolutionary shifts of terrestrials toward becoming the Fifth Root Race.

The mistake Universal Central Control made was in trusting the Earth's resident self-proclaimed gods to not overstep the boundaries installed in making North America their last frontier. The governing body's suppression of minds was not to interfere with the progress of the higher universal-mind's creation upon the web, nor the cosmic Earth-Mother's laws of consciousness that they had been trying to breach since the agreement was originally signed.

Valiant and the members of Universal Central Control had been waiting over 25,000 years for the races of Earth to enter this next level of evolutionary progression of consciousness.

The primary energy principle would soon be renewed when the awareness was danced in on the final days of the Ghost Dance. The sound frequency of the inner-Earth's crystalline structure has been raised sufficiently as the rhythmic beat continued to weave heartfelt cohesion across the land.

"These creatures have certainly been quite an interesting addition to the web's matrix! It will be a fortuitous time when people remember the words of spoken wisdom from the many great teachers," thought Valiant, as he teleported his being out of the shackles that held him at the table and went back to his mothership in the hot Arizona desert.

The reciprocating system of gravity, that of time into space, contraction into expansion, patriarchy back to matriarchy, is the in and out breath of the Cosmic Mother. And the children of Earth were now graciously connected through the awakening.

The Annunaki who had fallen from grace still fought with all their might to retain control of the advancing race's evolution. This need to quell evolution had always led them to problems with the council members.

Those of the Pleiades star system who sat with the Ascended Masters and the group of overseers of Universal Central Control had decided unanimously that it was essential to protect the evolution of humankind.

After watching the horrors of genocide inflicted upon the slowly evolving race of the two leggeds, they quickly threw a plasma shield of hydrogen quasicrystals to cloak and protect the teachings of wisdom at sacred sites across the lands. At the same time, the tilt of the axis mundi in Egypt let forth a fearsome tearing shift upon the land mass.

This alien race, whose return had been prophesied by the teachings drawn within all ancient writings, remembered the old days when they, as gods, had played upon the lands. At that time, the need to raise the consciousness of the Earth's cave dwellers became imperative in order for them to develop their fields of play upon the terrestrial planet. They built great structures upon the ley lines of the Cosmic Mother's grid known as the web's weave, which was a term those of the ancient race preferred to use to refer to the energy matrix. Now the very Earth herself was cracking along these lines of power just as before.

The Pleiadians' old home of Atlantis had just recently raised her head out of the icy ocean in Antarctica with the release of a huge iceberg, due to the warming of the Great Planetary Mother.

The terrestrials were once again about to be thrown down and suppressed by the Pleiadians' fallen brothers, the Annunaki and the Council of the Babylonian Brotherhood.

The cosmic story's unfolding was that the first people the Annunaki had encountered to work with were those of the great continent of Africa.

There were many people of the First Root Race that survived, and they soon dispersed to the lands of Australia after the flooding stopped and became the Aboriginals. Their descendants, those of the second race of man, began to develop without their gods at their side. They remembered some teachings of the ancient ones by following the path of the Rainbow Serpent, which was used by the wise to rediscover their place in relation to the sacred Earth they lived upon.

These people, with faith and knowledge, created a complex network within the patterns of life. And once laid down, they soon remembered the laws and customs of the land, people, plants and animals. The paths of the Rainbow Serpent were the ley lines of old and the people built many great temples along them. Various cultures had different names for the grid and many people of the lost races had forgotten the true purpose in the activation of the electromagnetic zones, causing their own disempowerment.

The gods who had survived the deluge, by remembering the practice in the teachings of Earth's sacredness, had ran and hid in Middle Earth during the upheaval. They had entered Middle Earth from an opening in the North Pole. The descendants of the fallen gods escaped in their aircraft's to hide on the dark side of Sister Moon until the Mother had stopped her upheavals.

In their new home in Middle Earth, they built honeycomb structures much like that of a termite nest while retaining the circular, crystalline architecture of energy in the Earth's teachings.

The skies of their inner world were a beautiful rose colour and the giant, 12-foot tall, Annunaki lived harmoniously within her confines. That is, until they were called forth to build new structures and to share the knowledge they had held sacred for so long with those of the upcoming Third Root Race. And so, with the gods that remained hidden for eons among icebergs and the beauty of the Aurora Borealis, they exited the center of the Earth with their guards in tow for protection. The mythical creature Big Foot was born at this time in order to protect the the Third Root Race from the fallen ones that had returned to Earth with a mission of their own.

The Hopi and Anasazi as well as the Tibetan and Mongolian people were much like the Aboriginals of Australia: they were of the great migration and held vast wisdom. Some were gifted a vision to retain the story of their beginnings, one that connected them back to the new realm of their old gods.

The Hopi remembered their birth story of crawling forth from the center of the Earth that was still represented and honoured in the sipapu of the kiva. As time passed, the people spread throughout the lands to all four corners of the planet. Great serpentine mounds were built, and stories of creation recalled through the new contact with these earlier gods. But, most important of all, the knowledge of the Earth Mother remained intact through myth and ancient stone etchings. The ritual honouring of the variations of corn, a reminder of the great variation of man, were held within the oral traditions as was the great tree of knowledge that held Earth's wisdom deep within her roots.

There were five sacred stone tablets created at this time, one for every colour of man and one for the gods to retain until the day when all would be united and Pahana would carry forth the missing tablet that spoke of the history of humankind—the time when all illusion would shatter.

The Tibetan buddhists taught of seeking Agharti and Shambhala, the sacred lands that were to be found within. Tibetan masters of the path still practiced acoustic elevation techniques, levitating boulders to dance, drumming and chanting song to create a weightless, parabolic flight upon the unified field.

The Dalai Lama, the terrestrial representative of the

ancient ones, spread his teaching in the sacredness of the mantra. Awaiting the time foretold to present the three lost notes that, when sounded together, would unveil the eternal nature and regenerate the world.

The mantra, "Om mani padme hum," was, at this very moment, being chanted along the heights of Mt. Kailash and lands throughout the Eastern realms:

"Om," chanted to purify pride and ego into the generosity of heart.

"Ma," purifying jealousy and lust into ethics.

"Ni," sounded to quell passion and desire, into patience.

"Pad," to release ignorance and prejudice, into self-diligence.

"Me," chanted for the renunciation of poverty and possessiveness.

"Hum," purifying aggression and hatred, into wisdom.

The spiritual master sat in bliss upon the lotus, a precious crystal-jewel of snow in the alps of his mind, intent on gathering the frequencies produced by the chant's vibration.

All was in preparation to awaken the grid's harmonics and pluck the lost chords of creation. The stone that the Tibetans had held for the yellow race of man had already been removed and placed at its home with the Hopi in the center of the four corners.

All were becoming one, flowing along the river of the

Red Path Way.

The fallen Annunaki of Marduk had tried for years to find the hiding place of the scared stones of Hopi legend. It was believed that the rejoining of the four races, the uniting of the four stones and the fifth that was held by the gods, would re-balance the Earth's spin after the tilt in her axis.

The fallen Annunaki had also done everything they could to stop the sounding of the three lost notes of the Tibetans, through the destruction and repression of the Tibetan people and culture by their minions. Their plans had never fully come to fruition, however, as the human spirit is industrious, patient and resilient.

The site where the lizard race had resided in secret watch for years had been discovered in 1909 by a man named Kinkaid. This halted the lizard race's ability to observe the elders of the four corners for fear of attracting more attention. The man had been traveling down the Colorado River while mining along Marble Canyon, when he found a cave that led to a parallel world of the Egyptian race. The aliens mistakenly believed that they were well hidden, since they had buried their station a mile underground. How Kinkaid found the entrance, 1500 feet down the side of a sheer cliff, was baffling.

The reptilian overlords had to act quickly when the mummified forms of their sleeping warriors were found along a passageway. The passageway was connected, like the spokes of a wheel, to an inner chamber at the hub. In this central chamber sat the lizard idol with yellow stones of cat's eye strewn around the impressive monument. From here, all of humankind was illuminated, from advanced ancient copper tools to the Akashic records.

The knowledge of the superiority of their race had to

be protected until the day when their massive hoard would crawl forth from the Earth to suppress the coming of the Fifth Root Race and the activation of the pineal gland—the all-seeing eye of creation, the pinnacle at the third eye—the opening of which would prove to be the apotheosis of humankind.

Once again, as had happened throughout written history, they activated a veil of illusion. Repression needed to be enforced by the mixed-ones in order to hide the truth of Kinkaid's discovery from curious minds, just as had happened with previous anthropological discoveries throughout the ages.

The Egyptian race was elevated to a higher vibration in the realms of creation and they were chosen to work upon the universal grid in harmony with nature, to avoid the trap of the material realm and greed's exploits. And the gods living within the hollow Earth shared their knowledge of the planet's need for a unified harmonic field to keep her energy vortex intact with the Egyptians.

They believed the best way to harness the necessary technology to do this was through the construction of a massive network of interconnected pyramids upon the ley lines. They placed these conductors across many lands on the European continent as a demonstration of the power that could be generated from the grid. They choose this part of the planet because of the high population density in Europe at the time. There were small pyramids built in Greece, Bosnia, Sudan and Indonesia and larger ones in Egypt, Russia and China.

Gaia was pleased with this work, and she allowed many delegates from across the universal realms travel through portals of time to come and experience her terrestrial beauty.

Many of those that populated Earth at this time began to document the vast knowledge shared from the universal mind, and with this knowledge Earth's children grew and developed in leaps and bounds.

The visitors soon came to be regarded as gods, and the people of the Third Root Race began to disconnect from spirit when they choose to embrace jealousy, vanity and greed. This transition away from spirit and the knowledge of the universal mind caused many of the advanced beings from other realms to leave the planet and Earth's people fell into a lower vibration of consciousness without the guidance of the cosmic universe.

This rejection of universal knowledge and the adoration of false idols and deities angered the Mother, and in her wrath she shut down the grid's torsion fields in the waves of time closing the gateways and burying them under mounds of sand and rock.

Humankind had once again forgotten the sacred power of the ground they walked upon and what Gaia had gifted them: life and the rich nutrients of her very blood—the waters of existence.

The wheels of time spun slowly. At times, vortexes upon the grid opened to offer the Third Root Race a glimpse of what they had lost. The records of universal knowledge would surface briefly, only to be buried again.

The human race entered a time of war resulting from the loss of gratitude and the disconnection from their Earth Mother, Gaia. The time of honouring the matriarch and understanding one's cosmic connection to the whole was contorted into a dark and repressive era of patriarchy that lasted for many centuries; it was an eon when humankind truly forgot its history and its destiny.

It was a time when numerous religions were designed to conquer the human mind by those of the fallen race of the Annunaki. Many of these new religions were based on ancient teachings, many of which contained hidden messages of universal knowledge within their symbols and practices, but these were mostly ignored and replaced with new ways of being that aimed to divide the human race. The shiva linga, benben, omphalos and baetyl stones could all represent the phallus symbol of patriarchy or the divinatory third eye; the phoenix, bennu-bird and eagle raising from the ashes were symbols of humankind's potential for reawakening. Stories were told and retold, all with truth, knowledge and the wisdom of infinity buried in a sepulcher of misinterpretation.

The Mother was tired of the violent games her children played, so she called forth the forces of the cosmos to help in the evolutionary development of the Fourth Root Race.

The Tuatha Dè Danann was the first group among many of higher developed beings that would help paint the picture in Earth's drama of evolutionary development. The tall, lithe and extremely beautiful race of faeries and deities brought a sense of mysticism back to the Earth, and the children of Gaia began to build temples in honour of her sacredness, raising the vibration of the web's weave.

A time of awakening was ushered in and the people were imbued with knowledge of the universe once again. This time was a time of magic and megalithic structures were erected across the lands through sound vibration. Vast, immovable stone structures were placed along the grid lines to remind humankind of its place in the cosmic scheme.

Stonehenge, one of many sites, became a school of knowledge for the children of the Tuatha Dè Danann, who later became known as Druids. The Druids were great scholars who paid homage to the processional impact of the stars and planets upon the Earth through rituals of gratitude.

Knowledge spread, as knowledge does. And people across all lands built observatories to peer at the heavens, following the cosmic path of the stars while their fear of the fall of humankind prophesied to come only grew. The people across the oceans with blood lines tracing back to those of the Third Root Race, the Aztec, Mayan and Inca, frantically tried to preserve and share their knowledge before all was lost. They created precise calendars of times past and times to come and a grid network of pyramids across the lands in a desperate attempt to retain the knowledge they had gained and protected for so long. In this attempt to hold on to knowledge, the human race became obsessed with honouring every god they could imagine in hopes of salvation and protection, while forgetting the mother of everything that is and ever will be, Gaia.

Their gods were of the Earth and nature, yet they raped the lands by their attachment to glorifying the ego. With the desire to beautify the pyramids and appease their many deities, they harvested and burned down forests leading to large-scale deforestation. Thus, the priests lost sight of Earth's intention, consumed in their own glorification.

War, famine and ritualistic human sacrifice soon befell the great nations. The final fatal blow to universal knowledge and connection to Gaia came when the religious factions came to destroy the writings, rape the lands and repress the last sacred rituals of cosmic gratification. The people of the Fourth Root Race had lost sight of the essence of being in this great repression of Earth's children.

The sacred structures that were the physical proof of humankind's rise and fall in consciousness and humanity were buried in a vast green sea of jungle growth, to be hidden once again.

Renewal became Earth's blanket of reprise from the abuse of her lost children, those that had fallen into the base instincts' primitive scope of fear and greed.

The people of the planet had so easily been fooled. Even when the detailed Piri Reis map was discovered and leaked to the public they still chose to ignore the truth because it was easier. The fact that there was a further advanced race of beings that came from other lands, planets, stars and galaxies, was hidden for hundreds of years.

Now, finally, the Fourth Root Race that still struggled spiritually and physically upon her living surface, was gladly awakening to the call and finally ready for the fifth shift. Gaia quivered in glory's delight as the children born from her blood, the keepers of her essence, sang forth creation's song of existence with hope.

The day dawned with the scream of Earth ripping open across her vast, undulating surface. The oceans, lakes, rivers and all the waters of the Earth rose to great heights, flooding the land with massive tsunamis while Atlantis rose from its frozen shackles under miles of thick ice. Mount Erebus erupted with a blast and the crystalline walls of the grand palace glittered through volcanic smoke and ash. The heat further melted the core of ice, releasing the 61 percent of Earth's fresh water held there as rivulets of healing elixir. The thousands of residents of the McMurdo station nearby ran screaming and tripping over one another in awe and fright at the beauty of the lands now suddenly above the cold ocean. The fallen had hidden the secrets of technology and understanding that these lands held for thousands of years.

The Aboriginal people in Australia had been gathering energy for this moment in the linear time of humankind: weaving along the Rainbow Serpent's winding ridge and following its rising back along a continuous, circling vortex, round and round in the long walk that they spun upon Mount Uluru and within the Kunoonda stone circles.

The great pulse of blue light emitting from the Pine Gap facility was losing its strength and the satellite pulse of the 380-nanometer wavelength that the lizards had once controlled was slipping away from them. HAARP was also losing control of the weather patterns, as Gaia began to expel the virus of reptilians that fed upon her.

The world's media network crashed, and Wi-Fi emissions that tracked and held the populous captive ceased to transmit.

The Mother breathed in and the freedom of awakening poured its long-buried love and faith across the lands. The people never felt so raw, so alive, so connected and complete. The world became smaller and reality, was again, the people's to create. Waves of time within the torsion field rippled and the old worlds of the Maya, Aztec, Olmec, Toltec and Zapotec collided, creating a cohesive unity, opening the doors of their portals.

Dolphins leapt from the waters of the Atlantic and Pacific oceans, beaching themselves along the shores before shapeshifting back to the form of their Mayan ancestors. These dolphin beings walked slowly along the raised white path of the sacbe roads of the Yucatán, weaving along the grid that connected an entire web of vortexes.   Millions of people gathered around numerous temples and ruins throughout Mexico and Central America for the five nameless days of Wayeb, the Mayan welcome of the New Year. The thinning of the veil between time-space and space-time came into symmetry with geometric harmony, as the crystalline structure of Earth lined up in coherence.

In Palenque, the tomb of Pakal shattered as the ancient Pleiadian stepped forth. The deity stood and with the raising of his arms drew forth his ship that was hidden beneath the ruin. He then opened the gates to the Underworld of Zimbaba and many beings from the priesthood of the fallen came forward in their ritual dress, alongside the Mayan feathered serpent god, Kukulkan.

Great lessons had been learned for the good of humankind; the cloak of mystery parted for all, as the truth of existence spilled forth.

Sacrifice, for many, had become a display of the lack of faith in the cohesiveness and purposeful intent behind all. And, with the remembering, more of the fallen began to rise through the gates of Tikal, a sacred entrance and exit to the home of the dead.

At Teotihuacán, in the East, ancestors of the Aztecs had been dancing for three days straight. The powerful allies present in the sacred peyote buttons were helping in the journey's crossover. The nourishing, yet intoxicating, pulque aided the sight of millions as they cheered and watched the spirit essence of Quetzalcoatl ride across Father Sun upon rolling clouds of red over fields of wavering pink skies.

In the lands of South America, various inland tribes of the Amazon sat within the trance of ayahuasca. They had sat quietly in their thatch huts for ten days while their shamans whistled the chanted song of the serpent's awakening; an awakening to life's purpose along the path and an end to fear's illusion.

The dark and muddy water of the great serpentine rivers of the Amazon that wound across the lands of the southern continent churned ferociously: on the Xingu River, the Belo Monte Dam was swallowed whole.

Thousands upon thousands of Indigenous people along the Xingu rode the tumultuous waves in dugouts, while smiles of victory over greed's backward progress played across their faces.   High in the Andes mountains of Peru, the Incans crossed back through hidden portals. Thousands marched along the gridwork of Cinque Terre roads to the numerous cities of gold throughout the region all heading toward the royal estate of Machu Pichu where the Incan god, Viracocha, awaited.

At the top of the world, on the shores of Lake Titicaca, the shamans guided their people in eating the San Pedro cactus and passing through the Aramu Muru portal that lay upon the dreamscape of their lands.

The blue waters of the lake parted as the ancient city of Wanaku rose from her depths. The Tiwanaku people along the shores joined hands and minds across the realms with the spirits of their ancestors and Pachacuti, he who transforms the Earth, was appeased.

Thousands also walked along the Nazca lines playing drums, singing and chanting with eyes cast to the heavens awaiting the Venusians of Venus' arrival.

In Tibet, the chant of oneness filled the skies. As the chant's reverberation across the land reached its crescendo, the Dalai Lama signaled the other Tibetan masters to introduce the last three notes. Another portal shimmered forth and the old wise man rose to float above the masses.

As the ley lines cracked along the axis mundi, a glimmering crystalline capstone appeared through a rip in the sky and landed ceremoniously upon the peak of the Great Pyramid of Giza. Then, in a crash of lightening, polished limestone appeared around the pyramid's exterior walls completely encapsulating it.

The light of Ta Khut was blinding and caused those that stood at the pyramid's feet to fall in praise at the base of the massive conductor. The ancient gods, Enlil and Enki, parted the veil that hid the mothership beneath the massive pyramid while the people stood below with mouths agape.

There were great throngs of people gathered around the Sphinx, Luxor Temple and Hathor Temple, all following the pathways of the ancient Egyptian god, Min, who also watched in awe as the mothership rose in the distance.

There were still thousands more, who practiced a variety of faiths—followers of the Bible, the Torah and the Quran—who climbed side by side in pilgrimage along the ridges of Mt. Sinai. All trekking upon the great mountain in an exodus from fear toward cosmic insight into the oneness of all. Judaism, Christianity and Islam had been created for the division of humankind; the fate of a choice between good and evil was reflected in the first deviation from the teachings of Zoroastrianism. In reality they all spoke the same truths, and all were to be judged for their mortal deeds.

The Church of Our Lady Mary of Zion, in Axum, Ethiopia, opened her guarded gates and the high priest removed the third stone of the Hopi prophecy, the one that represented the black race of humankind. The stone had been stored and hidden in the Ark of the Covenant for eons. The priest gladly presented it to the chariot of light that rode across the sky, high above a group of baffled onlookers. It was then carried upon wings of fire to its sacred home, into unity, placed in the puzzle of humankind's story with the Keepers of the Earth.

At the stone circles in Avebury, England, a mass of pagans stood to the calling of the summer solstice ritual. Many converged around England's sacred sites, all of which were linked along the 17 miles of roadway that formed the network grid of Stonehenge. There had been numerous crop circles reported in the three days leading up to the summer solstice. The Neolithic forms of the megalithic monuments were alight with tiny whirling spectrums of energy, creating magnificently intricate patterns of geometry's insight along the road's path. These balls of light gathered together creating a blazing spectrum that split the Earth to its core and the fourth stone, that of the white race, flew across the heavens on a direct path to the four corners that represented the four races of humankind. The great hoop was soon to be reconnected.

In Greece, the oracle, Sibylla, led her people along the sacred road of Hermes, gathering energy and the consciousness of remembering with every step taken.   On the scared mountain of Taishan in China, the souls of the dead returned, and the terracotta warriors of Xi'an came to life with the dancing of millions upon lines of magnetic force: the lung-mei, or the dragon's current.   The ancient Polynesians on the islands of the Pacific, shone from beneath the ocean's depths—glowing with the phosphorescent threads of the te lapa which they used to link those lands with the fortifying of the grid.   The huge monolithic structures of the Moai, the massive heads of Easter Island, stood, as they always had, at attention: a greeting party in honour and preparation for the return of their extraterrestrial forefathers.   The Aurora Borealis at the North Pole shimmered in such vibrant hues of green, that those who danced below the sacred entrance of the hollow Earth fell to their knees at the sight of its beauty.

Across the lands an overwhelming humming erupted from within the Earth as hundreds of flying machines manned by the ancients rose from their hidden lairs. The vimanas of ancient Vedic scripture hurled the Annunaki forth across the whole of Earth's surface.   The day of reckoning was here Gaia's children and the old gods had, once again, risen to help in the process of evolution: the awakening into awareness of a new world with the presentation of the fifth stone of prophecy.   In the North, the Ghost Dance continued into its fifth day. The Indigenous strongholds of North America had to catch the eyes and reach the hearts of their people.

The Keepers of the Earth had to hold their vision and keep their intent strong. Their unity was necessary to strengthen the web's fragile weave across the realms as foretold by the great seers of the secret and hidden knowledge of the red people.   The Earth trembled beneath their feet as it rolled and rumbled. Some cried out in fear, but they closed their eyes and gave in to the ecstasy of faith and continued the rhythmic dance upon the Sacred Mother.   In Oraibi, Arizona, the peaceful people of the Hopi exited through the ancient hole of emergence, the Sipapu, carrying the four stones forward to unite them with the fifth tablet that the ancient ones carried; the story of humankind was complete, and the people of all races who danced and chanted in a ritualized sense of oneness came to be of one mind with a shared remembering of the truth.

The prophets of the twelve great religions that had mistakenly divided humanity sat in council within the hovering mothership, high above the massive Pyramid of Giza's glittering capstone. Each sect sat in review of their respective "truths" and humankind's distorted view of the wisdom they had once tried to impart. The leaders now knew that each group of religious followers had forgotten that humankind could and should rise above all religious differences as co-creators of reality. They had all become archons: servants of the demiurge that divided the human race from the Goddess, instead of lighting the way to connection.

      The prophets held one another's hands in a firm grasp of respect as they formed a mindlink to review past and present atrocities. Each prophet's mind flew through the spinning reel of humankind's path through history.

      The wizard Merlin had manifested to represent a pantheon of deities from the Druids. The sorcerer of Arthurian legend smiled whimsically at the play of the prophets. With furrowed brow, he remembered with sadness how the peaceful religion of the Celtic people had become distorted. The introduction of a plethora of fear-based religions confused those that had once followed the ancient, mystical Earth religion. The eradication of paganism had culminated in the suppression and murder of over five million practitioners of natural medicine. The Christian's witch hunt had appalled the sage to no end, but he had no choice but to patiently wait for what was to come. He knew, through the realigning of consciousness, that the wisdom of the ages was now as it should be: there would be no labeling of sin, no blasphemy, no hearsay. The peace of nature-oriented ritual was, at this very moment, reconnecting the web in the fortification of Gaia with the blessing of her gifts.

Odin reviewed the laws of humankind's fate, its orlog, upon the mystical web of the wyrd. In his time, the children of northern lands paid homage to the nine noble virtues of being: their ideals forming a path to Asgard, a land of ease in the realm of the gods. The heathen customs of the Germanic, Wiccan and Norse people honoured the cycles of nature and all existence, understanding that the sentient beings that moved within the universe, and the Goddess Mother herself, had powers far beyond the ken of humankind. Sacred stories were told wherein one's ancestors became those honoured as gods and the tools of existence that were in nature were the weave of guidance provided to live by the organic, noble religion.

Neopaganism, a movement to return to the "old ways," was the resurfacing of these traditions. Much like the traditions of the Aboriginal peoples, the ways of being and honouring were not forgotten, they were protected by a select few who held the knowledge and bided their time. The majority had begun to worship what was formed from the breath. All the forces of nature were honoured until humankind began to see itself as a force that could control nature, forgetting the system of honour and the place where one's foot may fall.

Just as all stories manifest from a grain of sand in time, so the epic of Gilgamesh was created to warn of the times that were begotten from disconnection of the luminous self from An, the firmament. This was the time when Enlil and Enki were born. From this place of self-aggrandizement patriarchy was born and balance and honour destroyed. Man came to dominate humankind and control the teachings of the ancients. The Akkadians, the Babylonians and the Hittites separated at this time and their stories, told on cuneiform tablets, varied; however, in each history, a warning against the Underworld of Marduk and Nergal remained. The boat that ferried one across the river in "the wrongs" throughout time was full, and the many entrances to the gates of Hell were wide open.

The Ennead that formed the basis of interpretation of the nine deities failed to incorporate all the teachings, perhaps they were forgotten, or perhaps they had been stripped from the records when pharaohs began to view themselves as gods in the Pesedjet. The deities were created as an intermediary to maintain the order of the universe. They were present in nature and were formed to be a bridge between the world of humans and the world of the divine, but instead the representatives became engrossed in their own immortality. Respect for the properties of the Earth were soon forgotten as the people began to worship the Underworld in order to remain attached to the physical and material realm. The boat and the ferryman were revisited once again in myth as were the chariots of fire of the fallen.

For thousands of years the human race was formed and reformed. Myth and ancient teachings were at the disposal of humans, yet still they chose to focus on their own endless glorification. The universal Ma'at—truth, justice and order—had been under threat from the forces of disorder for eons and both the cosmos and human society had lost its cohesion.

The societies that were formed and resided in the

Middle East had decided long ago to continue with this division, no longer willing to cooperate or coexist in order to stave off disorder in the cosmos, and now the cyclical pattern of linear time was collapsing.

The Egyptian god, Atum, was now more than pleased to witness the restoration of the Great Pyramid of Giza to its former glory as a blinding beacon of truth shimmering in a white limestone casing.

The aion, Sophia, the deity of wisdom, a demiurge of the Gnostic school, played over and over again in her mind the script's messages hidden deep within the Egyptian library of the Nag Hammadi. The demiurge was a flawed being that emanated from the Monad (the one god) as the world, as all within the universe, had. The lower world of matter like the molecules of flesh and the concept of time were all part of the imperfect, ephemeral world within their mythological medium of thought. The practice of philanthropy, the shunning of the material and the embracing of the spiritual was the purpose behind the quest for gnosis (knowledge) of the adept. Their school of thought mixed philosophy and metaphysics, curiosity, culture and knowledge in the secrets of the universe, yet still the humans remained blind to the divine spark.

The Persian prophet, Zarathustra, perused the holy book of his teachings, the Avesta. The sacred poetry of the five hymns of the Gathas, those melodic songs of creation from the supreme god, Ahura Mazda, wove through his thoughts. Ahura Mazda spoke of the presence of good and evil and the division of humankind through the human's dualistic nature itself. Man was predestined to awaken to the righteous quest for the ethical existence of our cosmic nature, Asha, and the right of social justice for all. The five hymns were designed to help guide the people through the three eras of existence. The first era was that of creation. The second was the present, as far as humankind's evolution had come and the time when humans would be faced with the choice between good and evil, both of which resided within the divided soul, urvan. The third and final era was about to commence when the savior, Saoshyant, would appear to judge those who still choose to live in the division of humanity's dualistic nature and to precipitate the final renovation of human existence.

His religion was an optimistic, monotheistic faith that still recognized the power of the twelve commanders of light who resided within the Zodiac and around the table at which he sat. The reason for the faithful optimism was a firm belief in humankind's ability to choose to embrace good in order to ascend and reside on the final plane of unity in a paradise of love. But division was the test for the Fourth Root Race and divide they did.

Abraham wearily lowered his head in thought mourning the banal and convoluted ways of man. The philosophical study of the revelations and expression of Yahweh was a path designed to help humankind understand the dualism of spirit and flesh. The faith also provided a guide to follow the basic laws of ethics, those of Maimonides, that could sanctify humankind.

The Torah was an array of compiled oral stories that lost all intent when written down, as each scribe's version became infused with his own prejudice and interpretation. The traditional stories were meant to depart an awareness of the lessons that exist in the experience of struggle and the growth that comes from such living, not the personal human imprint that came to mark the teachings with each transcription. The one version was converted to the two Talmuds, and the study of philosophy and theology expanded as humankind continued to populate the planet. The division within humankind continued to grow as did the ego, leading to further separation and views of superiority as "God's chosen ones." The truth in the word was universal consciousness' concern for the world and Mother Earth, which was buried further and further below dogma, restrictions and judgment as patriarchy reigned.

Jesus sat and pondered his own teachings as all the others within the congregation had done. The loss of his message, even from the Essenes to himself, had massive consequences. The Bible, the new version, the old version, all had somehow, somewhere along the way, lost his message of love. The young messiah was baffled at this erasure and the distortion of his message. As Christians slaughtered a path through history, his heart had been broken.

The church's self-appointed role as mediary and the reliance on fear and the incorporation of the concepts of sin, evil and salvation had been the true blasphemy in the eyes of Jesus.

When the love for the all-encompassing Mother was lost, and the consciousness of she that birthed all was hidden in borrowed rituals, he had no choice but to wait for the day of his second coming.

Muhammad saw the struggle written on his brother's brow and held Jesus' hand firmly, attempting to comfort him. The utter safety and wholeness provided by the peace of complete surrender to Allah was the place where bliss lived. Since the revelations within the scriptures of the Torah had become distorted, he took it upon himself to try and reveal truth by guided teachings of the Quran. And yet somehow, once again, moral significance had become contorted through the worship of the Imam: they who were not gods, but humans. The time of judgment and resurrection, Qiyamah, was upon those who did not follow the five pillars of Islam. The angels would bring down the compassionate one in his excellence, and with him, with the power of prayer, his mercy.

"We all know humans are empty of Atman in this realm of existence," said Buddha, as he breathed in the calmness of his eternal contentment.

"We have all tried to end the suffering of these sentient beings with the elimination of ignorance and desire through the practice of mindfulness in meditation, prayer and contemplation. Whatever names that we have given these tools is of no importance.

"The simplicity in the dharma of the Four Noble Truths and the Eightfold Path designed to lead one to Nirvana has baffled humankind it seems. I believe the fault lies in their inability to see and acknowledge the three marks of existence. The first being the impermanence of all. Logically, this can only lend to a dependence on realism in the suffering of attachment. How can they not see that egoism is pointless and that nothing is independent from the whole?" Buddha asked.

Krishna had tried, as the others before, to lead by example and direct humankind toward the right path by illuminating the truth that all manifestations are of Brahman, the one ultimate reality. The Hindus did not need a formal god to submit to in order to find purpose in life on this plane. They had not one but four purposes: Dharma, to fulfill one's purpose with virtue and righteousness; Artha, the pursuit of prosperity in all its manifestations; Kama, obtaining enjoyment from life, relating also to desire and sexuality; and Moksha to find enlightenment with the release of karma.

"It appears," Krishna thought, "that humankind has preferred to focus only on the first three purposes of life, ignoring Moksha's call to freedom from reincarnation, samsara." The boundaries had been set forth in the ancient Vedic scriptures that was designed to lead one to the ultimate enjoyment: embracing the eternal soul. Yet again, however, humankind refused to adhere to the wisdom.

Confucius, like many of the prophets before him, believed in cultivating the practice of self-creation. He knew that there had always been an abundance of wondrous virtues available to humankind, ready to be applied.

There were five constants expressed in the ethical philosophy of Confucianism: Ren, the humanistic values of altruism; Yi, living righteously with consciousness in justice and honour in the rituals of life; Li, maintaining propriety and etiquette in the system of norms; Zhi, seeking knowledge; and Xin, living with integrity.

To Confucius, and those who followed his writings, there was no belief in any god or reincarnation, there was only how one lived in their moment with a focus on family, learning from one's ancestors and the pursuit of personal and communal endeavors with a virtuous heart. He had provided the five classics for direction. *The Book of Changes*, or the *I Ching*, was written to awaken humankind to the two energies of yin and yang that could easily provide powerful insight into the way of the universe. The divinatory art outlined in the book combined ethical insight with numerology and emphasized the truth that all will seek balance, with everything having its opposite or opposing force. *The Book of Songs* imbued one with poetic vision and an awareness of how music and prose could touch all of humanity with mutual responsiveness and feeling. *The Book of Documents* reviewed the government's responsibility to create trust in the processes that led to a covenant of social harmony. *The Book of Rites* outlined the four functional occupations of farmer, scholar, artisan, and merchant and the ceremonies intrinsic to each. Finally, *The Spring and Autumn Annals* honoured the ancestors, focusing on the significance of collective memory of community and the self-identification of one's role in the whole.

Now, it seemed to Confucius, that all of humankind had lost faith in their elected or instated governments and the unity of wisdom's teaching, that bound all religions, was lost in the concept of division—division of the Earth herself and Earth's people.

Merlin sent a telepathic prayer to the group mind. The prophets' retrospectives had cast a great blanket of sadness over the congregation. Merlin went on to address the group without words, "I honour all the paths at this table. I drink from the well of our Mother. I bring an unprotected heart to our meeting place."

Enlil's thoughts flowed to the group, "Let the light stream forth into human minds. Let the light descend upon the Earth. The primeval sea has existed before anything else, within this soup is the Heaven and Earth we've formed. Let us allow the goddess, Ki, to sing. Those who walk with truth will generate life. Who can compete with this righteousness?"

"An invisible mystery bore forth with the word. The beginning chant of vowels, 22 times each. Then the consonants came into existence next to the vowels and individually they were commanded, and they submitted. And the consonants, as well, are self-existent, and as they are changed they submit to the hidden gods," Sophia's words wove as a wisp through the group mind as existences' song. The song expanded and poured forth on a wave of sound across all the lands and a great light shone on the blessed goddess, Sophia.

From this blinding brilliance stepped White Buffalo Calf Woman, the matriarchal representative for Gaia, the truest of all powers. She was formed from stardust and the matter that all gods came from, except that *she* had always been. She was not dependent on the word, or stories for existence. She was existence, for she was the thought that came before the word. She was born of the essence of the primordial soup, from what became. Everything that existed upon her was dependent on her grace.

None of the hidden gods who had gathered, or those who had once manifested upon her bosom, could withstand the gaze of the forsaken Mother's messenger.

Atum bowed his head in respect and sent his message forth to ease the electric charge that poured forth from the group of Ascended Masters.

And then she spoke: "The true teaching is not an accumulation of knowledge it is an awakening of consciousness that goes through successive stages. Know the world in yourself; never look for yourself in the world, for this will project your illusion. The shortest road to the knowledge of truth is nature. Have the wisdom to abandon the values of a time that has passed and pick out the constituents of a future." The love of the universe poured forth across the land as she spoke to her children.   "Each of you, my children, the essence of life's longing for itself, has been a creator, a healer and the way for many. All of your teachings, in each and every one of you Ascended Masters, have contained some truth as well as some deception. That is all part of the duality you chose and agreed upon when you entered the realm of linear time, when I allowed you to manifest upon my being.

"Now, go forth and be the light you see in me and spread the true teachings that you all have in common, leaving division behind. Truth is one, sages just call it by different names."

Krishna rained his beatific smile upon those manifested at the table, "Truth cannot be suppressed and is always the ultimate victor. Life and death, joy and sorrow, gain and loss, these dualities cannot be avoided. Learn to accept what you cannot change.

"On this Earth do I stand, unvanquished and unhurt. Set me, oh Earth, amidst the nourishing strength that emanates from your body. Earth is my mother, her child am I," with that, Krishna nodded to the others and descended to his followers upon a bolt of lightning.

And awe was the sound as India's children of the Hindu belief beheld their master. He spoke to the disciples who had fallen by the millions at his feet, "One only sees truly when one sees the same light in every creature. Seeing the same lord everywhere, he does not harm himself or others. One who sees me in all things and all things in me, is never far from me and I am never far from them. Behold I am here!"

Buddha addressed those that remained: "You, yourself, as much as anybody in the entire universe, deserves your love and affection. The mind is everything: what you think you become. There are three things, my brothers and sisters, that can't be hidden: our sun, our moon and the truth. The only true failure in life is not to be true to the best that one knows. You cannot travel the path until you have become the path itself. How many holy words you've read, how many you've spoken, what good will they do if you do not act upon them?

"Now, let us walk upon the Earth, as no one saves us but ourselves. No one can, and no one may. We, ourselves, must walk the path of the Red Path Way."

With that, the Ascended Masters dispersed as one into the ether to manifest in the hearts of the lost followers of each discipline as hope.

At Pine Gap, the assembled group sat around the wide table still bewildered by the sudden disappearance of Valiant Thor. Why hadn't he left before, if he could?

The realization that fell upon them sent a ripple of fear through the group just as Zarathustra appeared before them.

Some of the congregation of spiritual leaders had chosen to appear before the fallen of the Babylonian Brotherhood as all sentient beings were being given the chance to ascend to the Fifth Root Race.

Zarathustra addressed the Pope directly, "I should only believe in a god that would know how to dance!" Then, he turned and addressed Marduk, the lizard king of the Annunaki: "You great star, what would your happiness be had you not those for whom to shine? Why would you choose to hurt these children, the only ones left to make you the god you seek to be? When power becomes gracious and descends to the visible it becomes what we call beauty. And there is nobody from whom I want beauty as much as from you who are powerful; let your kindness be your final conquest and leave this planet in peace."

Muhammad materialized at Zarathustra's side, adding, "Kindness is a mark of faith. Whoever is not kind, has no faith. Allah does not look at your appearance or your possessions, but he looks at your heart and your deeds. Your group has made this world a prison for the faithful, but a paradise for unbelievers. Your love of worldly possessions is the root of all evil."

Confucius then appeared alongside the other prophets and spoke in his gentle, solemn nature to those of the Bilderberg Group, the Babylonian Brotherhood and the Talisman Corp: "Never impose on others what you would not choose for yourself; real knowledge is to know the extent of one's own ignorance. Everything has beauty, but not everyone sees it. The superior man is aware of righteousness while the inferior man is aware of advantage: he who learns but does not think is lost. He who thinks but does not learn is in great danger."

The group's collective fear was palpable as Jesus stepped into the room through parting mists. He said, "Do not be anxious about tomorrow, for tomorrow will be anxious for itself. Let the day's own trouble be sufficient for the day. If you bring forth what is within you, what you bring forth will save you. What you do not bring forth will destroy you, for the one who is within you, is greater than the one who is in this world. Let me lead you to quiet waters that lie within the womb of the Mother."

"It is the stillest words that bring on the storm. Thoughts that come on dove's wings guide the world," added Zarathustra.

Abraham appeared imbued with righteousness, and with pointed finger on his raised hand he addressed the group: "Wonder, rather than doubt, is the root of all knowledge. As he thinks in his heart, so he is; as you teach, you learn! Yet you beings, although born of the Earth, do not realize that to have felt no pain is to have not been human. You have remained hidden within your own deceit!"

As Abraham's fury rose, his voice became the thunder echoing all around them. He continued, "I am Alpha and Omega, the beginning and the end, what is and what was, and what is to come." As Abraham's raised hand descended, the entrance to the cave that had housed the fallen for so many years collapsed, and the masters dispersed into thin air.

The Awakening

Old Joe felt exhausted yet also full of exhilaration for what was to come. His war paint had faded as had the fortitude it would take to complete the tasks set before him. He glanced at the beautiful woman beside him and saw the exhaustion in her stance as well.

The journey to the Three Sisters had been physically and spiritually demanding, especially for one who had not grown up with the stories to empower one's spirit. The quest to attain the crystal skull of pte had cost the small band of warriors supremely and the tribespeople dearly as it had the physical embodiment of the Way.

Willow was a beautiful specimen of a woman, he thought, so strong yet as fragile as the delicate flower of pte— one that transforms, as she had. She bore signs of her ancestry, but still it shocked Joe that a halfbreed would be the bringer of the dawn.

"She does bear quite a resemblance to her

grandmother," he thought with a chuckle. "And the old crow's fortuitous stubbornness as well!

"Okay, my dear, let us prepare, for we have little time before the sunset is upon us. Even though Father Sun comes down to rest in the bosom of the Mother's breast much later these days," said Joe.

"Yes, as in the expansion of the seasons, Grandfather," replied Willow, her exhaustion evident in her whispered speech. "The days seem to pass so quickly since our meeting this spring, Joe. Nothing is ever as one expects it to be."

"Ah, yes, expectations are like that my dear. The universe does not like stipulations applied to its workings," said the old seer as he swept the site clear with a cedar bow.

He put down his pack and proceeded to pull out his tools of trade. He drew forth a clay vessel from his seemingly endless bag. The vessel held embers from the sacred fire he had started at the base of the Three Sister's range to prepare the serpent elixir.

Willow had been gathering branches and laying them upon the hearth. She stacked each with intention: seven handfuls of dry kindling, seven small branches, seven medium branches and she finished with seven larger branches, just as she had seen the shaman do on their previous journeys.

When the fire licked to life from the embers Joe had brought, the two sat to rest in its warmth. Tendrils of orange, blue and white flickered and came to life under the fading light of dusk.

Sister Moon was just beginning to rise, her smiling face luminous, as her light poured down upon the sacred circle before the cave. She began to take on the deep, dark red hue of blood in her ascension to the sky.

The shadowing eve silhouetted the forest around them in a glow of deep indigo. The trees seemed to dance and sway to the rhythm of the fifth and final day of dance.

The shift was palpable: the air electric and knowing was complete. All the elements had risen and all danced together.

The shaman's eyes met Willow's across the flames and both smiled the knowing smile of one who is in complete acceptance of life's calling.

She stood and then bowed low to all the directions before moving to the mouth of the cave where the pulsing crimson of the womb's fold was inviting her home.

Old Joe also stood, wiping the tears from his eyes with the gnarled knuckles of his right hand, he turned away from Willow feigning smoke to be the cause of his red-rimmed eyes. Once again, he reached into his satchel and drew forth his war paint: the red ochre paste that had been applied with heart's insight to those lost throughout the centuries. The paint, a representation of the blood that had fallen upon the sacred lands of his people and the blood of all people lost in war and genocide, was mixed with years of salty tears. Slowly, he applied it to his face.

Willow stood in awe of destiny's course, as she embraced purpose in the wholeness of being. The glow of the cave's crystal walls beckoned her forward like the birth of a new universe—stars flickering to life in the deep, dark vastness. Her clothes fell away as she stood before the worlds of infinity that awaited her.

They both turned, as if the same internal clock connected them. The Wiyan Wakan and the shaman stood transformed into that that is the dance, that is life and that is death and rebirth.

Joe had already placed his tools and medicines upon the soft buffalo hide and its sacred symbols flickered to life, they too danced in the light of the fire's flames.

Willow moved forward slowly with determined intent in every step.

Joe had already called forth his guides and the air was shimmering in layers of existence beyond one's sight but within one's call.

The old man had drunk the visionary elixir and smoked the sacred herb, just as he had been drinking the tea of the little ones since he had been called forth to fulfill his path in the story that was written.

A song poured into the ether's of the air and whistled through the healer's missing teeth. It was a song of old, the one that held the last sacred note. The dance that throbbed from within the trembling Earth was carried forth to the universe on the wings of eve's breath.

The shaman moved forward until he was standing before Willow. His fingertips were warm and dry upon her skin as he applied the paste. The flowing symbols drawn upon her flesh were from the ages of all races: swirls became knots, then a circle with a dot, fish became crosses, stars, moons, a cup and a chalice. All flowed into one; all became one.

The cloying scent of the thick red paste sent their senses to the time of primordial beginnings; the smell was of a deep earthy musk, rancid blood, death and hope.

Willow swayed, deep in trance, and drank hungrily when the elixir was brought to her lips. She fell into Sister Moon's embrace; the deep red of her depths flowed through Willow's veins as the serpent raised its head among a thousand melding skulls on the plane below.

Old Joe knew the other side's magic had stepped forward to ease the physical vessel of the seer. He watched her transform into the Goddess, the one all had awaited.

White Buffalo Calf Woman stepped forth and spread out all the way across the perceivable universe. A luminous shawl shone as starlit ether upon her shoulders; her manifestation, a blinding beacon of light seen throughout the cosmos. Willow collapsed to the embrace of the soft, warm Earth as Sister Moon was eclipsed.

The Goddess looked down upon the throbbing masses of Earth's children. They were still searching the skies and not the landscape of their souls for gods they believed existed beyond themselves, while their archons strode with heads bowed among them.

The deceivers and those that had fallen prey to the falsehoods that befall all now faced them. The fear was tangible for when they looked in the mirror, it was the horrors of their own beliefs they now faced, along with the truth of their place within the matrix.

The Great Mother knew that she was also born from the black hole of the universal mind, one that existed beyond even her own embodiment. This level was a playing field of the gods created to watch the unfolding of evolution on this energy field of vibration.

She had no ego to behold, she just watched and hurt and prayed for those that had forgotten where they dwelt.

The shift to a higher frequency was part of this evolution, part of the plan. The dwellers of the Earth were meant to evolve this time around or fall down and into the abyss where they would have to try to elevate consciousness all over again.

As it appeared at this moment in time, all but a few

were likely to plummet once more.

White Buffalo Calf Woman continued to wrap her essence around the Earth and through the many layers that engulfed the Mother.

Oh, how beautiful she appeared from the heavens, but when the layers of illusion were peeled back scars could be seen, layer upon layer of scars. Clearcuts slashed through her forests, from North America to South, across Europe, Asia and Africa, across all lands. Islands of plastic formed an insidious plaque stuck inside her veins that polluted her arteries. Her blood was black from seeping oil spills. Gaping holes within her core had pitted her magnificence and drained her essence. The rivers of her tears were dammed, choking her pain's flow. A black acrid smoke sat thick in the atmosphere thinning her defenses and scorching her shell.

And then, finally, she rumbled a fierce resistance. The acid that lay in her womb's waters sprayed forth falling upon her children and scorching their skin as hers had been. Her fury exploded across all the continents. Yellowstone became the ultimate trigger.

All was connected within the web, and it had carelessly been weakened and stripped bare; now it was fortified once again with the unity of the Ghost Dance.

Gaia took no joy in the course the cosmos had laid out for her children, for she had manifested them all from her being, including this mind in the here and now that observed the fall and the awakening of a new dawn.

White Buffalo Woman appeared in a holographic form of the many relevant goddesses from all ages, of all races, across all religions.

The primal group mind exploded with fear and awe. Those who had walked the Red Path Way were protected under the shield of consciousness manifest in the knowing.

All ancestors, from all times of remembering, were cloaked and reunited across the realms with the grid's activation. The Earth was aglow in the red light of the luminescent path just as the Keepers of the Earth had predicted: A great blue light would come from the East followed by a red one that would bring with it destruction.

White Buffalo Calf Woman pulled her wrath within the confines of her shimmering buffalo hide cloak and returned to the woman who gave all to find the wholeness of self.

Willow lay prostate on the ground. Her pupils were dilated, and her shallow breaths barely sustained her.

"Come to me, child, our mission is not quite finished. Come back, for I am done with my wrath. Now I need you for the opening of the twelfth gateway: the door to the awakening and renewal," whispered the Goddess into Willow's ear, drawing her back to existence upon the physical plane.

The old man had been dancing for what seemed like a lifetime. He could see his ancestors before him gently strumming a thin gossamer thread along the web's weave.

Joe sang their song—it poured forth from his soul. The screaming, throbbing pain and suffering of all Earth's creatures shrilled forth like a heart torn, still beating, from one's very being.

Willow slowly drew herself back to consciousness. It was difficult to leave the warm bath in the waters of the womb.

The shaman carried on his entrancing chant as he lit the sacred pipe, the bowl filled to the brim with the smoldering little smoke.

All was raw and soothing in its depth: the song as well

as the smoke tendrils that kept Willow's mind wavering upon the precipice.

Old Joe handed the woman a chalice containing the warm tea of the red-flowered fungi, the flower that once grew abundantly upon the land the great pte had roamed. The shaman withdrew the fungi from his bag at his side, gently placing a fresh, moist bud between Willow's teeth. He tipped the chalice of tea upon her mouth to help wash down the helper with a nurturing warmth.

Old Joe was in trance as he began to dance again, never losing the song's rhythm or the steps that held the realms together. He bent close to the quivering ground, never losing a beat, and then came up with the crystal skull of pte in his hands. Round and round he moved in the figure of infinity.

In Willow's mind, the shaman grew as large as the trees that surrounded them.

He danced low, then high, like a cresting wave; the figure eight wearing deep within the Earth around the fire's perimeter and the cave's entrance. The Native elder was engulfed in the mists of passing layers—the ages of humankind.

Joe had changed through his endurance and belief; he embodied all the knowing of his ancestors and all the races of humankind. Red Hand had taught him well the duties of his lineage and the Wiyan Wakan was well prepared to follow through in the opening of the twelfth gateway. The grid could be fully awakened and held intact. The Mother's weakened threads in the web of life had been fortified with the dance and those who could hold firmly in the resolve to heal her; she was delighted.

After the final pass of the twelfth round of the Unity

Dance, Willow stepped forward and took the skull from the shaman's hands. She gently placed the sacred skull in front of its home at the mouth of the cave.

Willow shone ethereally as she bowed once again to Joe. "Tunkasila, I am ready to finish the Way. I thank you for being the noble man you have been. You have brought honour to your people, to me." She reached out, taking the old man's arthritic hands in hers and put them to her lips in the deepest sign of respect. She kissed his painfully gnarled knuckles and then placed the obsidian blade from her pouch into his hand. She grasped his hand firmly before letting go to give him her strength and permission for the deed that was to follow.

Willow knelt in front of the cave, bowing before the crystal skull of pte. She knew what lay beyond the beckoning darkness of the cave's depth. Its crystalline structures were vast stars that would pull her into the great black hole. She would soon awaken within the arms of her lover, Wahweyho, who waited in the next realm.

Joy imbued her very essence as she grabbed the glowing skull and held it high above her head toward the heavens. Her spirit rejoiced as she jumped on the back of the serpent and rode it through the mists of time.

The sound of the shaman's war cry pierced the air as he slit her throat from ear to ear. He held her head nestled upon his bent knees, falling protectively over her physical body in grief. In mourning awe, he lowered her delicate form gently to the ground and the Mother's trembling subsided.

The eclipse passed, and Sister Moon shone brilliant white. The eve was silent.

In the morning, all was quiet upon the web of life. Those that had shifted resumed life as usual; however, they carried a new knowing and a wonder at the beauty of life—a great sense of appreciation for all that surrounded them. No fear resided anywhere within the beings that shifted; no memory remained of what had befallen the people who had become the Fifth Root Race.

Gaia's veins, the waters of life, ran clean and pure. The green of all her forests renewed her breath. Her resources were safe within her womb where they belonged.

Gaia was anew—as she, as we, as all, are part of her sustenance.

And the raven flew through the realms of all the worlds.

When the blood in your veins returns to the sea,

And the earth in your bones returns to the ground,

Perhaps then you will remember that this land

does not belong to you.

It is you that belongs to this land.

-Native American wise man

A'ho

Kerri James is a Clinical Herbal Therapist that lives in British Columbia, Canada. She has pursued numerous studies along the esoteric path, embracing environmentalism and spiritual awareness. This is her second book.

Kerri's first book was based on her travels and study of medicinal plants while abroad. Her first book is called, *Ramblings of a Mad Woman: experiences in and out of mind.* She hopes to revise this read with an extension of short experiences, herbal folklore from the Amazon and future discoveries in travel, medicinal studies...delving into the withheld mysteries.